A Journey
into
the Fourth Dimension

A Journey into the Fourth Dimension

The Lasting Legacy of Derek Saul

W. Lawrence Miner, Jr.

Let me know your reaction.
Blessings,
Larry

Agents of Change
Columbus, North Carolina

Copyright ©2000 by W. Lawrence Miner, Jr.
All rights reserved.

No part of this book may be reproduced in any form
or by any electronic or mechanical means including information and retrieval systems without
prior permission from the publisher in writing.

Library of Congress Cataloging-in-Publication Data

Miner, W. Lawrence, Jr. 1926-
   A journey into the fourth dimension:
   the lasting legacy of derek saul/ W. Lawrence Miner, Jr.
   p. cm.
   Previously under the series; Derek: a journey into the fourth
   dimension--Publisher's info.
   ISBN 1-928992-01-3
   1. Brothers--Death--Psychological aspects--Fiction.
   2. Young men--Fiction.
   I. Title.

PS3563.I4648 J68 2000
813'.54--dc21
                                                                          00-027119

Manuscript editor:
Christopher Dailey

W. Lawrence Miner, Jr.
Arden, NC 28704

Agents of Change
P.O. Box 1429
Columbus, North Carolina 28722
An imprint of Granite Publishing, LLC
Living Lightly On the Earth...

Printed in the United States of America.

The famous mystic and clairvoyant Edgar Cayce (1877–1945), would put himself into an altered state and project his consciousness to the location of a person who was requesting a reading.

His reputation for accuracy, particularly in health readings, was phenomenal and his readings on spiritual matters were so enlightening that millions still study them today.

In one particular reading by Cayce, he was quoted as saying:

"The best definition that ever may be given of the fourth dimension is an idea." (Edgar Cayce reading 364-10)

Derek was a man of ideas.

Anything can be changed by changing your mind. All things in the physical are created first in the mind. Nothing in the mind is cast in concrete because we can fortunately always change our minds, but mind is the builder, the physical is the result.
—*Derek*

Part One

Chapter One

Letter from Michelle

Dear Ken,

Three years have now passed since Derek's death. I believe he was too great a soul to let his story drift into oblivion. Although he may not have made a mark on the globe, may not have set any world records, or made a million dollars, he did, however leave a big mark upon the hearts and minds of the people who knew him. He led the kind of loving, joyful life everyone admired. The kind of life that surely God wants us to live.

I would like to put the experiences that everyone had with Derek into a book so that others can get inspiration. I am contacting you, and a dozen or so others who were close to Derek, to ask if you would share the experiences you had with him.

I realize some of your experiences happened two or more decades ago and your memories will not be perfect. But, as much as possible, try to recount some of the conversations you had with Derek. Even Biblical accounts of Jesus were 35 years old when written. So just do your best to remember things and whatever you can recall will be fine.

Also, I know you probably didn't agree with everything Derek had to say, but try to report what you remember of his innovative thinking and philosophies. The idea for a biography of Derek is not to convince people to have the same beliefs as Derek, but to entertain readers with the joyful, active life of an innovative thinker and a loving man.

You don't have to rush off a reply. Please give it some thought and do your best. Thanks.
Blessings,
Michelle Saul Bassett

Ken's E-Mail Reply to Michelle

Michelle,

    I can understand why you would like to write a book about Derek with contributions by those whose lives mingled with his. I also understand why you ask me to write something, but you should remember I really only knew him as a child, a young child at that, 32 years ago.

    Don't forget he started school the year I started college and during my vacations at home I had my friends and spent very little time with him. I remember Derek as a cute, bright, and active kid, but I wasn't really very interested in him then.

    So, what could I possibly say that my parents and sister haven't already said? The above paragraph sums up about all I could honestly say about my brother.

    As you probably remember, I have spent the past 24 years as a journalist. I went from my second year at college, where I was majoring in journalism, into the Vietnam War, where I served as a secretary to high-ranking officers, then back to finish college. I was lucky and got a job with *The Globe* newspaper right away. Since I knew Vietnam well, I was assigned back there almost immediately. As a result, I almost never saw Derek as he was growing up and when I did, it was with a family group and never alone to talk seriously.

    Michelle, my thought is I might be of greater value to you with my journalism background, editing your book. I propose this to you because I think it would be great for me, too. I would finally get a chance to know who my little brother was.

    Also, it so happens that this might be an excellent time for me to come down to Falls Church. Jenny and I are going through a tense time with our marriage right now and it would probably be good if we had time apart. I could stay with my parents and, in fact, I would want to stay with them. I haven't seen them enough either.

    Having written this, I am excited about the prospect. Please call me collect. I am currently between assignments, so now would be a particularly good time for me to come down.
Affectionately,
Ken

Ken's Journal (March 27th)

This is the first entry in what will be a regular journal to record my thoughts and feelings.

I'm actually excited about keeping this journal. There's so much I want to express, but don't know whom to share it with at the moment. Recently, Jenny and I haven't really sat down and discussed anything. There's obvious tension between us, but neither of us wants to touch it. Everyday I start out planning to share some of my thoughts and feelings, but the day seems to pass before I get the nerve. I hate arguments when I'm not being understood.

I received a letter from Michelle yesterday. She's requesting me to write about my experiences with, and impressions of, Derek. Actually, she's requesting the same from everybody who was close to him. Although I certainly qualify as having been close to him by blood, I can't say I was ever very close to him otherwise. I don't know what I could write, except that Derek was my very unusual brother.

So, I sent her an e-mail to that effect today. Actually, I suggested I be involved in a much more significant way—helping put the book together. I think it would be interesting, but the biggest reason perhaps would be to get away so Jenny and I could have some time apart.

From Ken's Journal (March 28th)

As soon as Michelle read my e-mail yesterday, she called and invited me down. She told me she intuitively, and immediately, felt in agreement with my suggestion. She had recently sent a summary to a publishing company for review and received a reply requesting the complete book.

Since she's not nearly ready to send a completed book, she's very eager to get any help she can. It seems as though she's feeling rather overwhelmed in trying to assemble and edit all the separate accounts and didn't at first expect it would be so time-consuming.

So, anyhow, I'm now getting set to make the trip back to Falls Church to help out. And it really comes at a good time. Jenny and I don't seem to be able to work out our problems right now. The arguing has turned to silence and we're certainly not getting anything resolved that way. I told Jenny about my heading down there to help with the book and she thought it was a great idea. She says it will give her more time to focus on work with the tax season coming up. I wonder what else, or who else, it might give her time to focus on as well.

Never thought we would struggle like this. Maybe it really is as she suggests, and we're simply growing apart. I know I can be overly negative at times and I'm sure it does wear her down, but I sometimes think she just doesn't want to see things as they really are.

Right now she's in the kitchen talking to her mother on the phone. I know they've been talking about the problems we're going through. Her mother's probably telling her she deserves better. Maybe she does. Maybe I do, too. I don't know.

I do know I should wrap this up and go spend some time with her since I'll be gone for awhile. But I really don't feel like getting into another argument at this point. If we don't argue, we're likely to sit there in silence, staring at the TV. Guess I'll get started packing.

Chapter Two

Ken's Journal (March 31st)

As I make this entry, I'm sitting out in the sun deck of my parents' house. It's a lovely sun deck overlooking a small brook with woods beyond. Complete privacy. I arrived here late last night. Jenny and I said good-bye yesterday without saying hardly a word. It was more awkward than I thought it would be. As if we really weren't sure if we would still be together the next time we meet. Part of me feels as though I should call her, but I know we need this time apart.

It does feel good to be with Mom and Dad. Mom and I sat at the kitchen table this morning talking like we haven't done in a very long time. I really think this time is going to be good for me. I know Mom senses problems between Jenny and me, but she's not bringing it up, at least not yet.

Hopefully, I'll be able to sort a few things out while I'm down here. I have to admit I'm getting a little curious about the little brother I never really knew. Mom was surprised I actually came down to help out with this family project, considering how distant I've been much of my life.

Today, I read the first chapter about Derek. It was from Dad. Actually, I read it several times and even cried as I read the ending. I always knew that Derek meant a lot to Dad, but I guess I never realized quite how much and why. Or, perhaps, I never wanted to realize. The letter was very emotional for me. I can probably say for the first time, I actually felt the loss of Derek. Never having been around him much, I guess I didn't notice when he was no longer there. I knew he wasn't, but it was more of an idea than a feeling.

Dad's Account

We always realized Derek was precocious, but when he was about three and a half, maybe four, I really knew he was going to be different. I was reading the paper in my chair in the living room and Emily was preparing dinner. Derek and I were alone.

He was babbling away like a small child does and I was replying, "Uh-huh," "Yes," or "That's nice," like most parents have done, absorbed in my paper and not paying any attention to what he was actually saying. So, he walked up to me and, with his little arm, squashed the paper into my lap and with a firm, demanding voice said, "Asshole, I'm talking to you."

Flabbergasted, I reprimanded him, "Don't you ever call me or anyone else that again!"

"Okay, if you listen to me when I talk to you," he replied with a voice of assurance.

I agreed.

"Promise?" he said.

"Yes," I replied in a rather timid voice. I couldn't believe what I was hearing and that it could be coming from someone who was too young to be thinking, let alone talking, like that.

Then he continued, "And if you forget your promise, I'll forget mine."

Again, I agreed.

I had always been very proud of my young son, and knew great things were bound to come from him. Certainly, great things did come from him, but they weren't always as startling.

Derek was the apple of my eye. I loved everything about him. I was the passionately-devoted father. Yet, as the years passed, he proved to be so evolved that I don't know if I fully understood him…the inner him, that is. His head may have been in the clouds, but his feet were solidly on the ground. I understood the "on-the-ground" side best.

Emily and I had wanted two children about a year and a half to two years apart so they would be good companions for each other. Our first child, Ken, was seven years older than Maggie and eleven years older than Derek. So, there really wasn't companionship. As it happened, the last two came four years apart, which was a little like having three families of one child each. None of our kids were very close to each other. They weren't antagonistic, but just spread too far apart on the age scale.

Maggie and Derek were fairly close as they were only four years apart. Ken, however, was so much older, with entirely different interests and friends, that it was like two people passing in the night. During school vacations there was communication between Ken and Derek, but not much as I remember.

Between his sophomore and junior years at Tufts University in Massachusetts, Ken was drafted into the army and went to Vietnam in the signal corp. Because he was majoring in journalism in college he got a journalism assignment in Vietnam keeping records and stuff for the big wigs. When he graduated from college he got a job with *The Globe* and since he knew Vietnam so well, the paper assigned him right back there. I must say I was proud of Ken for doing what he did and so young. But the result was Ken and Derek never had much time together.

Still, Derek never lacked for companionship because our next door neighbors, the Bassetts, had a son, Michael, just two weeks older than Derek. Those two were inseparable, and even Maggie wasn't needed as far as they were concerned. Michael was Derek's best friend. Both were very active kids, but good kids.

One Saturday, when they were about nine, I introduced them to fishing and bought both of them cheap rods and reels. I am not much of a fisherman and was quite surprised at how they took to the sport. Many Saturdays they would dash off on their bicycles to a lake or stream to fish. When they were in their early teens, they would sometimes go off fishing and camp overnight, mostly in the summer.

I never worried about them when they were together. Michael was big and both were strong and level-headed. As far as I was concerned, their friendship was an ideal situation. They walked or rode their bicycles to school together until Derek bought his car; then they rode together. They were in the same classrooms in primary and middle school. When Michael and Derek studied together, I think it was more like Derek teaching Michael. Michael wasn't stupid, but Derek was just so quick.

I remember how Derek would close out the entire world when he was concentrating. Nothing would bother him. Nothing would reach him. He was completely oblivious to everything except what he was doing. That was his way of getting done quickly what he had to do. Michael couldn't do this. Maggie couldn't do it. And neither could I.

Once Derek overheard me from the next room bragging to my brother about how bright he was and how he got all A's on his report card. Derek came in and told me (he didn't ask me, but told me), not to tell people things like that. He told us, "Anybody could do it if they would just let their mind go blank. That's where the answers are." Then he left the room.

My brother just looked at me, shook his head and said, "Heavy, heavy." Then he smiled and said, "Who is that kid's father anyway?"

At the time when Derek first mentioned letting your mind go blank to find the answers, I didn't understand what he was talking about. I have came to learn over the years that he was talking about letting the conscious mind go blank and using the subconscious mind, which knows everything, as in hypnosis, sort of a self-hypnosis.

Later that same day, I mentioned to my brother that an old friend of ours had prostate cancer. Derek was in the room again and piped up, "I'll bet he has negative feelings about his sexuality or the cancer wouldn't have chosen a sex gland. Mind is the builder; the physical is the result."

My brother turned to me, put his hand on my shoulder and said, "What do you think, the milkman's maybe...?"

Derek loved to be read to and he loved to be held. I remember watching Derek read. He must have been nine or ten at the time when I first noticed he was almost turning the pages he was reading so fast. I asked him, "Are you reading or just skimming?" He didn't respond. In a louder voice I called, "Asshole, I'm talking to you."

"What?" he said, coming out of his trance.

"I said 'Asshole, I'm talking to you.'"

He replied, with his broad smile, "Don't you ever call me or anybody else that again."

"So, you remember that conversation," I said with a big smile.

"As if it were yesterday. It taught me a valuable lesson. It taught me that if I really want to get someone's attention or want to make a point, I should swear. And remember, you're the son-of-a-bitch who taught me that."

I repeated my question about skimming or reading and he replied, "When I was learning to read fast, if I'd try to think about what I was doing while I was doing it, I couldn't do it. So, I had to eliminate all thinking except what I was reading. Now when I read I have no idea what's going on around me. I'm not there."

"Where are you then?" I queried.

"I don't know. My body is here," he replied, "but my thoughts are in the book."

"Would you say you're in a trance?"

"How would I know? I don't really know what a trance is."

"What do you think a trance is?" I asked.

"When you're out of it, I suppose. When your waking mind is not working. I don't know. When I sit on the porch I get sort of like that. I'm wide awake, but I'm not thinking of anything in particular. I'm sort of listening, but not listening to, or for, anything. I'm expecting, but I don't know what I'm expecting. Then sometimes thoughts come and sometimes they don't. When a thought comes, it's as if it were given to me, not something I thought of by myself. I'm in a peaceful state, but I don't hear voices. It's more like a bubble coming to the surface. When it gets there, it goes 'pop,' and there it is as if I were remembering something, except it's new or something no longer buried in the past. I'm often surprised. Once the thought is there I can play with it."

The sitting on the porch that Derek mentioned refers to a screened porch we have to the rear of the house. There is a love seat hanging by chains from the ceiling. For years he would just sit there gently rocking for long periods of time, staring out into the yard.

Derek told me of a hypnotist he'd seen on TV or at school, I can't remember which, and how he put a woman in a trance so she could remember anything, even from when she was a little baby. Derek said that was what he thought he did to himself. He said the hypnotist had explained that everything is stored in the subconscious and it's just a question of accessing it.

The hypnotist believed in reincarnation and said that past life regression was no more than putting a person into a trusting, receptive state so they could remember back into their past lives. Derek said the hypnotist explained how some people can remember what happened in the trance after they came out and others couldn't. The hypnotist had also said that some people are sensitive enough that in that trance-like state they could attune to the subconscious minds of others, people like Edgar Cayce or Jesus. This opened a whole new world of understanding for Derek. He realized then he had been exploring his subconscious mind.

I used to ask Derek, even when he was a little tot, if he would like to help me do certain chores like wash the car, work in the garden, or run errands. He would always smile and help. When he was very young, he was more of a hindrance than a help, but I didn't care. We were together and I loved it. I think he must have felt good about it, too—doing "man's work" with his father.

I remember one time when he was about eight I arrived home with a muddy car. He asked me if I wanted help washing it, but I told him I was too tired. He asked if it were all right if he washed it. I was halfway up the stairs when he asked. I went down to him and sat so we were eye-to-eye and gave him a big hug as if to say I'm so lucky to have you as my son.

Later, years later, he told his mother how that moment was a turning point in his life because he knew that my expression of love was God expressing love through me. From then on, whenever he did anything for anyone, he would pretend he was doing it for God. I wish he had said that to me. It might have been a turning point in my life, too.

Derek was very quiet when it came to his private thinking about God, but I know he thought about it a lot. One time when he must have been about seven, he asked, "Is God everywhere all the time?"

"I think so," I answered, a bit nonplused at hearing a question like that from such a young lad. "Why do you ask?"

"Then heaven and hell must be everywhere," he said.

"How do you figure that?"

"I just know," he replied, enigmatically.

"How do you know?"

"Well..." he began with a sigh as if he really didn't want to get into it. "In Sunday school, Mr. Benson says the Bible says God is spirit. And spirit is spirit, not an object, not worldly, not matter. Spirit is everywhere. There is no place where it isn't. There is no such thing as three-dimensional space in the spirit world. So, if we are created in God's image like the Bible says, we also are spirit and when we die we leave our bodies and are just spirit. If we go to heaven or hell, they have to be spirit also or we couldn't go there, but if we do, they couldn't have any affect upon our bodies because we don't have bodies anymore. So, we couldn't burn or play harps. I think we make heaven and hell with our minds. Good thinking makes heaven and bad thinking makes hell. Like greed and selfishness, instead of generosity and kindness."

I know these are not Derek's exact words, but in essence, this is what he said in his young vocabulary and, needless to say, I was impressed. In effect, he was saying we are not our bodies and that our bodies are just how we get around on earth.

Another time, when he was in high school, Derek and I were talking about the Vietnam War and some of his older brother's experiences there.

Derek became impassioned and said, "War is insane. Problems are not solved. So, somebody wins and gets their way in the short run, but in the long run the real problems are suppressed into the subconscious. Ethnic rivalries, religious or tribal hates, and national animosities may stay hidden for centuries, but they still exist and threaten peace and harmony. Eventually, they will surface again so we can reap the harvest of the unfortunate seeds we've sowed."

"That's probably true," I told him. "But what do you propose we do?"

"Well, a psychologist tries to bring the unconscious or subconscious fears, tensions, hates, anxieties to the surface of the patients' conscious mind because, as long as they are buried in the subconscious, they can't be dealt with or resolved."

"Yes, but what does that have to do with war?" I asked.

"Instead of war, nations or ethnic groups should try national or ethnic psychology where those involved are required to join in groups with their opposition and an arbitrator. They should then express their fears, distrusts, anxieties, hates, and so forth. This should be done long before the real problems arise."

"Would you like to be an arbitrator for that one day?" I asked him.

"Maybe. I hadn't thought about it, but if I could help I would like to."

Derek believed a good way to arbitrate was for one person to state the problem and the other person to state back the problem. The first person would then know if the other understood. If they didn't state it back correctly, the first person had the chance to repeat it. Once the person that stated the problem was satisfied, then, and only then, could the second person give a rebuttal. Derek was afraid this technique wouldn't work, however, because both sides lack the patience.

As I like to say, the young man knows the rules, but the old man knows the exceptions.

Derek so lived that he never had regrets or guilt. I asked him about this once. Glancing at the floor he blushed, "You're embarrassing me." Then he quietly admitted, "God is my guide," and started to leave the room.

I suggested, "You mean God is your conscience?"

"Call it what you will. It works," he said.

"But how do you know it's God guiding you?" I pursued.

"When I learned to read without pronouncing words, I was on my way to thinking without thinking words," he explained. "This put me closer to living in my subconscious which is closer to the mind of God. Eventually, and unconsciously, my thinking has become pervaded by God. Not that I'm thinking about God all the time. I'm not, but it's as if His spirit is with me, through me. My actions and thinking become semi-automatic and in accord with God." Then he added, "Please don't tell anyone. They won't understand."

"Then why did you tell me?"

"Because you asked," he said.

Derek wouldn't express his innermost thinking unless someone asked. He didn't want to be like many religious leaders who proclaimed "this is the way." That's why he and Josh, Michael's younger brother, got along so well. Josh also had a questioning mind.

The other day I came across some old writings of Derek's and part of them included a time he had seen a movie on travel in outer space. The movie had talked about possible life on Mars eons ago and signs of apparent water erosion. Yet, the atmosphere there was now too thin to support life as we know it and there is too little water to generate rain. A little frost and maybe carbon dioxide frost, but no rain as we know it.

Derek wrote about the fixed mentality of some scientists regarding possible catastrophic events. In paraphrasing his remarks, he commented on the fact that scientists were assuming Mars always had the same orbit in the solar system that it has now. He suggested they read Velikovsky's *Worlds In Collision* wherein Velikovsky reported that the early Chaldean astronomers, about 3000 BC, had reported only four "stars" that didn't move with the rest of the heavens, namely the planets Mercury, Mars, Jupiter, and Saturn. Venus was never mentioned, yet Venus is now the brightest of them all.

Velikovsky researched volumes of ancient writings and myths and came up with a theory, a proof in his opinion, that Venus was a comet (or Derek speculated a planet on a very elliptical course), until it had a close encounter with Earth at the time of the Exodus of the Israelites from Egypt. A second close encounter occurred 52 years later during the battle of Jericho when the sun stood still for awhile according to the Bible.

Then, before Venus settled into its present orbit, it went on to encounter Mars, maybe more than once, knocking Mars out of its former orbit so that Mars had three close encounters with Earth before it settled down to its present orbit—which is elliptical. And, it could have been more elliptical centuries ago, making it the apparent threat to Earth as envisioned by the Romans.

A former atmosphere of Mars could have been gobbled up by Venus and Earth at those times of close approach since both have a much greater gravitational pull. The mass of Mars is only 15% and Venus's 85% of the mass of Earth. Derek conjectured another possibility, if Mars was knocked out of its old orbit, would be that its new elliptical course could have brought it close enough to the sun before it stabilized on its present course so that the sun's solar winds could have blown away the majority of its atmosphere.

Mars could also have been between us and the Sun before its planetary encounters. If these hypotheses are true, then Mars could have had an atmosphere containing water and would have been warmer, being closer to the sun. Therefore, Mars could have supported life and could have had rain.

Harlow Shapley, who was head of the Harvard astronomy department in 1950 when Velikovsky's book was published, wouldn't even read the book. "Either he's crazy or we are," Shapley said because Velikovsky had explained that myths and ancient writings say Venus comes from Jupiter.

Derek contended Velikovsky should have said that it seemed to come from Jupiter, because Venus could have come close enough to Jupiter to be affected by its gravity and have its course changed—much like our space probes going to outer planets use nearer planets to spin around. This changes the space craft's direction and at the same time gives a substantial boost in speed. If Venus used Jupiter the same way, it would have appeared to the naked eye to have come from Jupiter.

Some other questions I remember Derek raising at one time or another were: What would have happened if billions of years ago the earth rotated much faster than it does now? How would that have affected its magnetism? Would the movement of the crustal plates have been faster, creating greater catastrophes? Would this account for some of the extremely contorted strata in some metamorphose rocks?

As you can see, Derek was always thinking and ready to speculate from an early age. Like any father, I suppose, I was bombarded by constant questions. Unfortunately, I wasn't able to answer many of the ones Derek came up with.

In the early fall of Derek's senior year in high school, I took him aside one night for a serious conversation. My heart was in my mouth. I was nervous as I told him, "I want you to pay careful attention to what I am going to say. My father had this same conversation with me when I was your age. I am not going to repeat it because I don't want you to think I'm pressuring you. I want you to follow the profession you want to follow and you have greater potential than I ever had, but I want you to know that if you ever want to come into the insurance business with me, there will always be a place for you."

"Thanks, Dad. I won't forget. Right now I don't know what I want to do," he replied and then quickly buzzed off, leaving me a little embarrassed and downhearted. That was it. I felt relieved I had said it. Of course, I wanted very much for him to come into my insurance agency, but he had such potential in so many directions, I didn't think it would come to pass.

Then came that night in late November of his senior year. When he first called home, no one was there so he left a message on the answering machine saying he wouldn't be home for dinner. We were curious, but not worried because he was very responsible. However, when it turned ten o'clock and Derek wasn't home yet, I began to worry. Finally, the phone rang. It was Derek.

"I won't be home tonight. I'm staying at Michelle Duval's. Good night."

"Who the hell is Michelle Duval?" I tried to ask, but he had already hung up.

At that time Derek was only 17, just three weeks shy of his 18th birthday. He had never stayed overnight at a girl's house before. And who was Michelle Duval? Emily didn't know either. If he thought his call had kept us from worrying, he was 100% wrong!

"Well, at least he called. I'm sure everything will be all right," I told Emily, though I wasn't at all sure. Neither was Emily, although she also tried not to show it. I tell you, we didn't sleep much that night.

Derek had dated girls, mainly Jan Hall, but not all that often and mostly to high school functions or athletic events. I don't know why, but I was pleased he didn't get serious with Jan. She seemed nice, but something about her grated me. She seemed to me to always want to be right. Jan was with Derek in his fatal accident and died instantly. None of us knew why she was with him.

The next morning, Derek's car pulled into the driveway. He popped out and went directly to his room and changed clothes. Then he flew down the stairs and was about to leave without saying a word.

Emily stood at the foot of the stairs as he descended. "Well…?" she said.

"I can't talk now or I'll be late. Tonight…," he said as he raced past her out the door.

That afternoon, Derek called Emily and asked if he could bring Michelle over for dinner. He said he wanted us to meet her because he thought they were in love. Or, actually, I believe he said he knew they were in love. Of course, Emily consented and immediately called me to deliver the big news and make sure I would be on time.

Six o'clock rolled around and no Derek. At 6:15 his car pulled into the drive. Even through our window I could see Michelle was cute, well proportioned, a little shorter than Derek and dressed in a smart-looking red dress. The style was flattering and her pearl necklace accented the outfit to give her a simple elegance. Her brown hair was almost shoulder length. She wore low-heeled black shoes and a white cardigan sweater over her shoulders.

"She's dressed to make a good impression," I said to Emily and Maggie who peaked out the window just as curiously.

"I can't believe it. Do you know who that is? She's the new French teacher who is tutoring Derek," Maggie explained.

"Oh, God!" Emily sighed, expressing my thoughts exactly.

In they walked, Michelle entering first. "These are my parents and my sister, Maggie. This is Michelle Duval," said Derek with a smile stretching from one ear to the other, full of pride.

Michelle graciously shook our hands and politely said hello while Derek continued, "I tried to tell Michelle we were simple folks and not to dress up, but she insisted. I must say she looks beautiful, don't you think?" Derek looked at her adoringly. It was obvious he was out to make sure we saw things as he did.

"Beautiful is too shabby a word. Divine would be better," I responded.

Michelle, although a bit nervous, certainly did radiate beauty, poise, intelligence, and joy. Emily was more reserved in her opinion, probably because she was a woman and Derek, her youngest son, was still just 17.

Emily politely ushered us into the living room where she had already set out appetizers. After we were seated Emily started in, "Derek hasn't told us anything about you, Michelle…except that he's in love."

"We're in love," Derek quickly corrected, and he was about to say more when Emily raised her hand.

"Why don't we let Michelle tell us?" Emily said.

So, Michelle proceeded to tell us about being born in Washington, her father being with the French Embassy, though now remarried and back in France, and her mother dying during childbirth with her younger brother. She told us about going to Middlebury College, graduating last June and now being in her first job teaching French at Derek's high school.

"How old are you?" Maggie asked bluntly.

"Twenty two. The same as you, Derek tells me."

As Maggie delivered her best glare in Michelle's direction, I figured it was my turn to chime in.

"How did you two meet and become such good friends, may I ask?"

Derek decided he would field that one. "Well, Michael and I were walking down the hall on the first day of school last September when this beautiful woman walked by in the opposite direction. It was Michelle, of course. I turned and watched her go by and she turned her head around and looked back at me. She quickly looked forward when she saw I was watching her. She was embarrassed and I was excited. I'd never been affected by a girl like that before. I told Michael right then she was the girl I was going to marry."

With that remark I shuddered and glanced over at Emily who was nearly choking on a bite of food.

Derek continued, "When I found out she was the new French teacher, my heart sank. I had already taken third year French which she was teaching, but I persuaded my student advisor to let me take the course again because her accent was so good and I was going to major in French in college, which was a lie. At that time I had no idea how good her accent was, but I convinced my advisor and he let me take her course."

I could hardly believe that my son had fallen in love. We all sat there listening to Derek and not knowing what to think or say. Derek took a deep breathe and started in again, unable to hold back an irrepressible smile as he relayed the story.

"Michael, as you know, is the football team captain and our best player. However, he was doing poorly in French II and Rusty Bianchini, the coach, was worried Michael might flunk his mid-term and would be ineligible to play out the season. Michael's French teacher, who is old enough to retire and not athletically friendly, had warned Rusty. So, Rusty approached Michelle about tutoring Michael. But, since Michelle is already working with many students, she suggested that I tutor Michael. You should have been there when she asked if I would have a problem working with him. I jokingly told her I didn't know, but I would give it a try. So, during a mutual free period Michelle gave me instructions as to Michael's assignments and how to tutor him and that's how it all started. We immediately hit it off extremely well. Michelle said she owed me a favor for tutoring Michael and I suggested private lessons in oral French. You can figure out the rest."

We continued to sit there, stunned, but listened politely as talk about the two of them continued into dinner.

Then Derek dropped the bomb. He announced that when he turned eighteen in three weeks and became legal age, he and Michelle were going to get married. I was about to explode, but, thank heavens, it was Emily who spoke up first.

She started in a calm voice, "It's one thing to fall madly in love with a woman who is four years your senior when one is much older. But, at almost 18, it's very unusual, to say the least. Also, to be madly in love when you're young is not uncommon, but to remain in love for a lifetime is again unusual when so many youthful marriages are ending up in divorce. Michelle seems to be a wonderful young lady, but we have only known her two hours, and you only two months. Don't you think you ought to know each other a little better? Maybe even live together a while. What's the rush?"

Emily's suggestion of living together came as a jolt to me. I had no idea she could think that liberally even when she was between a rock and a hard place.

But, then the second bomb fell.

"Michelle is pregnant and an abortion is out of the question," Derek explained, not sheepishly, but with enthusiasm.

A long silence ensued, until it was broken with an expletive from Maggie. "Asshole!"

I couldn't have agreed more.

Derek pleaded for understanding. "Have I ever gotten into serious trouble? Have I ever, ever given you reason to mistrust me? I even called you last night and told you I wasn't coming home and where I was, so you wouldn't worry...much," he added with a sheepish grin. "If you love me, you'll trust me now. I need your support."

Emily burst into tears. She got up, walked over to Derek, hugged him and kissed him on the forehead. "I love you, Derek, but you must know you have shaken me to my core. I want to, but it's very hard for me to trust." Then she paused, still crying, "But I will try."

I told Derek I loved him and I felt exactly like his mother. I assured him I would never desert him, even in times of trouble, and that he always had my support.

That must have reassured Derek enough to proceed with the third bomb of the evening.

"Also, I'm not going to college next fall," he said. "Two months ago you told me there would always be a place for me in your insurance agency. If that's still open, I'm going to take you up on it."

, wishing I had never said anything about that. Yet, with... , I said, "It's open Derek, but a man with your potential ...ollege."

...worry, I will go to college, but not in the fall. With the baby coming in July or August, and with learning the insurance business, I figure I'll enter the spring semester. I'm going to forget Harvard and Stanford and go to a local college where I can take some courses at night. After all, I have to earn money. I'll have a family to support and Michelle, with a new baby, won't be able to teach any more, at least not until the child is in school. I gotta work."

He seemed so mature, so responsible. He had it all figured out, but would the changeover from a carefree youth to a responsible adult, a working man, husband and father, break his youthful spirit? That was my greatest worry at the time. His only big mistake was to have accidentally impregnated a young woman. I realized he had worked two jobs to buy a car, managed the football team for four years, gone out for wrestling in high school, while also doing gymnastics at the Y, and still managed to get all A's on his report cards, but.... Could he make such an early shift to adulthood and be happy? This was such a giant step. His youth would be over. My eyes watered. I stood up and looked out of the window so no one would notice. I remember how my heart cried out in pity for him and how devastated I felt that night.

I assured Derek we were ready to extend help if needed. I knew he had never asked for anything, always relying on himself. I told him, "We want to do something, Derek, but what can we do?"

"You're already doing a lot. You've given me a job. I know you'll want to train me, so that's going to cost you something, but if you still want to do more, why don't you put me on the payroll for a dollar a month until I can work full time. That way I'll be on your group insurance policy in case Michelle's health insurance with the school is not enough. She has signed up to teach for one year which ends the last week of August, so her insurance should cover through the delivery."

I agreed to put him on my payroll. Then, if all that wasn't enough, the fourth and final bomb came, although we shouldn't have been surprised by anything at that point.

"If you still want to do something else, there is one more thing," Derek said. "Michelle's lease runs out in August. We can live there until then. What I would like to do is convert the third floor attic here into a four-room apartment for us. I'll do the work and pay for the materials and anything I have to hire to be done. In the end, you will own it all and, when you go to sell the house, it will be worth more. I'll share the utility bills."

Emotionally, I was drained and couldn't have said no even if I wanted to, which I didn't. I will never forget that night!

Derek had no fear. He figured everything would work out okay as it always did for him. As his quick and easy smile would suggest, he was very happy-go-lucky, but focused.

Our old home was a turn-of-the-century house and the third floor already had one finished bedroom (for a maid, I guess), and an old-fashioned bath with a tub on legs which Derek quickly replaced. He built a small kitchenette on the other side of the bathroom wall in a large storage area, which also became their dining area and living room.

In a large dormer he replaced a single window with two larger windows plus a windowed door which faced south and opened on to a small sun deck which he built. It was a small, but very attractive room. Next to the bedroom, Derek walled off a little room for the baby.

The apartment was finished before the baby arrived in late July. So, young Mike was able, just like his father, to move into the same house straight from the hospital.

Much thanks should be given to Michael for all the help he gave Derek in building the apartment and moving in. You would almost think it was he who was moving in with his new wife and child. Derek was so lucky to have such a devoted friend. Michael left for college in late August with a football scholarship, but visited every time he got home.

When Mike was a year old, running around, crying and, in general, disturbing the peace above us, we wished they or we weren't there. We finally realized that, with Maggie graduated from college and working in Boston, we no longer needed a large house. So, we bought a smaller, one-story house on the edge of town. We took out a 50% mortgage on the old house and gave that money to Maggie and gave the mortgaged house to Derek, reminding them both that it was part of their inheritance. Fortunately, we were financially able to do this. Ken was financially established so we didn't include him. He would have to wait for us to kick off.

Derek learned the details of the insurance business faster than he thought he would. By September, he had changed his mind and decided he could enroll in American University in Washington and take a light schedule with some evening classes. Combining a new job, new wife, new baby, and college took its toll on Derek and he got his first and only 'B' in one of his courses. Poor thing!

Derek's career in insurance was unusual in that he was only 18, yet, he was quite successful. He had taken insurance courses provided by the insurance companies in the spring of his senior year. Then, he started delivering renewal policies and getting to know our assured and sometimes getting an increase, or maybe a new policy on their auto or business. He also called on the parents of his classmates who knew he was valedictorian at graduation. There is no question in my mind that Derek's good looks, winsome personality, and beautiful smile were definite assets. The fact that he was the son of the agency's owner didn't hurt either.

On the night of Derek's auto accident, we were out. Upon returning, I went to the answering machine to see if we had any messages. There was a message from Michelle. Her voice trembled as she told us, "Derek's been in a serious auto accident and he's being taken to the hospital by ambulance. Michael was here when the police called. We are leaving now. I'll call you from the hospital."

I immediately yelled for Emily to come quick and began putting my coat on to rush out the door when the second message came on.

"This is Michael. We're still here at the hospital. We're going to stay awhile longer in case you're already on your way. If you're not here in 10 minutes, we'll come over. So…I guess we'll…. Well…we'll just talk to you then."

I know Michael didn't want to tell us over the phone, but I could hear Michelle sobbing in the background and I knew by the tone of Michael's voice that Derek had not survived the accident.

Emily had come rushing into the room and listened with me, but she had not heard the first message. "What was that all about? Who's in the hospital?" she asked with the concerned look of a mother who intuitively knew something was very wrong.

I couldn't talk. I was in utter shock. I played the tape back for Emily, holding her in my arms. She knew as well as I did, but was not about to accept it. Choking back the tears, she frantically began looking for her coat. "He's going to be all right. He has to be all right. Let's go to the hospital now! Let's go!" she shouted.

I can still hear Emily crying now just as though it happened yesterday. Our life has never been the same since. It seemed so wrong that such a fine young man with such promise should die so young, only 33. I have only to think about it, and I do often, and I choke as anger fills my soul. I will let Michelle and Michael tell the rest.

Chapter Three

Ken's Journal (April 2)

I was impressed and choked up as I read Dad's chapter. I have a feeling dinner with the family tonight will also be very emotional for me. We're headed over to Angelo's, the Italian restaurant where I took Jenny and the whole family the first time I brought her home to meet everyone. We really were in love. It was such a beautiful time, but it seems so long ago now.

Derek was still alive then. He and Jenny hit it off so well they sat next to each other and talked all through dinner. Part of me wishes she was here now. Maybe it would revive something that's missing.

While editing Dad's account last night, I began to wonder who the hell Jan Hall was because her name was so familiar. So, I asked Dad and he said she was the friend who died in the accident with Derek. At first, I figured that's why the name was familiar, but it still rings a bell with me for some other reason…but I'll be damned if I can place it.

Janet…I certainly didn't know her when I lived in Falls Church. I somehow think what I almost remember is important. I don't think it is favorable either. I mean not flattering, maybe sub-rosa. Maybe some article in a newspaper—maybe even in one of those scandal sheets. I don't know, but I eventually want to check it out.

Anyway, this morning I was all set to dive into another account about Derek, but, before I could get started, Mom presented me with her account. She told me again how happy she was to have me home and to see me helping out with this "family project." She appeared to be getting emotional and gave me a motherly kiss on the forehead. I looked up at her as if to ask why and she smiled, saying, "The answer is I love you. The question doesn't matter."

I know she thinks it's wonderful, although long overdue, that I'm getting to know my brother. And I am.

Mom's letter affected me much as Dad's did and sheds more light on not only Derek, but my parents as well. If I had known this would be such an *emotionally-involved project, I wonder if I would have still decided to come down, but I'm glad I did.*

Mom's Account

My pregnancy with Derek and the birth were uncomplicated, as it was with my two older children. He weighed 6 pounds 8 ounces and was normal and healthy. As all babies are cute, so was Derek, but he remained cute all his life. I say cute, rather than handsome, much like Michael J. Fox is cute, but Michael Jordan is handsome. I nursed him. He was a good baby. I had no complaints.

Derek went through the various phases of infancy that all babies do, except he walked and talked earlier than most. He loved to be read to. I don't know whether he memorized the stories or learned to read early, but he certainly knew when to turn the pages.

Maggie, his sister, was four years older than Derek and was very possessive of him. It worried me when she played with him as if he were a live doll, but he survived her sisterly affections. Her devoted attention ended when she went to school the next fall, and definitely was over when Derek was about one and walking and talking. After that it was a normal brother/sister relationship. A few squabbles, but not many. They didn't play together much, which was probably because Michael Bassett lived next door and was Derek's age.

Ken was eleven years older than Derek and the two of them were not close at all. They didn't argue or torment each other, but had totally different interests and friends. After all, 11 years is too many to hurdle and when Derek was old enough to be of interest, Ken was already at college or Vietnam.

Derek was always neat and organized. He kept his room in order and toys put back in the toy box when he was through, all without being asked. When he had chores to do he did them without a fuss and yet he found enough time to do the things he wanted to do. He wasn't a fuss-budget.

About the time Derek was in first grade, he started his habit of gently swinging on the swing on our back porch. He would just sit there and stare.

"I'm thinking," he would say.

Once I asked him what he was thinking about. He replied, "School."

"What about school?" I asked.

"It's a waste of time."

"Is that so? What makes you say that?"

"I already know what they're teaching."

I had always known Derek was bright, but we didn't think it was wise for him to skip grades. Socially, we felt he should stay with his age group, particularly since he was smaller than most of the boys. It's all right to be at the top of the class we thought, which he always was.

It was about that time, when he was in first grade, that he shocked me with some sound advice about the way I scolded his sister. "Don't make a big issue out of a little issue or Maggie won't catch on when you scold her for a big issue," he said.

I sometimes would call Derek "the thinker." He told me not to call him that.

"But you are. That's a compliment," I told him.

"Don't call me that, because there is derision in your voice."

"Derision? Where did you learn that word," I asked him, not believing my ears.

"I guess I made it up," he replied.

I looked it up to find out it means "an object of ridicule," so he had used it correctly.

Needless to say, raising Derek was always full of surprises. When he added such words to his vocabulary at such a young age, I wondered if he knew them from a previous incarnation and was just re-remembering.

In addition to being bright, Derek always had a sharp sense of humor. I remember one time around the dinner table I questioned Roger about what he thought was killing a bush by the front door.

Derek quickly replied, "A squirrel pissed on it…or was it Maggie…or Dad, or maybe even you, Mom. I know I didn't do it."

Derek quit Sunday School when he was twelve after an argument with his teacher, but he continued to do Sunday-school type reading and thinking on his own. In effect, he became his own teacher.

One day he was sitting on the swing again and I asked him my usual question, "What are you thinking about today?"

"Life," he said.

"What about life?" I asked.

"You wouldn't understand," was his flattering reply.

"Oh, really. How do you know?"

"'Cause you don't think like I do."

"Try me," I challenged.

He smiled and started in, "Close your eyes and concentrate on the front of your brain, not thinking of anything, just being quiet. I am very much awake when I do this, but it's like listening for a thought, not creating one. Like straining to see what's beyond the horizon. You try it."

So, I did. Maybe not long enough, but I couldn't eliminate thoughts. One thought would come up and then another and so forth. I told this to Derek and he replied, "See, I told you that you don't think like I do."

"So, what are you saying? I'm scatter-brained?"

"You said it, Mom. I didn't," he replied. "The only thing I can't stop being aware of at first is my breathing, but finally even that goes. After my mind gets still, I start to feel a pulsing in my forehead just outside my skull. Sometimes this happens quickly and sometimes, when my mind is active or I have other things I should be doing, it doesn't happen at all. I tend to think, when I feel the pulsing, that it is God knocking. If I don't feel it, I'm tempted to say 'Where are you God?' but, instead, I say 'Where am I, God?' for God is always there. It's me who is distracted. After the pulsing, I move my attention to the top of my head and then upward, as if I were following up a straight horn like a unicorn's horn. Following a horn, I know is a gimmick, but it works for me so I use it."

"A horn?" I questioned, jokingly giving him a look like he was crazy.

"If it doesn't work for you, don't use it. Instead, just raise your consciousness above your head. Actually, that's a gimmick, too, because you aren't out of your head."

"Maybe you are," I suggested with a grin.

"The whole purpose of all this is to stop conscious thinking and let all my thinking be almost unconscious, like involuntary," he explained. "When I get to the end of the horn, I think my mind is out of my brain, so, I can't think. If I do, then I am back in my brain and I have to start over again."

It was fascinating to sit there and listen to Derek talking about all this, although I have to say he lost me on some of it. I can remember how excited he was and how his eyes used to light up.

"So, tell me what it feels like when your mind is out of your brain," I said, encouraging him to continue.

"When I am out of my brain and not thinking my own thoughts, I am in what I call 'God's country,' the infinity of God, and I try to let God take over my thinking. I smile slightly because, unless I am joyful,

I can't experience God. When I'm in God's country, all I'm aware of is my breathing, so, I imagine I'm breathing in the God force; his love, pure energy, and joy. I either store it in the top of my head or breathe it out to the world. When I feel connected to God, I shower that feeling of connectedness back into my body from head to toe. I almost tingle. It's very serene. The more I do this, the quicker it happens. I suspect, eventually, I will be there most of the time, whether I am sitting or not. I just listen. I'm working on being able to get in and out of God's country quickly. I try to think only what He wants me to think which is usually nothing."

"What's the point of thinking of nothing?" I asked.

"It's great!" he said with enthusiasm. "It's so peaceful. It's like God, with all His love, is right there all around me, through me, as if He were me. I feel as if I am radiating God's love to the world."

"Maybe that's the Holy Spirit," I suggested.

"Maybe, but I don't like to think of it that way," Derek explained. "If people thought of God as the universe and the Son as this world and the Holy Spirit as the God within us that we can contact, it might be all right, but people don't think of it that way. Anyway, the three are all one. We should think of God as the 'Wholly Spirit.'"

"Yes, well..." I began to say before another idea quickly jumped into Derek's head.

"That reminds me of Mr. Benson at Sunday School," he said. "He talks, using other men's words, about what he's read or been taught. I don't think he ever had any personal contact with God."

"And you have?" I questioned.

"Yes," was his startling reply. "If God is spirit, He doesn't have a body. He is everywhere. If He is everywhere, He is also in my brain and yours, too. So, if we can get rid of our thinking, we can open ourselves to His thinking."

"If He is everywhere, then Mr. Benson has had contact with Him also, hasn't he? Hasn't everybody?" I replied.

"I don't believe so. The fact that he is everywhere simply means that anyone can have contact with him, but they must first open their minds to Him. It's our thinking that gets in our way, keeping us separated from God. God won't compete with us. He has given us free will. We have to let go and let God. Mr. Benson says it's my thinking that's going to send me to hell. He wants me to accept what he says. I say it's my duty to think things through for myself. God doesn't want a robot or puppet to play with. He gave us free choice to be separated from

Him or not to be. It's our choice. No one can do it for me just like no one can die for me. I gotta do it for myself!"

"That's very true," I remarked, not knowing what else to say.

"This business of Jesus shedding his blood for us and, therefore, we're saved is very incomplete. It's not automatic. We have to follow the teachings of Jesus. You know…love, forgiveness, service. A spiritual law is 'as you sow, so also shall you reap.' Jesus knew this law and, therefore, knew he would have to die or shed blood, or something of equal personal harm if he was going to attack the wrong teachings of the religious leaders of his day. He would refer to the scribes and Pharisees as hypocrites, saying one thing and doing another. 'Don't follow them!' Jesus was saying. He attacked the errors of the church of his day. So the harvest he reaped was that he was also attacked, crucified. Yes, he shed his blood for us so that we might know the errors of the old ways and how we should live. However, there is nothing automatic about our being saved if we don't follow his teachings."

I was always so proud of my son. I also learned a lot from him. I used to always look forward to our little discussions, although many times they weren't so little.

Derek had worked out a system of understanding God that he described to me, "The first and foremost requirement to experience God is to believe God exists. Not just to say 'Yeah, I believe it,' but to really know that God exists and is right here all the time, right here in my brain, as well as everywhere else. I've got to feel it. I've got to know it, really know it. I've got to believe it. When you've done that, you've completed step one. Then you've got to desire to access God by letting go of anything the ego wants and allowing God to come through. Be detached from all worldly things and happenings. This isn't easy because the ego wants to be there to see what's happening, to control what's happening. This is why I can't ask questions of God when I'm in God's country because that's the ego asking the questions. God already knows what we need or want to know. That's what I'm working on now."

"Do you ever hear voices when you're working on this?" I asked.

"No, I don't hear voices. I sometimes think I'm given thoughts, which I sometimes doubt. Sometimes I get a feeling, which, again, I sometimes doubt. I never want to be in touch with the spirit of someone who is dead. I do not want to be a channel for some entity I can't see. It could be right, but it could also trick me into error. I want direct communication with God. If God chooses to send some discarnate soul, or an angel even, to help me, that's up to God. But I hold God responsible, no one else."

"What about holding yourself responsible? You said he gave us free will."

"That's true and I do. Actually, getting back to freedom of choice, let me give you an example. There is nothing evil about a gun. It's lawful when the trigger is squeezed for the firing pin to hit the bullet. It's lawful for the powder to explode. It's lawful for the bullet to follow a curved trajectory. It's lawful that when it hits a body that the flesh break apart and that the body may no longer support life. So, what is wrong? What is evil? It was the freedom of choice to aim the gun and pull the trigger. We have the freedom to believe what we want to believe or to follow a misinformed leader, but it is always we who are responsible for our choices. It's not just what you have been told is truth, like Mr. Benson believes, it's what you have come to know through personal study, what you intuitively know, the truth you're really conscious of."

Then he added, "God speaks to you, too, Mom, but you don't listen. We all have that potential. God is God, everywhere and everything, and we all are a portion of that oneness. It's subtle, but there is no way we can be outside the whole even if we feel we are. We have to step aside and watch. That is, our conscious mind has to step aside. In nature there are neither rewards nor punishments…only consequences."

In another discussion, Derek claimed, "Jesus should have his second coming right now. A thousand different sects of Christianity can't all be right. The Christian religion has strayed so far from Jesus' teachings that we need his help right now."

"Maybe He is coming," I offered.

"Maybe. Yet, if He were, would the leaders of the various sects or denominations recognize him? Would they accept his right thinking and drop what they now think is right? Or would they crucify him again. Would some radical fundamentalist shoot him? I think the latter, I'm sorry to say. I hope I'm wrong."

"Well, I hope you're wrong, too," I agreed.

"If he were to come and teach us how to experience God directly, individually, each on his own, and not preach the church's old set of right thinking and behaving, then he might have a chance to get his message across and not be done away with."

"Do you really believe that? Why do you say that?" I asked.

"Let me give you an example. Martin-Marietta, the defense contractor, is allegedly working on a very secret project, above top-secret. It was reported that two of their scientists were caught talking about the project out of shop. They both were murdered. It was called suicide, but their boss is scared to death for her own life. She knows they were not the suicidal type. If that's how bad it can get in this country's scientific/military community, why should we think radical, fundamentalist men in the religious community would behave otherwise at the time of the second coming?"

"Well, I hope it would be different because everyone would know it was the second coming," I said, debating the possibility in my mind. "But maybe it's possible everyone wouldn't know that."

"That's right," he exclaimed. "And even if everyone did, there could be a lot of people unreceptive to Him. I think the second coming will be a soul who will come to unite all religions. For Christians it will be a soul with the message of Jesus. For the Jews it will be their Messiah. For the Buddhists it will be "a holy one, a supremely enlightened one, with wisdom embracing the universe." For the Hindus Vishnu said, "When evil is rampant on the Earth, I will assume a human body to restore tranquility." For the Moslems Mohammed said "the Guided One of great power, wisdom and knowledge" will come. Sathya Sai Baba, currently alive in India, says he is the one who is to unite in peace all religions. You should read at least one book about him, Mom."

Derek was only 13 or 14 when he discussed most of this. His voice had just changed. Obviously, I was surprised and impressed. I wondered how I came to produce such a remarkable child. I know I have written as if Derek was saying everything in a long speech. He didn't do it that way. Some of these ideas would come out one day and another maybe a month or even a year later, but this was his thinking. I can't possibly remember which thought came first, or how old he was when he said it, or his exact words any more than the writers of the Bible could about Jesus when they wrote the Gospels some 30 to 60 years after the his death. Most of the Gospels were not written by Matthew, Mark, Luke, and John. Rather, after they had already died, the Gospels were then written by their followers.

I remember another time I interrupted Derek's back porch swinging.

"What's it about today?" I prompted.
"Shadows."

"What about shadows?" I pursued as I settled into a chair for one of our "little" discussions.

"If I put a three-dimensional object, like a box, in the sun," he began, "it makes a shadow which has only length and breadth, but no depth; in other words, two dimensions. If I could take a shadow, like a piece of paper, and stand it on end in the light, it would make a line for its shadow, that is, one dimension or length only. If I were to take a line and aim it at the sun, it would make a point for its shadow. That would be no dimensions, not length, breadth, nor width. Anybody can understand that. My problem is trying to understand what it is that makes a shadow that has three dimensions like us or a box. It's easy to conclude that a four-dimensional object would cast a three-dimensional shadow, but we three-dimensional creatures with our three-dimensional mentality, find it very difficult to envision what a four-dimensional object looks like. What is the fourth dimension?"

"I don't know. I never thought about it. What do you think it is?" I asked.

"Imagine for a moment being in a two-dimensional world of only length and breadth. Now someone throws an object, say a ball, into your dimension or plane. As it enters your plane it is first a dot, then rapidly it becomes a small circle, then larger and larger circles until the ball is halfway through your dimension. Then the circle becomes smaller and smaller until it becomes a dot again and disappears. Think how difficult it would be for a person with a two-dimensional mentality to visualize a three-dimensional ball, instead of all those smaller and larger two-dimensional circles."

"Well, I guess it would be pretty difficult," I said, having no idea how else to respond.

"I read somewhere," Derek continued, "that someone thought time was the fourth dimension, but I can't go along with that. All the other shadows of the one, two, and three-dimensional objects are in the here and now, but time is always a variable. Time does not cast a shadow."

Then Derek again talked about Sathya Sai Baba, the spiritual leader in India, who is known to have materialized the sacred ash of the Hindus, as well as rings and trinkets, out of thin air.

"Sai Baba claims he merely thinks on what it is he is going to materialize and there it is," said Derek. "Jesus changed water to wine and fed a multitude with a few loaves and fishes and gathered up twelve baskets full of scraps when the meal was over. If Sathya Sai Baba makes these materializations and says he does it by thinking, then I am going to believe him. I am certainly not going to believe a scientist, who can't materialize anything, anymore than I am also not going to believe Carl Sagan, the astronomer, when he says he doesn't believe in UFOs because 'they can't get here from there'—as if our technology were perfected."

"So, you believe in UFOs?" I asked.

"UFOs have been photographed and videotaped and seen by millions. Even ex-President Carter has documented he saw one when he was governor of Georgia. Just two hundred years ago a similar remark to Sagan's would have been made by many so-called brilliant scientists about airplanes, automobiles, electric lights, and television. If Sai Baba can cast a three-dimensional shadow—that is materialize an object by thinking—then thinking, or mind, or thought, or an idea, must be the fourth dimension. What I am trying to work out now is what controls thought, or rather, what is the fifth dimension that creates the four-dimensional shadow of a thought or an idea."

"What do you mean?" I asked.

"Let's see. I know that if you gave me a loaded gun and you had a loaded gun and you told me that if I didn't shoot you before you counted to ten, you would shoot me, I still couldn't pull the trigger. Why? Because my mind couldn't conceive you would do such a thing, because I would never kill anybody. Because the standards by which I make my decisions precludes killing people. My ideals do not allow me to do away with someone for my personal benefit, or because I don't like someone, or because I am fearful of this or that. My purpose in life is to be peaceful, thoughtful, and helping; none of which allows killing. I, therefore, can not engage in the kind of thinking that is against my standards, my ideals, and my purposes in life. So, if something has a control of the way I think, then it must be related to the fifth dimension which casts a fourth-dimensional shadow, which, in turn, casts a three-dimensional shadow, and then, of course, a two-dimensional shadow like that which we see all the time."

Then Derek added, "Thinking the way I do, I can't conceive of being pushed into or attracted to a situation like that."

"I'm glad to hear that," I said. "So...."

"I don't think I have ever done anything in this life, or past lives, that would lead me into a situation like that where I needed to learn that kind of a lesson. Of course, one rarely knows about past lives, but everything is going so well for me this time around I just don't believe I've got that kind of skeleton in my closet. I could be wrong, but...."

"Well, I hope you're right," I told him.

This gave me another insight into Derek's mind. It made me wonder how I could be his mother. He was probably in high school when he said all this. Of course, as I have said before, these are my understandings, not his exact words. I keep saying that because I remember how much it aggravated Derek that the authors of the Bible had not said the same when writing about Jesus' life.

I don't know if it was how we raised Derek, or if he was just born that way. I tend to think the latter, but, just to give some background, I'll write a little about our family life.

Roger and I have always had an excellent, happy marriage. A few disagreements to be sure, but never a fight. Our children were not exposed to constant bickering. Roger took care of his insurance business, came home at a reasonable hour, maybe even early by some men's standards, worked around the house and yard, and tended our garden. He also helped with the children and cleaned the dinner dishes while I took care of the housekeeping, laundry, cooking, shopping, and the babies. Roger and I played bridge at least once a week. After Derek was in school the full day, I went back to teaching.

Marge Bassett, Michael's mother, lived next door. She and I were the best of friends. We were about as close as Michael and Derek. She was also a teacher in the same school where I taught. During the years before our boys were in school full time, she and I got together for coffee every morning while our boys played and we also took our boys on excursions to the park or swimming, usually when we went shopping. Sometimes we even went on family vacations together. Roger and Ralph Bassett were also good friends. It was an ideal two-family setup.

Shortly after Derek and Michael were a year old, Marge became pregnant again. Josh was born a month before Michael's second birthday. Although Josh went with us on our get-together, he was, for several years, too young to be close friends with Derek and Michael. Michael would tend to exclude Josh and even tease him, but Derek would protect him and include him when he wanted to come along.

Josh had a vivid imagination and didn't seem to mind playing quietly alone. He was, by nature, a quieter person than his brother. By the time Josh was old enough for the Boy Scouts he accompanied Derek and Michael much more frequently. About the time Michael got tied up with high school athletics and girls, Josh started coming over frequently to talk with Derek. This developed into a very close friendship. Eventually, he shared the house with Derek and Michelle, living in the third floor apartment and later, after college, he worked for Roger and Derek in their insurance agency, but I'm getting ahead of myself.

Derek and Michael were both athletically inclined, but Michael was 6'2" in high school while Derek was only about 5'6". They were frequently called "Mutt and Jeff" after the comic strip characters.

Roger introduced Derek and Michael to fishing when they were quite young and it stuck. Michael's father on several occasions took the boys, including Josh, on weekend backpacks in the Blue Ridge Mountains of western Virginia which the boys loved.

After my mother died, my father came to live with us. One day Derek told me that Grandpa was going to get more forgetful if he used those big pillows. He said they put his brain higher than his heart and then his brain gets less blood.

Before Grandpa died, Derek came back and explained that maybe Grandpa wasn't really forgetful, but was using his right brain more now than before, the left brain being the one that involves speech and reasoning and the right brain being more intuitive. He wondered if this might be true for most people as they grow older, becoming more right-brained and less left-brained.

"Maybe we become more intuitive and less language-orientated with age," Derek said. "Maybe it's easier, requiring less energy and we get lazy." Then he wondered if it was because old folks thought they were getting more forgetful that they started a self-fulfilling prophecy about helplessness in old age. "After all," he said, "mind is the builder. We attract to ourselves what we think—good or bad." Derek often said this.

"Even the Bible tells us," he reminded me, "'for as a man thinketh in his heart, so is he.' The stronger the desire, or fear, the more potent it is and if we are doing something we know we shouldn't be doing, the more potent the reaction. What we do innocently has much less of a reaction. It takes less energy."

Another time Derek commented that Grandpa had said he doesn't pay attention to the words of a song, but just listens to the music. Derek wondered if this also indicated Grandpa was using more of his right brain instead of the word capacity of his left brain.

Derek thought a lot about Grandpa. He once told me, "Unless Grandpa develops a purpose in life, he won't live long." And he didn't. Shortly before his death, Derek told me we can't heal Grandpa by praying because he has already decided to die and he has that right.

Prayer, Derek believed, isn't usually effective because it has no "juices" in it. The person praying doesn't really believe his prayers will be answered, so they aren't. If one doesn't have faith in what he's doing, it won't work. God doesn't give us anything. It's because we get in accord with truth, love, and law that things can and do happen.

That's why group prayer is more effective. It's not because more people praying give it more power, because one person, like Jesus, could do it alone with enough faith. But in group prayer, people are apt to have more faith in the prayers of the others than in their own prayers alone. It's their faith in the group that makes the difference. I strongly believe this, too.

A smoker can't effectively pray to stop smoking if he wants to smoke more than he wants not to smoke. It's a question of energy. The universe says mixing this energy with that energy produces this or that effect. To pray that a lawful effect will not follow a cause is a waste of time. God doesn't play favorites. The law of cause and effect is a truthful principle, a cosmic law. Actually, Derek believed every thought is a prayer of sorts because it sends out energy to effect change or to keep things the same. Thoughts are things.

Derek said it often appears that we do not have freedom to choose because we wouldn't choose to have poor health or poverty. The question is when did a poor person choose to be poor? Maybe it was when that person decided not to study or do homework. Maybe it started when a person rebelled as a teenager against parental authority. Maybe it was when a person took what was supposed to be a temporary job to earn beer money and beer or drugs became a debilitating habit. Maybe a person was born into a family where there were no incentives and never learned anything but negative attitudes; or maybe a child is born with an older sibling and believes subconsciously that he is inferior with no self-esteem because he can't do what his older sibling can do—not considering the difference in their ages.

When we choose is not always apparent, but it usually comes early. We have developed attitudes, habits, and priorities that head us in one direction rather than another.

A friend of mine was over one afternoon and Derek was listening to her complain about what the schools were and were not teaching. Derek jumped in, "The schools teach us a lot of facts and ways to do things, but 50% of our teaching is done at home like values and attitudes. The question you should be asking is 'What am I teaching?'"

Derek confided he thought drugs should be legalized to give people a freedom of choice. When we try to take away freedom of choice we create a desire. He wrote a poem about that.

> When Eve offered Adam the apple red,
> She didn't say eat and come to bed.
> But placed it coyly at his feet
> And said "Of this fruit you must not eat."
>
> Millenniums have passed,
> But one thing's for sure,
> 'Must not' and 'Can not'
> Remain the best lure.

Derek said, "Think of all the money we spend now trying to enforce the drug laws which could be spent, instead, on education against drugs or healthful programs for youth. Teaching some youths about the evils of drugs may entice them to use drugs because they are rebellious or have lost self-esteem and want to escape or self-destruct. They might be just bored without purpose or direction and think if drugs are really that bad, they must be exciting. The thought of taking a chance is exciting, gambling proves this. Therefore, the teachers against drugs, or any crime, should emphasize the potential that can be lost, that every soul has a niche, be it big or small, to do good. *It's not what you do, it's why you do it.*

"If we're going to keep drugs and drug dealing illegal, then the punishment should be commensurate with the rewards. This business of putting someone in jail for a few weeks or years even, is nothing. The dealers get out and they are often right back dealing but being more careful not to get caught. I say castrate them. If the offense is not horrendous just take one testicle the first time. Castration should be used for all felonies. No male wants to be castrated. Legislators talk about 'three strikes (felonies) and you're out' (imprisoned for life). With castration you get two strikes before you can't reproduce and go through an unwanted personality change, then on the third strike you get jail for life. Believe me, many a youth will not start on the road to crime or drugs if he knows the consequence is castration. After the loss of one testicle a male will really think twice before he takes the chance of losing the other one. A man can still lead a normal life with one testicle, but with no testicles it's a very different ball game. With women it would be the ovaries."

"Do you really think that would be the thing to do?" I asked.

"Sure. Can you imagine the disappearance of crooked politicians, bankers, lawyers, stockbrokers as well as drug dealers? Castration is the answer for punishing felons of all types. It would be so simple and so inexpensive."

"Well, I'm sure it would be a much more effective deterrent," I said. "But it's hard to imagine our legal system going to something like that from where it currently is."

"Yes, it may be hard to imagine," he replied, "but there is another good effect from castration or sterilization. That person can't reproduce when the second testicle is gone. The kids in this screwed up world who are most screwed up come from screwed up families. Sterilization will keep many of these kids from being born, not just off the streets like jails do.

"If an unmarried mother on welfare has another kid, sterilize her. Don't just take her off welfare because that is punishment to the kids and not to the willful, unmarried mother on welfare."

"That really is punishing the child," I agreed.

"Rape and certain sex crimes like child molestation would mean total sterilization on the first offense," Derek continued.

"Don't you think that's a bit severe?" I asked.

"It would work," he simply replied. "Believe me, it would work. Yet it would not be death or as expensive as life imprisonment, and afterwards these people could still care for the kids they already have and do meaningful work. They could still be an asset to society."

Another time I asked what was on Derek's mind he replied, "Gene mutation."

"I should have guessed. What about gene mutation?" I replied, checking my watch to see if I had time for one of our discussions.

When he was asked something, Derek could talk, but he was unwilling to promote or even discuss his ideas unless he was asked. I mentioned this to him once and he replied that more people should do that before they sound off. He was constantly on guard against becoming like those many past theologians who created dogma. He didn't want to find out he was wrong and find out that people had accepted what he said was truth.

This time he wasn't reluctant to explain. "All matter is energy. Einstein postulated this and it was proved when the atom bomb went off. So, our bodies are nothing but energy. Since brain waves can be measured, they must be energy also. Nothing happens, but thinking makes it so. So, if you have the energy of thought impinging on the energy of our DNA, or our cells in general, is this enough to cause gene mutation? Scientists seem to think the gene mutation comes first, but I wonder. Psychosomatic illness is caused by thinking. But scientists are rarely quick to stray from traditional perceptions. Courage is the power to let go of the familiar."

"I believe that," I agreed.

"Biologists claim they have discovered a gene for homosexuality. Did the homosexual tendency come from the gene or was the mutant gene created by homosexual thinking, activity, and desire? Also, if gene mutations are created by our thinking, did this happen in this life or in past lives?"

Derek believed in reincarnation. He believed that too many very intelligent spiritual leaders, particularly in other parts of the globe, and early Christian theologians in the first and second centuries believed in reincarnation for him to say they are wrong just because the greater body of Christians today don't believe in it or don't want to believe in it.

"Besides, reincarnation explains so many inequities like why one person is born deformed and dumb and another healthy and bright," Derek said. "We are attracted to the lessons we have to learn because we flubbed up last time. All great ideas first come as blasphemy."

Given Derek's strong feeling about sex being reserved for one's spouse, the biggest shock of my life came when he brought Michelle over for dinner for us to meet and then announced they were going to be married because she was pregnant. I know Roger wrote about that night and his commentaries on that evening echo mine, so I won't go into it further.

Even though I was shocked at the time, I easily grew to love Michelle. She is a wonderful, thoughtful person and they were, as Derek often said, meant for each other.

Even though I know Derek believed death was simply passing through one door into another room, his death was extremely painful for me. I did so love Derek. He was the perfect son, the perfect person.

I know Derek believed that mourning over a deceased person makes it harder for that soul to adjust in the life to come, but I couldn't help myself then and I still grieve. However, I do say, "I love you, Derek, and I miss you, but I have released you. Go in peace." For the time being, that's the best I can do. He is released. Still, I am crying as I write this.

Michelle and Michael told me, even before the funeral, that Derek's last words were that he wanted them to marry before their second child was born so the baby's last name would be Bassett.

I think they should have realized Derek was in a coma when he said this and could not have been in his right mind. I wanted my new grandson to be Derek Saul, Jr., not Derek Saul Bassett.

Nevertheless, I dearly love my grandsons and I must say Michelle still is as close to me as if I were her own mother. Thank God. I love her so. And I love Michael. I always have. He's like a third son.

In closing, let me say that Derek was right in encouraging Michelle and Michael to marry. Children do better with two parents. But, did it have to be before the baby was born? Although Derek never could be replaced in Michelle's heart, she needed Michael, and Michael worshipped Michelle. I am sure they will always be a devoted couple and will be the best possible parents for my grandsons.

Chapter Four

Ken's Journal (April 2nd, late)

After we got back from dinner at Angelo's, I headed off to bed, but found myself reliving all the conversations of the evening. Then I began reading Maggie's account about Derek. And now I'm wide awake.

Dinner was very enjoyable. I had the chance to see people I haven't seen in a long time as a good bit of the extended family showed up. I had no idea so many people would be joining us. Even Aunt Maureen, who's now 89 years old, was there. She's still as quick as ever.

As I expected, it did feel a little strange going to Angelo's for the first time since Jenny and I went there together. With all that's going on between us right now, I couldn't help but drift back to that time throughout the evening. It struck me how different I was back then.

I certainly had more enthusiasm for life than I do now. And, unlike Derek, I still have a chance to enjoy the many things that do bring me happiness in this world.

It's beautiful here tonight! I think I'll sit out on the sun deck and enjoy it while I finish editing Maggie's account.

Maggie's Account

My point of view, as Derek's sister, would probably be a lot different if I had told it when we were young, rather than now, after I have turned forty and he has passed on. I will try to write from the viewpoint of a child when I write about our earlier years. Use your imagination and bear with me.

I can remember Derek when he came home from the hospital as being just like a live doll. I remember always wanting to play with him as if he were a doll. Mother was protective of him, of course, so I was as careful as a four year old could be and he survived.

I cannot remember thinking that I was being neglected when he was a baby because he got more attention than I did, which he, of course, needed since he couldn't do anything for himself. Yet now, being a mother, I'm sure I knew I wasn't king pin anymore, or queen pin. This is bound to have had some affect, but I have no conscious remembrance of it.

When I started school, Derek was a year old and starting to talk quite well. I played less with him after that. He was walking and into everything of mine and not at all careful. I ended up having to pick up after him. In short, he became more of a pain than a pleasure.

Then, too, Michael was always around for him to play with and he preferred Michael who was the same age and lived next door. Sometimes, when I was at school, the two of them would get into my things and make the worst kind of a mess. That really pissed me off.

As he grew older it was obvious that Derek was very bright. He would come up with questions that I would never think of, even though I was four years older. I remember one. It will sound dumb, but you have to remember he probably was less than 15 months old at the time.

It was a foggy morning. Derek looked out the window and asked, "What's that?"

"It's foggy out," Mother replied.

"Can I go out in the foggy?" Derek asked.

"Sure. It won't bother you," Mother told him.

But Derek replied, "Might I get loose in the foggy?"

I remember once he walked under the belly of a horse, but that certainly doesn't show brains. He must have been about one then. Dad panicked running around the horse to get him as Derek nonchalantly walked back under. I grabbed him before he could do it again.

Derek never seemed to get into trouble and I always got the blame for anything that went wrong or was left out of place. Of course, I often was the guilty party, but all the brothers of my girlfriends were the ones who caught hell, even if it was my girlfriend that did it.

But not Derek. It's not that he was sneaky and got away with things, he just never got in trouble. And it's not that he always sat around watching TV, most of the time he was running around like crazy. He and Michael, what a pair!

Derek had a good sense of humor and was always smiling. He was cute and people used to call him cute. Nobody ever called me cute. I guess you can see why I took to playing with my friends at their houses. I didn't dislike Derek. I liked him. But I guess you could say I resented him a little.

Another thing, after that baby stage, he was neat. I wasn't. He always hung up his clothes and put away his toys. By the time he was in school, he made his bed before he came down to breakfast. He even pinned his socks together when he put them in the wash so he wouldn't lose just one sock. I asked him once, "How come you're always so neat?"

He said, "That way I don't get shit from Mom and Dad like you and Ken do."

Ken was our older brother, seven years older than me. Derek was smart and this was the way he thought, and Derek did say "shit" often. Oh, yes, Derek liked to swear. He swore all the time even in front of our parents, but as long as he didn't say the "f" word, they wouldn't object. But could I swear? No! It wasn't lady-like. When our parents weren't around, we both swore like troopers!

One nice thing about Derek was he never squealed on me, or anyone else as far as I know. He would just laugh at us and call us stupid. Derek was far from stupid. Almost never doing homework at home, he still got all A's. Not that my parents rubbed it in about Derek's great grades, but it was hard to know you're not as bright as your younger brother.

As we got older we would sometimes go to the movies together. Derek would cry in movies during the highly emotional scenes. Not the sad scenes as much as the ones which showed great achievement or great joy. You know, the scenes that if you were there you'd think "great going!"

He even took me fishing once, but I didn't like it. I didn't like standing around doing almost nothing and then end up not catching anything. With Derek and Michael, it was not only a contest between them, but a contest with the fish to see if they could outwit them. Dull, dull, dull was my reaction and Ken's, too.

One summer we were having a drought and the town asked everyone to conserve water; no watering lawns or washing cars and so forth. One afternoon the bathroom door wasn't closed tight so I just walked in and there was Derek pissing in the sink.

"What the hell are you doing?" I demanded.

"Conserving water," he said, quickly turning his back towards me. "What the hell are you doing?"

"What do you think? I need to use the bathroom. Why are you pissing in the sink to conserve water?" I asked him.

"Because I can rinse this sink with three cups of water whereas it takes three gallons to flush the toilet and, besides, this way I don't have to wipe off the rim of the toilet when I splash."

"But think of all the germs," I complained.

"Piss doesn't have germs if your kidneys are working, only dissolved salts," he replied.

I complained to Dad and he told Derek to stop, but Derek said he wouldn't. Dad finally acquiesced as long as Derek used a bottle and poured it directly down the drain and then ran the faucet. I never caught Derek pissing in the sink again. Derek and Michael were always pissing in the yard. It was too much trouble to come inside and what difference does it make anyway they would say.

The same fall I left for college, Derek entered high school and we only saw each other during vacations. He was always curious about what I was studying and I was always impressed with all he already knew. "How do you know all this stuff?" I asked.

"Pick up a little here and a little there," he replied.

"Come on," I said. "What do you read? Text books?"

"Naw. A lot of things you could figure out yourself if you'd take the time to think," he said with a grin.

All I can say is Derek was very bright. His mind was like flypaper; everything stuck to it. "Is that what you do when you sit on the porch?" I asked.

"Sometimes. But, what I really do on the porch is not so much figuring things out as it is figuring out a new way of thinking."

"You gotta be kidding! What do you mean 'a new way of thinking'?" I asked incredulously.

"I don't expect you to believe me and I am not going to try to convince you," Derek explained, "but there is a part of our minds which knows everything already. The problem is accessing it. It's related to telepathy, but it's not telepathy. I figure that if I want to access something which is not physical, then I had better get out of my brain which is physical. This is what I'm working on when I sit on the porch. I told you that you wouldn't believe me."

"I do...maybe I do, but it's so far out I can't take it in all at once. I think you're a little crazy, but...." What I was also thinking was how could a fourteen-year-old boy think up things like this. "So, how do you get out of your brain?" I finally asked.

Derek replied in great seriousness, which was not like him because he usually wore his joking smile.

"You have got to remember you're asking the questions and as long as you do, I am willing to tell you what I believe. I have promised myself I will not try to convince anyone that what I believe is truth. If it doesn't ring true to you, discard it. So, when I say 'get out of my brain,' this is just so I can express what I am doing and so you can understand better. What I'm doing is like putting my brain to sleep, or better yet, not using it to think with anymore, but just to watch. My conscious mind is more or less dormant."

"Okay, I'll buy that," I said. "Maybe."

"Do you want to hear or not?" he asked, getting annoyed with me.

"Yes, I was only joking. Go ahead."

"Then, what I think psychiatrists call the subconscious mind comes through and all that which has happened previously in this life and past lives, if you can believe in past lives, comes through; or is available for recall. Our subconscious mind has access to other people's subconscious minds, but only to the degree that we have accessed our own subconscious. Putting our conscious mind and our physical consciousness in a dormant state is not easy and that is what I am working on most of the time."

"And all this time I thought you were just sitting on the porch vegetating," I joked.

Derek continued on ignoring my attempts at humor. "I do this not just when I sit on the porch, but when I'm wrestling, for instance. I listen for what I should do next or for what my opponent is thinking so I can have the jump on him. Sometimes I have better success than others. The hardest part comes when I think I have accessed my subconscious mind and feel pleased about it. Then I know I haven't accessed it because feeling pleased is of the ego which is of the conscious mind—a 'Catch 22' you could say. My ego is my greatest enemy. It doesn't want to give up any of its control."

"I can believe that. Especially, considering how big it is," I said, failing to remain serious. "So how do you know when you have accessed your subconscious mind?"

"To know when I am in my subconscious mind or the 'Mind of God,' which is still higher and harder to access than our subconscious mind, I need to feel that all thoughts are being fed to me, that I am not, or that my ego or conscious mind is not, thinking them up. It is also very difficult to be out of the conscious mind and ask a question, because my ego has to be in operation to ask the question. Recognizing the ego is needed to give up the ego is the only way the ego can help with the process. The only desires it can legitimately have are to be in God consciousness and to love God, which is a serene state to be in."

"Sounds good. I'd like to feel something like that, but how...?" I asked.

"It's easier, I think, to access the mind of God than to access the minds of others and when you have accessed it enough it becomes easier. All your thinking is influenced by the mind of God without your being aware. That is really saying universal law is always functioning. This is really the only purpose of man coming to earth, to bring into the physical world the practice of the mind of God. We are separate from God, but we can be one with God if we get rid of the barrier, the ego, and make our wills one with the will of God. Then we can say like Jesus, 'I and my Father are one.'"

"What do you think about hypnosis? Don't you think that can help someone gain better access to their subconscious, too?" I pondered out loud.

"A hypnotist helps his subject relax into the subconscious mind, which never forgets. Then the subject can be guided to a very early age and/or asked questions, the answers to which he would not remember in his normal waking state. But it takes the hypnotist to ask the questions. I believe if the hypnotist didn't ask a question, the subject would just sit there speechless and eventually fall asleep. Upon awakening he would be in his normal conscious mind. I believe that with careful practice, and by not allowing the ego to take over, self hypnosis is possible."

"So you're saying you perform self hypnosis?"

"Sometimes I feel I can let my subconscious mind take over my physical body while I move about, write, or read. In this state I can read very fast and retain what I read. It's as if I were not doing anything myself."

"C'mon, are you serious? Who's doing it then?"

"Well, let me explain. I sit back and watch it happen. I have no ego involvement. I'm not asking questions. Life's a bowl of cherries. Everything works out. Things get done and done right. I don't have any problems. I don't get into trouble."

"Tell me about it," I said sarcastically.

"Things flow. I'm happy. It's like watching a movie and wondering what's going to happen next. Only, it's what is going to happen next to me?"

"So what is going to happen next to you?" I prompted.

"I don't know, but I can't say it too strongly that stepping aside and watching myself is the key to letting God run my life. It is detachment from the things and experiences in this physical world. Letting go and letting God, knowing that things will work out well. Having faith. Not storing up treasures on earth. However, I don't sit around and do nothing. I'm not in this observing state all the time like when I'm running around, joking, or conversing casually. When I'm not in the subconscious mind, however, I tend to behave in the way my subconscious mind has taught me. The subconscious mind doesn't teach me bad things, only good, because, as I said before, what I'm tuning into, or trying to tune into, usually is the 'Mind of God,' as I call it. Although, to say God has a mind is limiting God. To describe God with our limiting words, to describe his limitless existence is beyond our capability. Others who know it may call it something else."

"Some would call it tuning in to craziness, you know?"

"Yes, I know. There are a lot of people who don't want to try to understand. I could tune into the evil thought forms floating out there if I wanted to. Many people do. A lot of blame can be put on the newspapers, magazines, TV, and the movies in creating these thought forms. British propaganda about things the Germans had not done during World War II almost certainly pushed the Americans to side with the British sooner. The Americans tuned into the thought forms the British gave us. It is the ego which runs the conscious mind and teaches us greed, lust, self-indulgence, selfishness, control of others, power, and so forth. We tune into negative thought forms and accept them."

"You must tune into them sometimes, too. Don't you? Isn't it nearly impossible not to?" I asked.

"I can tune into anything I want—good or bad. My ego can tune into God or good thoughts or just as easily to thought forms sent out by wrong thinking, evil thinking, or whatever, or to hopeful thinking which, unfortunately, can be either perfect or imperfect. When we tune into wrong or evil thinking, we are in a state of rebellion against the perfection of God, whether we realize it or not. We could then be said to be harkening to the devil. That's all the devil is—a state of rebellion against the will of God. The devil does not exist as an entity, just as rebellious thought forms man has created."

"But a lot of people think he is an entity," I reminded him. "Down below in that fiery hell, all dressed in red, with a pitchfork in hand."

"If you get enough people thinking alike, the thought forms are stronger and it's harder to tune them out. That's how ordinary people become followers of demonic leaders. That's how come for generations there is ethnic rivalry and hatred. You'd think that, after a generation or two, all these hard feelings between two or more ethnic groups, races, communities, or nations would have dissolved, but the thought forms are perpetuated. They are hard to destroy. Forgiveness is the answer, the only answer. Forgiveness is the name of the game and that amounts to standing back and letting the love of God flow through you and watching as it does."

"Easier said than done though, wouldn't you agree?"

"True. Unfortunately, we become habituated to our way of responding to thoughts or actions or situations. In effect, we have given away our freedom of choice to our habits. Even though we think we have ourselves under control, we may lose it when subjected to an old stimulus. Just ask a reformed alcoholic how hard it is to stay reformed, or a reformed anybody for that matter."

"I know that. My friend's mother had a lot of trouble with drinking. She has quit on and off so many times, but just can't seem to beat it. It's terrible to watch the effect that something like that has on a person and everyone around them," I told him.

"But, if we were to attune to God, there would be no problems in the world. There is one problem, however, and it is a big problem. Until we learn to subjugate the conscious mind to the subconscious mind, we are stuck in the conscious mind, the ego mind, and, unfortunately, this includes all but a handful of people throughout the ages. And, if we cannot subjugate the conscious mind to the subconscious mind, then there is no way we can fully access the 'Mind of God.' We may have the desire to do God's will, but the ego which operates the conscious mind is limiting."

"How?"

"The ego thinks it knows God's will and is often wrong, frequently accepting previous wrong thinking of others. Throughout the centuries well-meaning men and women have given their own interpretation to what they think is God's will or Jesus' message as I have hinted at before. They are doing it from the perspective of the ego and conscious mind which is far from perfect. Even the subconscious mind is not perfect since it is the sum of all previous experience, but the 'Mind of God' is perfect. It is on the level of spirit, as God is spirit and we, the real us, is created in His image. These religious thinkers were convinced they were right, but…."

"But how can they all be right at the same time?" I asked. "They all say their way is the only way."

"Exactly. All 2000 denominations or sects professing to be Christian can't all be completely right. This is where the ego of a leader has set up thought forms and convinced others to tune into his thinking. And, this includes the apostle Paul who never heard a word Jesus said, yet wrote a lot of things Jesus did not say, including the downplaying of womanhood. Paul's writings are Paul's interpretation of the truth Jesus taught and, I must say, a lot is right on target."

"So...."

"So, what these leaders should have done is to simply show their followers how to tune into the 'Mind of God' by first subjugating their conscious minds to their subconscious minds and then dissolving that and their egos into the 'Mind of God' and universal consciousness. It's not easy to do and even more difficult to teach. But then there would be no Bible lessons to learn, no catechisms to memorize, no dogma, no affirmations of faith and so on. As the Bible says, 'Let that mind be in you that was in Christ Jesus.' That's why I quit Sunday school. The teacher was trying to force down my throat what he had been taught, some of which, I was convinced, was made up by man and didn't ring true to me."

"Sometimes I kind of felt like that, but I guess I didn't think about it as deeply," I told him. "I just didn't believe everything I was told to believe–but I also didn't care like you do."

Derek paused to gather his thoughts and then continued, "Another thing I have an objection to is the use of the name 'God.' It's been used by so many different people in so many different ways."

"Including you," I reminded him.

"Yes, but I think most people don't really know God. Theologians say 'God is love.' That's fine, but what is love? Ask ten people and you'll probably get eight different answers. If you were to say that love is that force which brings all things into manifestation, I can't argue, but I don't think most people think that way. I have heard someone say that God is a verb. In my opinion that's error. The Native Americans call God the 'Great Spirit.' I like that if they know what spirit is and don't think of the great spirit as a great, good someone up in the sky. Edgar Cayce often referred to God as the 'Creative Forces.' That's a good way of expressing the nature of God. Joel Goldsmith, a very gifted spiritual author and speaker, used the words 'Infinite Invisible' which is fine, but vague. Another expression for God I've read is the 'Great Unseen,' which I think is also okay, but also vague."

"It's amazing how many different names people have come up with to try to describe the same thing," I said, stopping to ponder potential names.

"Most Christians believe in the Trinity, that is, the Father, Son, and Holy Spirit; three in one. I think the two words 'Holy Spirit' is fine, but 'Father' and 'Son' anthropomorphizes God, which greatly limits the understanding of God. Since the 'Holy Spirit' has such widespread usage in the Trinity, I believe that if it was used alone it would be confusing to many. I, therefore, prefer the 'Great Spirit' or 'Creative Forces.'"

"What's wrong if you still want to call Him, or whatever it is, God?" I asked.

"I would prefer to think of God as law and truth. I don't mean man-made laws, I mean universal laws such as like attracts like, cause and effect, 'as you sow, so also shall you reap,' 'what goes around comes around,' and what we think we become. The Lord's Prayer says 'Thy will be done.' God's will is the law of the universe, or spiritual law. God is that law. 'We cannot mock God' means we cannot avoid the universal laws. We can only watch them at work.

God doesn't punish us. We punish ourselves when we try to avoid universal law or set our minds and desires on something other than the will of God. When we choose poorly we attract misfortune to ourselves. If our lives are in accord with universal law, we can only experience good. In accord includes love and joy, service, forgiveness, helpfulness, kindness, peace, and friendliness. We attract to ourselves pleasant or unpleasant experiences by our in-accord or out-of-accord thinking, not just by actions."

"That's kind of scary, but I suppose it could be true," I said, beginning to wonder if Derek was trying to say something about the way I was living. Derek never commented on the choices I made in life unless I asked him. But I was usually afraid to.

"In effect, we cannot break universal law," he continued. "We can only observe its outworking. However, you can change the results of the outworking by changing your mind and, thus, changing the energy patterns you previously set in motion. If you look at God as simply love, then you must realize that God would be very unloving if the universe were not lawful. It's like if one day you threw a ball up and it came down, and you threw it up the next day and it didn't come down. There could be no science if there were not lawfulness that could be relied on all the time. So, to manifest love, things must be lawful, never capricious. Love is the glue that holds the universe together. Destiny is not a matter of chance. It's a matter of choice."

"I agree with that," I said, happy I could finally respond to something I entirely understood. "Do you know of anyone who has reached God consciousness?" I asked.

"Jesus certainly did," Derek answered. "Jesus said, 'If you have seen me you have seen the Father' and 'I of myself do nothing; it is the Father in me who does the good works.' Since God is spirit and has no body, what Jesus is saying is that the 'Mind of God' is in Jesus' mind and does the good works. To try to define God with finite words is to limit God. So, we can only hint at some aspects of God. Jesus had completely subjugated his ego, his will, his conscious mind, even his subconscious mind to the 'Mind of God.' Jesus also said that 'All I do you can do and more.' Now there is the challenge for everyone. That is the real purpose of our being here in earth, to put into practice God's will or law in this three-dimensional world. But, what a mess we're making."

"How true. Something has to change," I responded with a newfound conviction. "I wonder if anybody else, besides Jesus, has been able to do that…you know, reach God consciousness."

"Certainly Sathya Sai Baba, sometimes called 'the man of miracles,' the avatar living in India, is in God consciousness all the time. He was once asked, 'How can you say you are God?' to which he is reputed to have replied, 'That's only half of it. The other half is so are you. The only difference is I know it and you don't.' And, Paramahansa Yogananda, who wrote the *Autobiography of a Yogi*, was in that state of God consciousness often, maybe all the time near his death in 1952. In his book, he tells of a number of others who had reached God consciousness. He used the word 'enlightened.' I am sure there are many Christian saints and other saints from India and other religions who have reached that state of consciousness."

"Have there been others that you know about?"

"When Edgar Cayce, the psychic/mystic, put himself in an altered state of consciousness to give a reading as he called them, he had access to this state of consciousness, but when he came out of his altered state back to his conscious mind, he could not remember what he said in his altered state. He'd have to read what his secretary had transcribed."

"Are you serious? That's pretty incredible."

"The only person I have personally met who, I think, reached the Mind of God or God consciousness was Brian Tamini. He picked me up hitching through Asheville, North Carolina, a while back when I was returning to Virginia after backpacking alone in the Great Smoky Mountains. In the course of the conversation, I had told him I had been hiking alone to tune in on a new way of remote thinking. He encouraged me by describing his experiences of tuning into God where he had all knowledge and all power, that is, he could not tell the difference between himself and God. His mind would go out of body when he did this. His wife, and probably family, couldn't accept this which led to a divorce."

I vaguely remember Derek's meeting with Brian had a profound effect upon Derek for he was a person having reached God consciousness, at least part of the time, and he was just an ordinary person, not a saint or spiritual leader. "If Brian Tamini could do it, so can I," Derek asserted.

I never made time to try even the first steps towards God consciousness. I believed Derek, but I wasn't motivated. Life was already crowded with things I had to or wanted to do.

What I've said above didn't occur in one conversation, nor is it Derek's exact words, but the ideas are his.

My relationship with Derek remained about the same during his high school and my college years. I had admired his participation in wrestling and gymnastics. I thought this gave him balance instead of being too intellectual. His love of fishing and backpacking also kept him in balance.

Undoubtedly, the most unforgettable single experience with Derek occurred when I was 20 and had just bought my first car, a used Ford. Derek was 16 and had only recently gotten his driver's license. He wanted to test drive my car. Naturally, I went with him. After driving about town a bit he headed for the open road and stepped on the gas. A blue light flashed, then a siren, and Derek pulled over. Derek liked to speed and had already been ticketed once. Up strode Ronnie, the local trooper.

"Hello, Ronnie," Derek said meekly.

"Hello, Derek," Ronnie said. "You were speeding again."

"Ronnie, please don't give me a ticket. This is my sister's new car and I just had to push it to see if it would be safe if she had to go fast sometime," Derek pleaded. He was clearly gobbling humble pie. "There is no traffic. The weather is clear. The road is straight and in good shape. Ronnie, I wasn't being reckless."

Ronnie listened patiently and, I would think, with a bit of glee seeing a youngster squirm.

Derek continued, "Dad will take my license away until I'm 18 if I get another ticket. Please, Ronnie, don't give me a ticket. I promise I won't ever speed again."

Ronnie tried to hold back a grin and shook his head, "You're a nice kid, Derek, but I don't believe a word you're saying." He paused. "However, I want to believe you. So I'm letting you go this time, but only this time. Now, get the hell out of here."

"Thanks, Ronnie," and with that Derek started the car. He had pulled off the road on to some gravel and when he started forward his wheels spun, sounding like he was peeling rubber. I leaned forward to see out of the side view mirror and there was Ronnie with one hand on a hip shaking his head, but smiling. Only Derek could get away with something like that.

Then just the following week I was going a bit too fast and Ronnie pulled me over. "I have to give you a ticket, Michelle. I don't want you growing up like your brother."

"Grow up like my brother? I'm four years older than him!" I retorted.

"Don't try to confuse things," was his reply as he proceeded to give me a ticket.

I was livid. When I got back to the house I lambasted Derek up one side and down the other and he made me all the madder by rolling on his bed in laughter. When I got through he asked, "How much was the ticket?"

"Twenty dollars."

He pulled out his wallet and handed me ten dollars, "Let me pay half." That's the kind of a guy he was.

After these two experiences Derek was determined to get the law changed from "speed limit" to "suggested speed limit" or "reckless driving." His reasoning was obvious. That's what the arresting officers were doing anyway. Even officers driving nowhere were driving 10 to 15 miles above the posted speed limits. Anybody could do this without getting arrested if they weren't endangering others or driving recklessly, unless of course, they were juveniles or blacks, who Derek was convinced were both discriminated against.

Then I don't know how he did it, but he talked Ronnie into arresting him for going two miles above the posted speed limit on an Interstate highway at rush hour. His case went to court and Derek represented himself. The judge listened to the court clerk read the charges, then asked Derek how he pleaded.

"Guilty," Derek spoke up loudly, "to a law that should be changed from exceeding the speed limit to reckless driving."

"How old are you, Derek?" the judge asked.

"Sixteen," Derek replied.

"I know how you feel, Derek," the judge said in a kind, fatherly voice, "and you may have a point, but I am not going to open a can of worms you cannot close. Case dismissed."

Derek was furious. "You can't do that. I have my rights," he insisted.

"But I have done it," the judge said, standing fast. "Next case."

The media thought it was very newsworthy. Derek got good press locally and even made the local radio and TV, maybe nationwide. The reporters were encouraging this young kid to stick up for his rights, continue his fight, and to appeal the decision.

However, a couple of days later, he suddenly announced through the paper, "I must quit. I am experiencing anger and hate and my calling is to further love and peace, compassion and forgiveness. So, I quit and I forgive the judge." Again, he got good press. I was very proud of him.

Needless to say, Derek's announcement of his engagement came as a devastating shock. It was so out of character. I was angry. Derek was the brother who never got into trouble, always did the right thing. I mean here was a guy who was working with God consciousness for Christ's sake!

How could he, at 17, knock up a teacher four years older than himself? I would have guessed him to be a virgin. Here was my little brother, with all the potential to be a Ph.D. college professor, throwing it all away to marry an older woman, probably a mentally disturbed slut who loved having sex with teenagers. I was home from college and met her when Derek made his announcement during my Thanksgiving break. Michelle made a good first impression, but I felt sure she was two-sided.

I came home for the wedding prepared for the worst, but, I liked Michelle. However, in the back of my mind I was still thinking that she can fool some of the people some of the time, but not all of them all of the time. As time went by, it became obvious they were meant for each other. He probably had thrown away a chance for a distinguished career, but he was happy, in love, a great father and, as always, he was doing and living what he believed was right.

After my graduation, I got my first job in Boston and I didn't see much of Derek and Michelle, or Mom and Dad. I did get to know my older brother, Ken, better as he lived about an hour away. Then I got married and had a family which further reduced my mobility.

The news of Derek's death was the worst shock of my life. I did not want to believe it. I dissolved in tears. I could not believe the world was robbed of such a wonderful person. So young. Thirty three is just too young for anyone to die. I still tear up inside when I think about it. I realize now how much I really loved and admired my brother.

But, I have to admit, in those early years…it was kind of hard to live with perfection.

Chapter Five

From Ken's Journal (April 4)

Mom and I were talking about Jan Hall this morning at breakfast, and why she was with Derek in the fatal accident. Although Mom said she really never knew that much about her background, except that Derek dated her in high school, and worked for Michelle so Michelle could go back to teaching.

She knew she had recently moved here to take care of her mother who was in the early stages of Alzheimer's. She had joined the Army from high school and had been stationed in Saudi Arabia. She had never said anything about her experiences there except that it was hot and she never wanted to return.

I thought we could try to get some information from Jan's mother. I asked Michelle if Jan's mother was still around or if she might be in a nursing home somewhere. Michelle wondered why I might ask that, and actually I have to wonder myself. She questioned if I was getting psychic like my brother. The last she heard was that Mrs. Hall had moved north to live with her son, but she had no idea where and she also couldn't remember her mother's first name as Jan always just called her 'Mother.'

I don't know why, but I just have this gnawing feeling that there's something I once heard about Jan that I should be remembering. Somehow, I'm going to recall it.

I went over to Marge and John Bassett's today to pick up their accounts of Derek which they had just finished. It was a nice visit. We ended up sitting around talking for nearly three hours. I didn't know them well when I was growing up, simply because I wasn't as close to their children as Derek was. But they certainly knew me by way of my parents and had plenty of stories to tell—stories I had completely forgotten. They even had me sharing some of my stories from Vietnam.

They mentioned how different I seemed when I returned from the Vietnam War. They thought I seemed more pessimistic and cynical about life. Perhaps more realistic, or less juvenile, I would say. Who knows, just different I suppose. I was older. What did they expect...a kid?

The thing is, it's just as Derek had said—nothing permanent was solved by that war, or any other war for that matter. And when I went back to Vietnam working for The Globe, *I began to look at the United States from a journalist's perspective. Perhaps, along the way, I lost the idealistic visions I had as a youth.*

They asked about Jenny. I reminded them we were both seniors in college and were considering marriage until I went back to Vietnam. Marge said she remembered the look on my face when I came over to say good-bye. She knew she would not be looking into the eyes of an innocent, young man the next time she saw me.

Marge was disappointed when Jenny didn't wait for me and got married within a year. I told them I guess absence doesn't make the heart grow fonder at age 22. I said it as a little joke, but I can vividly remember how crushed I was when she wrote she was dating a guy named Scott and then shortly announced their engagement. About a year later, Jenny gave birth to a deformed little girl who only lived a few months and an infection made future pregnancies impossible without an operation—which she didn't want. I thought back to my first reaction. I was glad she couldn't have a child with him. I felt terrible for her and terrible for thinking that way, but I was so resentful of the fact that she could leave me so easily.

I don't know if I've ever tried to look at the situation from her point of view—having the man she loved taken to the other side of the world, not knowing when, or if, he would return. I know now she really needed somebody at that time of her life and I wasn't there for her.

I remember hearing through the grapevine how she panicked at the thought of a second deformed child, even though the doctor told her it was very unlikely. I wasn't surprised when I heard Scott divorced her. She was being the same unrealistic self I'm dealing with now and Scott really wanted a family. Maybe I should have gone after her then. No doubt I was happy to hear about the divorce, but I had too much pride to go chasing after her right away.

I'm sure Derek would have said to forgive her. He might also have said that maybe she was meeting a trauma from a previous incarnation. And maybe I was making it worse for her.

Marge says Mom used to say she hoped we'd get back together again, or at least that I'd find another woman. They knew I wasn't very interested in a family. I had always said I probably wouldn't have been a good father since I was always traveling for the paper for months at a time to all parts of the globe. And now I'm not even being a good husband.

It was also interesting to hear from Marge that Mom intuitively knew Jenny was going to be at our 20th college reunion and she was hoping some-

thing might happen... although she never said a word to me. I can still picture clearly when Jenny and I spotted each other at the reunion. It was love at first sight all over again. It felt as though hardly a day had passed. I wonder if Jenny ever thinks back to that now.

I remember Mom couldn't have been happier than she was at our wedding four years ago. It truly was a wonderful marriage...until recently that is.

The Bassetts asked how Jenny was doing now and I tried to make it seem as though everything was wonderful between us, but I'm not sure I was very convincing. But I have to say I went through quite a catharsis in my bedroom the other night.

Perhaps our troubled relationship has simply been the closest thing I could point to without taking a look at myself. I should have realized sooner she's been one of the brightest spots in my life.

The one thing that stands out so clearly about Derek is how strong his spiritual side was and how much clarity of vision it provided him. He always stayed positive. He truly believed everything works out for the best. I envy that. Today is the tomorrow we worried about yesterday.

Oh Jenny! I don't know what's wrong with me sometimes. But I'm coming home soon and I'm going to make it up to you. I really am.

Marge Bassett's Account

There is an additional bonding between two women who are pregnant at the same time, particularly when their due dates are almost the same. This was the case with Emily Saul and me. "Will our babies be born the same day?" was subconsciously stirring in our minds.

Not only were we best friends, but we lived next door to each other. My pregnancy was my first. Emily already had a four-year old girl and an 11 year-old son.

My son, Michael, arrived two weeks before Emily's son, Derek. On the way home from the hospital Emily first brought Derek into our house to introduce him to Michael. From the very start, the two boys were inseparable and remained best friends for life. It was a great relationship. Since they were very active with each other, they kept out of trouble for the most part.

They were never deprived of parental love, which included discipline, the necessities of life, and a few luxuries. This meant they didn't have to go through the trauma of a broken home or parental fights, or any kind of child abuse. They were fortunate, happy boys in a good, upper-middle class home—not too much and not too little.

The boys developed their own language with each other before they accepted our version of English. It was great fun listening to them. Emily and I used to get together for coffee most mornings, usually at her house because she had four-year old Maggie. We would put the babies on the rug and just watch. Often Maggie would snuggle up to her mother and watch, too.

Emily and I had been teachers in the same primary school and independently had decided not to go back to teaching until our children were in school full time. For me, that was two years after Emily because I had another boy, Josh, two years after Michael. Fortunately our husbands earned enough so we could live on their salaries. My husband, John, was the assistant administrator at a local hospital.

Emily and I used to do much of our shopping together, taking the kids with us. We also would frequently go to parks or playgrounds or for walks together with the kids. It was a good life. Several times we, our families that is, rented a cottage at the seashore for our vacation. John and Roger, Derek's father, were close friends also, but not as close as Emily and I.

John took the kids to the mountains several times hiking and camping. They rode their bikes all over. They were also in the YMCA, Boy Scouts, and Church School together, although they quit Church School abruptly after Derek had an argument with the teacher and called him an antichrist. I would have loved to have been there. Derek was a clear, innovative thinker even at an early age. We sometimes called him the little philosopher…much to his disgust.

From time to time, I would draw Derek into conversations when he was at our house and wasn't running around with Michael. I never ceased to be impressed. He had opinions on everything. I once asked Derek where he got all his ideas. He nonchalantly explained that we are always training our minds to think or avoid thinking. What we do or the way we think can easily become a habit. Even if these habits turn out to be unrewarding, they are still hard to break. We have to develop a new habit, an acceptable habit hopefully, to replace the old one. To just give up a habit leaves a hole and it's easy to fall back into a hole if it's not filled up. Such observations coming from a 12-year-old astounded me.

Derek was death on politicians. "They are all dishonest crooks," he would say. "Dishonest because they don't vote for what they believe in, but vote for their party's approval and endorsement without which they'd have trouble being re-elected. And crooks because they look after the welfare of the special interest groups who pay for their campaigns. Look at Congressmen from North Carolina, for instance. They stand behind the tobacco industry, which contributes generously to their campaigns. Yet, tobacco is the cause of much ill health for their other constituents who don't contribute or don't contribute as much."

Derek was adamant about not taking away a person's freedom to choose. God didn't create men to be puppets or robots, so He gave us free will that we might choose to be one with Him or not. Derek claimed religions are trying to take away people's free will all the time through fear and guilt: "Do it our way or you'll go to hell." His opposition to this kind of thinking was what got him kicked out of Sunday School when he called his teacher an antichrist.

Derek had the same feeling about our nation trying to decide what other nations should believe and do. We impose economic sanctions or worse. We have stationed our military in or near countries that disagree with us and where civil outbursts or aggression are probable. Derek pointed out that the cold war is over, so wage peace by example, like Switzerland, Sweden, and Spain. Demonstrate to the world our desire for peace. This would be far more effective, and a lesson to other nations, as opposed to military intervention or the threat thereof, which creates fear and hate for us, as well as for various factions in that country. Our intervention might appear to quiet life in that country, but the underlying feelings and hates last until forgiveness quells them. "Forgiveness is the name of the game," Derek often said.

It is wrong, evil, and sinful, Derek would insist, to try to force our will on others. God doesn't do this with us. So, if nations go through distressing ordeals, that's their own fault because of their choices, their desires, hate, greed, and refusal to compromise. We can't, by force, impose new desires, new motivations on people or countries even if we try. The old patterns still lurk in the background and will re-emerge when we leave. It's their free will to stick with the old or change and they have an eternity to decide. It is we who are impatient, not God.

But what about the poor, innocent individuals who have to suffer in the process, I asked him. Derek said it was more comprehensible if you believe in reincarnation as he did and I do now. Those who get killed can reincarnate. Death is not the end. There is always another chance. Besides, Derek believed, we choose on the soul level, before birth, the circumstances we now find ourselves in because we deserve or need those circumstances to understand the effects of our actions or thoughts in a previous incarnation.

Another cogent belief of Derek's was his insistence that we could drastically reduce our military to perhaps 10% of what it currently is. We used to have a lot of discussions about that. But, of course, Congress seems to feel that would cause national economic distress and we wouldn't be ready to stop aggression. Derek contended that economic distress could be relieved by paying salaries for two to four years to the military men and women who were discharged to help them retrain for peace.

Also, production of military equipment should be halted on the spot, but the profits should be paid as if the equipment were produced giving the companies income while they re-tool and retrain for peacetime pursuits. Suppliers and subcontractors should similarly be paid their profits by the general contractors.

To be sure, it would be complicated to administer, but within ten years we would be clear to demonstrate peace and at the same time vastly reduce our annual budget and easily eliminate our national debt. Any company caught cheating would be cut off from further reimbursement.

Derek would say we must always be ready to help others, but if they don't want it, don't impose it on them. Everybody isn't ready to think as we do, nor is it necessary that they do. They have freedom of choice. As the saying goes, "A man convinced against his will is of the same opinion still."

Just as teenagers experiment with different forms of behavior, so do nations. There is nothing wrong with many of the concepts of communism and socialism, but they were carried out wrongly in the past. The masses got hurt. So, now we refuse to study good ideas that would put the rich and the poor on a more even basis. We're willing to throw out the baby with the bath water.

Derek pointed out that the Republicans, particularly the rich, think they need to have their money so they can invest in factories, shopping centers, and the like to create jobs for the rest: trickle-down economics. Give the rich tax breaks, but then the executives usually squeeze the poor workers to please the stockholders and their own pockets, instead of sharing the profits with them, thus making the rich richer and the poor poorer.

Derek said the biggest criminals in the world are the rich because they are always thinking of themselves, taking more from others to increase their wealth and, thus, their power, prestige, and the luxuries that go with wealth. Of course, not all the rich because many are very generous, and a few even humble.

I remember Derek used the example of one company that is building plants all over the world so if the workers of a plant in this country want to strike for better wages or benefits, management says, "go ahead strike, we can produce overseas for our markets here and abroad." That way they can make the workers here accept less, which leaves more for the bosses and stockholders—that is, the already rich, the ones that have the clout to maintain their control.

I suppose some would have considered Derek a socialist. He felt half of all corporate profits of all corporations should go to the workers, not top management as it does now, but equally to all employees. And the other half of the profits should go to the stockholders, or for bonuses for those who made the company profitable, but half in equal shares to every employee. Until we learn to share we have not learned a spiritual purpose of life here on earth.

Derek insisted we must accept the responsibility for our thoughts, actions, and attitudes and not try to blame it on others. We attract to ourselves all that happens to us by our conscious and unconscious thinking. The best way to know a right way is by the fruit it bears.

Derek's belief in reincarnation implies that to get the right understanding of our actions might take several lifetimes. This is why a particular life might seem unfair, but it isn't. We get another chance to perfect our decisions and our motivations. Our souls live on seeking perfection and reunion with God. Reality is always open to revision.

An example Derek used was a man born into a wealthy family who felt he was elite because of his wealth and developed into a snob looking down on others. In a future life he may be denied all that wealth to learn humility. His wealth wasn't wrong, it was his attitude toward having wealth that was wrong.

Derek said too many people think this life is so very important. Keeping the body alive has too great an emphasis in our culture with our use of life support systems after the quality of life has gone. Also, keeping the fetus alive has too great an emphasis. To want to make the unwanted baby suffer the distress of being unwanted or to make the aged and debilitated body suffer by keeping it on machines, helpless and hopeless, are sick points of view. Although some souls need to suffer not being wanted because it's the harvest of seeds they sowed in a previous life.

The knowledge of one life occupying many bodies one at a time is not sick. The body is the vehicle, not the soul. The soul is spirit as God is spirit and does not die with the death of the body.

That's about all I can remember of Derek's metaphysics. Of course, the words I used are my words, not Derek's, but the concepts are his. I thoroughly enjoyed our conversations and learned a lot from him.

When 17 years old and in his senior year of high school, Derek announced that he and Michelle were going to get married because she was pregnant. I couldn't believe it. I was in shock. Derek insisted he wasn't marrying Michelle because she was pregnant, but because he loved her and the fact that she was pregnant only gave him a good excuse to marry her then.

It was so unlike Derek. If Michael had come up needing to get married, I wouldn't have been surprised, but not Derek. I knew Derek very well and I can't remember him ever doing anything wrong. His thinking, his actions, his attitudes were beyond reproach. He reminded me of the Bible passage, "Be you therefore perfect even as your Father in heaven is perfect."

I lost most of my contact with Derek when we sold our house to Michael, who was then playing professional football, and moved into the country near Emily and Roger who had recently moved. Although we missed having Josh around, I was glad he continued to live next to Derek in Michael's house as caretaker when Michael was away playing football. This meant Josh could remain in Derek's influence. I knew they discussed metaphysics a lot, but they rarely discussed it with me. Why I don't know. I was always interested when they did, as you can gather from what I've said above.

I was pleased, too, that when Michael rented his house for a few months to a friend, Josh moved into the third floor apartment in Derek's house. I was pleased when Josh joined Derek and his father in their insurance agency after college.

When the news reached us that Derek had been killed in an auto accident I was traumatized. How could God recall such a great soul! I could only console myself by saying it must be part of a larger plan that we humans cannot see. Our vision is so limited.

The news that Derek had asked on his death bed for Michael and Michelle to marry before the baby was born did not set well with me or Emily. Yes, we thought it was fine for Michael and Michelle to get married, but not before the child was born. In the back of my heart I knew it didn't really matter, but my emotions were twisted. Michelle needed Michael and he dearly loved her and was, by then, ready to be a good husband and father, but it still seemed too soon.

I shall always miss Derek, but so many things remind me of him, I feel he is right here, just around the corner.

John Bassett's Account

I have read what Marge, my wife, has said about Derek and concur with her recollections. I have only a little to add.

I knew Derek right from the start. I wasn't home from work for the now infamous introduction of Derek to my two-week old Michael, but I did see Derek at his home that night. He seemed like a normal, healthy, red-faced baby.

Most of my early knowledge of Derek came secondhand from Marge. I watched Michael and Derek grow and play with almost excessive energy. They were good boys.

I was fond of Derek, but didn't know him well enough during the early years to make big judgments about him. I knew he was bright, talked early, and had an unusually large vocabulary for his age.

As Derek and Michael grew older, I took them a half dozen times to the Blue Ridge Mountains to hike and camp. Usually Josh, my younger son, came also which slowed us down a bit because he was two years younger. Eventually Josh grew taller than Derek, but he was never as tall or as muscular as his brother. Still he kept up. They were a very compatible threesome. Ken was too much older to come with us.

On one trip I remember Derek surprising me with a theory I would not have expected from a ten or eleven year old. We were crossing a bald in the Blue Ridge Mountains, that is a field on the top of a mountain, no trees or brush. We stopped for lunch and to enjoy the view.

Derek was studying the grass when he said, "There is a lot of surface area on these little blades of grass and they are very close together. I wonder if you measured all their surface area and compared it to the surface area of the leaves on the trees in the tropical rain forests which would have the larger surface area. I bet they would be pretty much the same. In the rain forests, aren't the tall branches separated so the leaves would be far apart? Then don't the leaves keep the sun from coming through which prevents or slows growth on, or near, the ground? If there's no sunlight on the low-growing vegetation can there be much photosynthesis? Therefore, how could there be the production of a lot of oxygen? Could it be that the cutting down of all those rain forest trees isn't going to be as disastrous to the oxygen supply as the environmentalists think because low growing vegetation will take over when the tall trees are cut? Also, doesn't all the dead stuff on the ground in the rain forests rot and doesn't rotting take oxygen?" He paused a moment and continued, "I wonder if the spring spurt of growth of leaves and branches produces a spurt in photosynthesis and thus a spurt of oxygen production which offsets the lack of leaves in winter?"

All I could say was I didn't know. Derek said we may never know since trees are usually replaced with houses, roads, concrete, and other infrastructure, rather than low-growing vegetation.

Derek's brain was always running full tilt and he seemed better informed than most adults, but he wasn't somber. He was a joker, filled with humor, laughter, and smiles.

A few years later when many people were getting flu shots because of an epidemic, I asked Derek if his family was going to get shots. He answered, "I don't know about them, but I'm not."

"Why?" I asked curiously because Derek was always logical and thoughtful and I really wanted to know how he was thinking—even though he was a third my age.

"Well," Derek started, "we can choose to be well or sick. Since we don't usually choose to be sick, the choice to be sick is unconscious. So, the choice to be well is almost always unconscious, too. I feel that if I think positively and attune to the creative forces, or God, I won't create negative energy that could lead to sickness and I'll remain well. It's that simple."

He stared at me quietly and I stared back wondering what to say. Even if he were all wet, he had logically thought it out. He was probably a sophomore in high school then. His voice had only recently changed. He was growing a pathetic fuzz on his upper lip. Yet, he spoke with authority. I was so impressed and didn't want to end the conversation.

"Suppose you've been naughty and God feels you need to be punished?" I asked lamely.

"God never punishes," Derek explained. "God forgives. Actually, God doesn't forgive either because He doesn't see anything as right or wrong, good or evil. God gave us free will to choose this way or that way, and we need to experiment to learn what works out to be good or bad and experimenting isn't wrong. It's the only way. If the fruit of our choice is pleasant, then we chose rightly and set up good energy. If, however, our choice was not for the benefit of all, if it was selfish or self-glorifying then it was a bad choice and we've set up bad energy. Good health or, sooner or later, bad health is the result of the energy patterns we've stored up, which could be from just thinking—like an attitude, a desire or a fear or by our actions."

"I see what you're saying," I told him. "We would probably all be wise to keep that in mind whenever we think or do anything."

"It's not sensible to keep doing whatever turns out to produce bad fruit," he said. "But again that's our freedom of choice. Our accumulated bad energy can come back to haunt us such as an accident, poverty or misfortune as well as sickness. Likewise our good energy comes back to bless us in many ways."

"Where did you read all this?" I asked.

"I didn't."

"Well, who told you?" I continued. "This is pretty deep to just think up."

"Thoughts like these would come to you, too, if you would just sit quietly, let go of your own thinking and let God do your thinking. I call it retreating into God's country. All you have to do is listen. But it takes time and practice, because God doesn't speak in words very often. He first allows us to experience the fruit of our actions and thoughts or, secondly, we get feelings, and, less frequently, we get words which we usually do not hear with our ears, but with our brains."

"Does Jesus or some spirit talk to you?" I asked.

"No, I go directly to God. God is perfect truth. Others are apt to be partial truth or even error. If God sends someone to me, that's His decision, but I trust God completely. Jesus said, 'Ask believing and you shall receive.' If you don't have enough faith, it's okay to rely on Jesus' faith and ask in his name."

Derek was deep, but he horsed around like any other healthy kid. While I sat pondering what he had said, Derek went outside and was throwing a frisbee with Josh.

Derek's marriage to his French teacher, Michelle, was a shock to me, as to all of us, but it turned out fine. His death was a much greater shock.

If it weren't for my faith in Derek, his deathbed request that Michelle and Michael get married right away would have seemed entirely wrong. There again it worked out beautifully.

Michael adored Michelle and Michelle needed and loved Michael. Michael knew he could never replace Derek and I don't think he wanted to. I am sure Michael reasoned, like Derek did, that to marry Michelle would be the best thing for the two of them and Mike, particularly since Michelle was pregnant again.

I am proud of my son. God bless him and Michelle.

Chapter Six

Ken's Journal (April 5)

    I started on a trail to find out more about Janet Hall today. I don't know what's gotten into me, but I'm determined to learn more about her.

    The trail started with the town hall, trying to find out her mother's name by checking the ownership of their old home. The house belonged to James S. and Catherine B. Hall. It was sold to a Richard Bales. I thought Mr. Bales might know what happened to Mrs. Hall, but he only knew that her son was going to take her back with him to someplace near Boston. Bales couldn't remember the son's first name. The lawyer had just called him "Mr. Hall." But he thought the real estate agent might have his name and address, and maybe even his phone number.

    When I checked with the real estate company, I found that the agent, Simon Bentley, was away on vacation, skiing in Europe until April 15th. The secretary couldn't find the file. She said, "It should be right here, but it's missing." Strange? Probably not. But, she remembered dialing Jan's brother for Bentley at area code 508.

    So, next I tried to locate Jan's brother through the phone company. I called the operator and eventually got the supervisor. They both said that area code 508 has so many Halls that, without an address or a first name, they could be of no help. I figured that might be the case. I'll have to find another way.

    Had a long talk today with Michael Bassett. I edited his account about Derek after we went out for lunch. We had a nice time and it was good to get to know him better. I must say I, too, thought Derek's request on his deathbed was rather strange. I could understand Derek wanting to make sure that Michelle and Mike were taken care of, but requesting them to marry, even before the birth of the second child, seemed unnecessary. I suppose I wasn't as friendly with Michael in the past as I could have been. But, he really has been incredible to Michelle and my nephew.

After listening to his story and what Derek said before he died, I can understand better why things happened the way they did. It's truly remarkable how Derek was able to look beyond selfish, prideful interests, and retain focus on the bigger picture of what was really important. How many people would, on their deathbed, request their best friend to marry their wife and become father to their child? It still sounds strange, but Derek looked at things a little differently than most.

I can't wait to talk about all this with Jenny. I was going to call her today, but decided to wait until at least a week has passed. I'm a little surprised she hasn't called, if just to make sure I arrived okay. But, I suppose she's also thinking we need this time apart.

Michael Bassett's Account

I was two weeks older than Derek and lived next door to him from his birth until his death, except while I was at college and playing professional football. There could never have been two closer friends than us.

There is no remembering life without Derek. I was lucky to have known him. As a matter of fact, I'm willing to admit it was probably Derek that kept me out of all serious trouble, except with women. I had all the potential of being a hyper-energetic beast.

Mom told me that before Mrs. Saul brought Derek into their house on the way home from the hospital, she brought him into our house to introduce Derek to me. "This will be your closest friend," she prophesied and how right she was.

One summer, when we were quite young, our mothers had taken us to a lake to swim and fool around on the beach. Derek had knocked our beach ball too far out and was going after it when he got in over his head. Being taller than him, I could touch ground and I pulled him into shallower water. Then I got the ball which the wind was blowing closer to shore anyway. No big deal, but I remember it because I thought I had saved his life. I probably hadn't, but who knows. Our mothers never knew about it. We were afraid they might restrict us if we told them. Derek's older brother, Ken, was there, but he was too busy with the girls to notice. He was in high school by then.

For the most part, Derek and I would build sand castles and roads for our little cars, construct buildings with our blocks, and have wars with our toy soldiers, tanks, and airplanes. All those things little kids do. Later, we built a tree hut in my backyard. It was really just a platform using an old door.

We would go down to the brook and play with our boats. It was only ankle deep so we built dams and stuff like that. We would often hike in the woods and climb trees. I remember climbing up some small trees which would bend with our weight so we could get into the branches of the next small tree and keep going.

Often in grade school, we did our homework together. I never knew anybody who could read as fast as Derek. He told me not to pronounce words, just look at them, but I never could do this. When I thought about not pronouncing words, I would be thinking about not pronouncing the words and not about what they meant. So, I read a paragraph and would not have pronounced a word, but I also wouldn't know what I had read.

After we got to high school we didn't study together much, if at all, except for French in my senior year, but I'll get to that story later. Mainly it was because we didn't have the same classes, but also our lives were on different schedules. Up until high school we were always in the same rooms. In high school, Derek would try to get a study hall his last period so he could complete his homework and not have to bring his books home.

Although Derek was a brain in school, out of school you'd never know it. He was always smiling as if everything was a bucket of roses, as if everybody was doing him a favor and he appreciated it. Almost as if he were constantly in love, in love with life and everybody.

Derek's father taught us how to fish and we did it a lot. I mean a lot. Maggie, Derek's sister, joined us once. Dull, she said. Sometimes in warm weather we would go hiking over a weekend and bring our fishing gear with us.

One warm spring day in our junior year in high school when the water was still cold, we went fishing at one of our favorite spots, a deep pool in a fairly fast-flowing stream. Derek hooked a large rainbow trout. It was one of the largest he'd ever landed, maybe the largest. He was in ecstasy. He was so proud of it. Moments later, I landed a big one.

"Let me see yours," Derek demanded. I handed it to him and he held his beside mine.

"You son of a bitch," he exclaimed. "Yours is bigger than mine," and he threw mine back in the brook.

"You bastard," I yelled, "Go get it." I grabbed him to throw him overboard. I should say here that Derek was a wrestler. He had just won the high school state championship in his weight class. However, he was only 5'6" tall, weighing 145 pounds. I was 6'2" and 185 pounds. I was captain of the football team and strong, but Derek was quick. When I carried him squirming to the water's edge, he spun around so quickly I didn't know what hit me and we both went tumbling in, going totally under. The water was freezing. We came up breathless and crawled out as fast as we could.

Derek stood there smiling and wiggling his fish in my face. Through all that he had held on to his fish. He offered it to me, "Here, you can have it. It's yours." I took it and tossed it back in the stream. Now it was his turn to yell, "You bastard. You go get it."

I was ready for him. With smiles on our faces and growls in our throats, we went at it. Even with my 40-pound and 8-inch advantage, I could not keep him from eventually throwing me overboard, but I brought him with me. I found out what a scrapper he could be if he wanted to. We had never really fought.

On the bank he offered me his hand, "Truce?" We shook. No more of that cold water for us. We laughed all the way home, soaking wet and freezing.

Derek was always wise cracking and spouting crazy puns. He would even do it in class. I can't remember the complicated ones, but it wasn't usually the kind of humor where you'd roll on the floor in laughter, more like you would just sort of moan.

For instance, someone would say something in class and Derek would ask, "Are you serious?"

And, of course, that kid would say, "Yes," or "I'm serious."

Then Derek would say, "Great, I'm Roebuck. Let's form a company. Serious and Roebuck, get it?"

The summer before he married we took an overnight bicycle trip. It was a hot dry night so we didn't bother to set up the tent and just slept on our tarp, looking up at the stars. Derek asked how my date went with Cindy the previous Saturday.

"It was great," I admitted.

"How great?" Derek asked inquisitively. "She's got quite a loose reputation. Did you get in?"

"None of your business," I told him.

"Come on," he continued, "I know you got in. I know your reputation, don't forget, and I know women can't resist you. I want all the juicy details step by step."

I enjoyed reliving my experience so I began relaying the story. "Well, after we left the movies, on the way to the car, I had my arm over her shoulders. I pulled her over and gave her a kiss on her forehead as we walked. When we reached the car, I unlocked her door and opened it, but before I let her slip in, I took her in my arms and gave her a real juicy kiss. Once in the car, I said we should go for a ride and she didn't object."

Then I told Derek where I drove and how I spread out the blanket so we'd take advantage of the view of the river, which we never even noticed I might add, and how I had trouble making out in the car because I was too tall. Then how we necked and I let my hands run over her back first, then in front, and eventually undoing her bra and so forth and so forth and eventually slipping down her panties, letting my hands explore.

"You can stop now," Derek interrupted.

"But I haven't come to the orgasm part," I protested.

"Well, I have," Derek said.

"You slob! Derek, get yourself a woman," I advised. "The women love you, too. They think you're cute and your cock ain't that small."

"I'm going to keep myself for my wife," he explained, "And you, you son-of-a-bitch, just because you're hung like a horse doesn't mean I'm not adequate. The vagina lips and the head of a cock are the most sensitive parts and they are the first to meet, so size makes no difference. It's the gays who go for the big cocks and you can have them. I won't be jealous."

Derek and I always walked to school together or rode our bikes and we also went to Boy Scouts, the YMCA, and Sunday school together. The Boy Scout Troop we joined was sponsored by a church halfway to town. We knew a bunch of the guys who went there. That's why we picked that troop. We enjoyed it for a couple of years while we were in seventh and eighth grades.

Derek and I were a little disruptive, I should add, particularly at meetings because we were a bit more adventuresome than our scoutmaster had planned. Hyperactive, you could say. Our scoutmaster was all for teaching skills for tests and merit badges, a lot of which we knew, and he would do them over and over again for new kids or because he couldn't think of something else.

We went on all the campouts and hikes, but even that was often old hat for us—the same places over and over again. Except for the other kids we would have been bored out of our gourds learning stuff we already knew such as fire building and outdoor cooking. There wasn't enough time for games like capture-the-flag or duck on a rock or just plain hiking in the hills. We quit when we got to high school since there was simply too much else to do. Besides, we figured Scouts was for younger kids.

We started at the YMCA at an early age because our families had family memberships. Our parents had done this primarily because of the family swim on Friday evenings. Eventually, we got involved in other Y activities. Derek and I both got involved with the Y swim team. I swam freestyle sprints and Derek became their star diver.

In high school, when he went out for wrestling, he still continued with the Y gymnastics team, but gave up diving. If there was a conflict in meet times he would choose wrestling as it was for the school. He was good at both, but preferred wrestling anyway.

In the fall of our freshman year at high school I went out for football. I was already over six feet and had a strong build. I was a natural, you might say. Derek on the other hand was only 5'6", if that, and probably weighed no more than 120 pounds soaking wet. He thought he could play in the backfield and not get ruined. The coach thought otherwise, and suggested he be the freshman team manager. Derek grabbed the offer and did such a fine job he became varsity manager the next three years.

As to Sunday school, we started there when we started regular school. Derek had a hard time accepting the idea that Jesus was God. He reasoned that if Jesus was a man with a body and God was spirit without a body, then they had to be different. He also thought that if, in the Trinity, there was the Father, the Son, and the Holy Spirit and if God was the father and Jesus was the son, then they couldn't be the same. He also had trouble with the idea that, if God was forgiving, how could he punish us by sending us to hell. If God loved us, He would teach us how to stay out of trouble and Jesus would be our teacher. Yet, suffering is everywhere. Why?

Derek explained that maybe suffering was God's way of teaching us, to let us experience the distress we cause others and in time we'll learn and change. Derek said this was cosmic law. We must experience what we dish out sooner or later.

Sometimes Derek got on a Bible-reading kick, particularly the New Testament, and didn't always like what he read. Like in 1st Peter, "Likewise, you wives, be in subjection to your own husbands...." So, Derek felt the Bible wasn't entirely the inspired word of God, and that, well-meaning men often used it to keep people feeling fearful and guilty, hoping that would inspire them to be good. And, thus, the power struggle.

Everybody should figure truth out for themselves, Derek believed. We should not just accept what somebody says is truth. He felt that truth can be broken up into relative truth and absolute truth. Relative truth is what man accepts as truth, but can change with time—like the earth is flat, for instance. Absolute truth does not change, like two plus two is four. To know the difference in complex matters is our dilemma and our decision because we have freedom of choice.

This religious stuff wasn't all he thought about. Derek told me once it's better not to fight a habit because, by thinking about the habit, you give it energy. For instance, if I say don't think of a green rabbit, what's the first thing you think of? A green rabbit, of course. The subconscious mind doesn't understand the negative. It would be better to think you are being possessed and being made to do whatever the habit is. That way you are fighting the possessor and not the habit. That makes it easier because nobody wants to be told what to do or think all the time.

Derek had a strong opinion about killing animals. I remember when I got a .22 rifle for my 16th birthday and asked Derek to go hunting with me. I remember him saying, "As long as you hunt to eat, it's okay to hunt, but, if you hunt for the love of killing, it's not okay, even if you eat what you shoot." Once he looked at a dying squirrel I had shot and said, "I think I'll become a vegetarian."

Later I asked him why he hadn't become a vegetarian and he said it was because it would disrupt the family and that's more important.

After Derek was kicked out of Sunday school for calling the teacher an antichrist, he rarely talked about his "thinking" sessions. Derek said that episode was a turning point in his life. It happened when we were twelve. I was there.

We had Mr. Benson as our Sunday School teacher. He was a man about 45 to 50. Things were either black or white in his book without leeway. He and Derek were always arguing. Derek said there are many inconsistencies in the Bible because it was written so long after Jesus' death. He took the position that many Biblical expressions were ancient idioms or that words had different meanings than now and should not be taken literally. One such example was a virgin meant a young woman and could even be a married young woman.

Another example, Derek wondered if the use of the word "Father," meaning God, was good. Derek claimed that "Father" made God sound like a good human instead of spirit and even the best human father would be putting a very severe limitation on God. Derek said that spirit, not having any substance, doesn't dwell in a place and heaven was made to sound like a place, instead of a state of consciousness. Then, after Mr. Benson disagreed, Derek added, "Well, maybe two thousand years ago those were the right words for the people then, but they certainly are not today."

Mr. Benson said the Bible is the inspired word of God. The time Derek was kicked out, he pissed Benson off by saying, "Since the Bible wasn't written in modern English, which translation of which translation of which translation are you talking about?"

"The word of God is the inspired word of God. I sometimes think you are possessed by demons, Derek," Mr. Benson said with his black and white mentality.

"If I am," Derek responded, "I'm not going to kick them out because who would teach them? Certainly not you."

Trying to conceal his rising anger, Mr. Benson replied, "Derek, watch it! You're paving your way to hell."

Derek countered, "Well, I won't see you there, 'cause hell isn't a place. Jesus never said that we go to hell. Other men like you did. You should study your ancient languages because the original Bible wasn't written in English. In Jesus' time, hell was an idiom. It was where King Ahaz sacrificed his son with fire. Later, it became the place where they burned the bodies of those who died of the plague. Hell is a figure of speech."

I don't know where Derek got all his knowledge, but he spoke with assurance and authority.

A bit flustered, Mr. Benson sputtered, "Derek, I've been studying the Bible since before your father was born. I know what it says and if you don't believe what the church teaches, you *are* going to end up in hell."

Derek came right back, "God is not going to send me to hell because I don't go along with what you say. Jesus says God is loving and forgives us seventy times seven times. Apparently, you and Jesus are in disagreement. That makes you an antichrist."

Old Benson turned beet red. In a burst of anger, he ordered, "Get out of here, Derek, and don't come back until you can apologize!"

As Derek left he muttered audibly, "Antichrist, antichrist. I'm never coming back."

I left with him. Once outside, Derek said, "I really appreciate your support, but I can't talk right now."

We must have walked an hour in silence. We were in the woods by then. He stopped, looked at me and gave me a hug—the only hug I can ever remember him giving me—and said, "I'm so lucky to have a friend like you."

We sat down in a grove of large pines with our backs to the same tree so we couldn't see each other's faces without turning our heads, but I could hear him okay.

"I'm not going to allow myself to get angry like that again. When I get angry I am the loser, whether I win my point or not. What I am really doing is separating myself from God. With you as my witness, I vow I will not try to convince anybody that what I believe is truth. If someone asks questions and I have an opinion, I'll talk about it. I will not argue because 'a man convinced against his will, is of the same opinion still' and all I have done is create anger."

"Yeah, old Benson sure was angry, wasn't he?" I said with a laugh.

"I will not try to lead a person to a place where they feel uncomfortable, even if I don't feel uncomfortable being there myself. Making people feel guilty is a trick the churches have used for ages. People have the right to be where they need to be, so I'm not going to try to move them to where I'm coming from, without their wanting to."

From that day on, Derek became his own teacher. He did go to see Mr. Benson and apologized. I wasn't there so I asked him what he had said. Derek told me he apologized for being discourteous and told him he didn't see how either of them could benefit from his coming back to Sunday school. After that he never went to church either, except for weddings or funerals.

Our parents rarely went to church, but they felt we kids ought to go to Sunday school and be exposed. When Derek explained his argument with Mr. Benson, they didn't make him go anymore. His sister, Maggie, had already stopped going.

From time to time I would question Derek, "What's the little philosopher thinking about today?" He'd tell me if he had anything special to say, but I usually couldn't think of what to ask him. Being a more typical twelve year old, I wasn't into metaphysics, or spiritual matters, as Derek preferred to call it.

My younger brother, Josh, was quieter and more contemplative than me and the two of them had lots of deep discussions over the years, which was good because Derek needed someone like Josh to stimulate his thinking and Josh benefited greatly from Derek.

By the time I was a sophomore, I was as tall as I am now and weighed almost as much. I've never had a problem with fat. Neither did Derek. We could eat whatever we wanted and our stomach muscles still rippled much to the annoyance of some people who easily put on weight.

It helped to be lean at the beach or around the pool. I used to wear my tee shirts cut short, exposing my midriff to attract the girls. Derek wasn't so brazen. I was never at a loss for dates and I played the field. In our class yearbook I was rated "the best physique," "the best athlete," and "the most likely to succeed (with women)." Derek was called "the class brain" and "the most likely to succeed."

Both of us had our drivers licenses before Christmas of our sophomore year. Derek had worked harder in the summers than me and spent considerably less on dates so he had saved enough to buy a used car that winter.

During the summers, he had a yard care company and would get younger kids to work for him. He also worked at Wendy's behind the counter. The manager had told him that any time he had free time, he had a job. I preferred to date and loved the challenge of making out with different girls. As Derek would say, "God gave us the freedom to choose." So, I chose females and had to use my parents' cars. On rare occasions I borrowed Derek's car.

Derek once said something like, "Nothing makes me happier than to see others happy and I can't do this with a solemn face. There must be joy and where there is joy there are smiles and laughter. A fake smile won't do because it has no joy. Compliments create joy for the receiver and keep the mind of the giver attuned to the good he sees. If, when I sit on my porch swing, I do not feel joyful, then I had better not pay much attention to my thoughts because they will be my creations and not given to me from on high. So it is with everything I do. If it is not done joyfully, God is not acting through me. I have walled God out."

Derek always looked to do the little things that made a difference. Things I never thought of doing. At a rest stop on the way to a football game Derek and I sat in stalls next to each other. I noticed Derek picking up scraps of toilet paper some slob had torn off and left on the floor. I said something like, "They have a janitor, Derek. Do you want him to lose his job?"

Derek replied, "I don't like messes. When we see something that needs to be done, just do it because it needs to be done. No one need know. If I do something to impress people, I do it for the wrong reason. It's better to do wrong things for the right reasons than right things for the wrong reasons." And then he added, "Service is the door to the future." You figure that one out.

On another football trip we again stopped at a rest area. Several of us took leaks, including Derek. When finished, Derek walked directly to the bus without washing his hands. One of the players teased him saying, "My father taught me to wash my hands after pissing."

Derek replied, "That's great, but my father taught me not to piss on my hands."

In my senior year, I was taking second-year French from old Mr. Shea who was about to retire. He was anything but inspirational. He was a bore. As a result, I sometimes fell asleep in class which, needless to say, didn't ingratiate me to him. In fact, Shea threatened to flunk me, "Football or no football, the big game or no big game," he said to Rusty, our football coach.

Rusty panicked. I was his star player. Our biggest rival game was only three weeks away and mid-terms were just two weeks away. "I'm going to see if I can't get that new French teacher to tutor you. I know you'd pay attention to her," he told me. He was right. That cute, new French teacher was Michelle Duval, who, of course, is now my wife. Rusty convinced Michelle, and I went to her room to set up an appointment.

Let me insert here how Derek and I first noticed Michelle. We were walking down the hall the first day of school our senior year. Derek was the first to see her coming towards us. He exclaimed, "Look at that cute chick! She's new. She's gorgeous. She's..." and so forth. I had never seen him so enthusiastic about a female before. He ended up by saying, "She's the gal I want to marry." The chemistry was right between Michelle and Derek from the very start.

Michelle gave Derek a glance as she passed us. He whispered, "She looked at me." He stopped and watched her go down the hall. Then Michelle turned her head and briefly glanced back at Derek. Derek went crazy. In his excitement he pounded my arm with his fist. "She looked back! She's in love with me! I'm going to marry her!" He only cooled off slightly when he learned she was the new French teacher and was four years older than him though she didn't look it. "Poor Derek," I told my folks at dinner that night, "he spotted the love of his life this morning and it turned out to be a new teacher. Poor Derek."

However, that didn't stop him. French III was one of the courses Michelle was teaching and Derek had taken it the previous year. However, he went to his advisor and somehow convinced him to allow him to repeat the course as an extra subject 'because she has such a good French accent.' He didn't know if she had a 'good French accent' or not, never having heard her speak French, but he convinced his advisor. She did, of course, speak perfect French since her father was French and they spoke it at home.

When our free periods didn't match, she suggested I come to her classroom right after school. I told her I had football practice right after school and asked if we could meet after practice. She paused and then made a mistake no experienced teacher would make, at least not with me—particularly if they were young and cute. She told me her apartment was right across the street and I could come over after practice.

I was there freshly showered. We sat at her kitchen table next to each other, she on my right. I had my text book to my left and my open notebook in front of me. Michelle stood up to point out something in the text she wanted me to work on. I moved my shoulder slightly away from her so she would come closer since the text was on the other side. When she bent closer, I slowly moved my shoulder back against her and slowly rotated it against her body while I let my hand fall limply to my crouch. She went into the other room while I translated some sentences. After I had written out what she wanted me to, I went into the living room to tell her I was finished.

Michelle put down the newspaper and came back to the kitchen table and sat in her chair. I pushed the notebook in front of her, but remained standing next to her as she read my work, deciphering my penmanship. First I put my hands on her shoulders and then started to gently massage. I didn't want to appear too forward and scare her, but I did.

The next day at school, I got a message to report to Michelle's room. She told me that because of what happened yesterday afternoon she had arranged for her best student to tutor me. "Derek Saul, you know him don't you?" she said. "I think I've seen the two of you together."

"Yeah, I know Derek. He lives next door," I quietly admitted.

"He's very competent," Michelle assured me, as if I didn't know.

"But he isn't you," I complained.

"There is a time and place for everything and this is not the time for anything but your learning French," she sternly reminded me.

Derek was excited about tutoring me because this gave him the opportunity to see Michelle about how and what he should be doing. A close bond continued to grow between them. He exuded the good vibes that everybody enjoyed. But, to win more brownie points, that son-of-a-bitch asked Michelle to speak to him in French. There was no way I could compete. It was during these few weeks that they fell hopelessly in love—hopelessly.

Derek quit tutoring me after midterm exams and Michelle invited him to her apartment to work on his oral French because she owed him a favor after he helped her out by tutoring me. The next thing I knew they were engaged, Michelle was pregnant, and Derek wanted me to be his best man.

The wedding was held the Saturday after Christmas. That way Derek's sister, Maggie, could be home from college on her Christmas break. Derek's older brother, Ken, flew down from Boston where he worked. It was a small wedding held at a country club in the next town.

Although her pregnancy went smoothly, Michelle was given a hard time by the other teachers at school. Derek and Michelle tried to keep their marriage quiet, but somehow the word got out as Michelle's stomach expanded. She was then considered a slut. Derek had always been such a pure kid that everyone, including the students, believed Michelle had seduced him. Derek didn't receive any of the disapproval.

Michael Duval Saul arrived August 8th, ten days late, although they told everybody he was six weeks premature. I don't think anybody was fooled. He weighed almost eight pounds. Derek was the perfect father right from the start. Two weeks after Mike was born, I was off to college. Football practice started about two weeks before classes. I got home for Christmas, then spring break and, at last, summer.

I had not done well in college scholastically. The courses were harder, demanded more time, and I was heavily into athletics, football, basketball, and baseball. I had done famously in football, and also with women. I was very popular. There are advantages and disadvantages to being good looking and well built. All kinds of opportunities opened up and the temptations were irresistible. At least I used a condom.

I had been introduced to a professional football scout, Richard Short, around Thanksgiving in my freshman year. He was there scouting an older player and had given me his card saying, "If you ever decide to leave college to play professional football, give me a call."

I had kept his card even though I had no inkling then that I would consider quitting college. Later when I knew I was in danger of being ineligible to play sports because of poor grades, I found his card in my desk and transferred it to my wallet. I actually had become ineligible my freshman year, but they had winked and let it pass.

When I called up Richard Short that summer it was mainly to keep in touch. I did not want to be forgotten as the years went by, because I definitely had my eyes on professional football after college. He remembered me. He quizzed me on how I was doing, how well I made out in football last fall, and about my grades. I had made first squad the last half of the season. He seemed impressed and we got together.

I asked about starting salaries. I became excited. I started bargaining for a higher salary. He jumped up 25% so quickly it made me suspicious. I suggested maybe I'd do better if I played another year at college and got to be better known. He said, "Go ahead and try it. Make sure you don't get injured." Or something like that, but making sure he had planted "the get injured" germ. When he offered a signing bonus, I grabbed it. I decided to quit college and go into professional football.

But, then came the unpleasant task of telling my folks and facing their criticism. I can still hear them screaming, "What! Quit college! You must be out of your mind! Football is such a short career. What will you do then? A high school won't even hire you to coach without a college degree," and on and on. But it was too late. I had entered into a contract. The pay was good, very good, and I wanted to do it.

My parents' remark about a short career and Richard's remark saying you might get injured made me realize I had to put something aside. I was worried I might blow the $15,000 signing bonus. I decided I didn't need a new car. My old clunker would do for the time being. Right at that time the Sauls were planning to sell their house to Derek and were moving out into the country.

Mom was particularly upset about their move as she and Mrs. Saul were best friends. I suggested my parents sell me their house at fair market value and move near the Sauls. After all, I had $15,000 as a down payment and a salary to support the mortgage.

They immediately liked the idea. We all thought it would be excellent for me to make a sound investment with my cash and a house would be just that. Also, I would have to become responsible being a property owner and having a mortgage to pay. I was particularly delighted to be living next door to my best friend, his wife, and their cute son.

Josh agreed to continue living in my house while he was still in high school. He could take care of it while I was away during the football season and he didn't want to move. He was close to school and his friends, including Derek with whom he had become very close while I was away. It all worked out so smoothly it seemed as if it was destined.

Derek, more than once, had said that when our motivations are pure, things work out for the best. He had explained, "We are not our bodies; they are our vehicles; we are not our minds either. We are our motivations and that controls our minds, which in turn determines or limits our actions, for mind is the builder and the physical is the result."

Derek's thinking continually amazed me. It just wasn't like anyone else's I knew, certainly not like Mr. Benson, our old Sunday School teacher, or any of the churchy church people I knew. That's what made Derek so special. God blessed him.

My first year in professional football was mostly a learning experience. At my parent's and Derek's prodding, I went back to college for the spring term during the off season. I decided to go to American University, the same college Derek went to nights and sometimes during the day, so I could live in my house and be close to Derek, Michelle, and Mike.

My second year with professional football went very well for me. I got to play every game and towards the end of the season I played at least half of every game. By the end of the season I must have been considered a potentially valuable player because the team owners wanted to tie me up with a five-year contract at double my salary.

I was only 21. In five years I would be 26 and many, maybe most, players are through their careers by then. I wondered if I would be wise in signing up for that long a time. Suppose I became a big time star.

When they offered an annual review of salary with arbitration, if needed, and retained the right to sell me to another team, I knew then they thought I was valuable, and not just another player. I was money in their pockets. Then, I figured it was all right to sign.

About this time, while on the road, I met Diane. She was beautiful by anyone's standard, well-shaped, athletic, and an outdoors person. We hit it off famously right from the start. I forgot about other women. I felt wholesome.

Diane wasn't Phi Beta Kappa, neither was I, but she was alert, loving, humorous, compassionate, and I felt she truly loved me. We spent a lot of time together that summer, including some backpacking and traveling in my new car. She quit her job as a secretary to spend the summer with me. We spent over a month at my house in Falls Church next door to Michelle and Derek and young Mike, whom I loved as if I were his father.

My parents loved Diane and Michelle and Derek approved. We were married in October. On our short honeymoon, because the football season was underway, we had our first unprotected sex and by early November she was pregnant. This wasn't exactly what we had planned, but we were delighted.

In late November, during a crucial football game, I was tackled by two players from opposite sides as I was receiving a pass. One tackled low, getting only my left leg, while the other tackled high, pushing my upper body sideward, although the first tackler was still holding my lower leg firmly. It almost seemed planned to eliminate me.

The result was my bones ripped apart at the knee. A wicked injury, excruciatingly painful, involving ligaments, tendons, cartilage, and muscle. I passed out. It would have been much better if I had broken bones. They heal much faster and more completely. With my kind of injury there was no way of telling how long it would take to regain the agility and strength to walk comfortably, let alone run and play football.

In the next six months, I had three operations, each trying to mend something else. Physical therapy was very painful. The results were not apparent to me, although the doctors said they saw increments of improvement between visits. I thought they were lying.

I was extremely depressed. Sex was so painful to my knee it was impossible. Even though Diane always wanted sex, I just couldn't. I couldn't even snuggle up to her at night. I had to lie on my back with a pillow under my knee. Sometimes Diane would snuggle up to me, put her head on my left shoulder while I put my arm affectionately under her neck. This was nice until she accidentally hit my left knee in her sleep. Then I would gasp with pain and the damn knee would ache all night.

I felt guilty leaving her unfulfilled. We switched sides of the bed sleeping on the other side of each other, her on my right. That proved better, but sometimes my knee would ache anyway, a dull ache. I was never really comfortable. I was grouchy. I could see my lucrative football career going out the window. I started losing weight.

I had to get out of the house. I just couldn't stand lying around doing nothing but reading and watching TV. I started hobbling next door on crutches to play with Mike, who was then two and a half. He was a joy. Michelle was a joy and very understanding and sympathetic.

Once in a while Diane would come over, too, which I enjoyed thoroughly, but she couldn't develop the same joy playing with Mike that I could. Michelle and Diane got along well, but the more I saw them together the more I realized Michelle was a superior person. Derek had given up a potentially great career to marry her, the woman he loved. Not because she was pregnant, but because he loved her. He was—they were—so happy. I was jealous but I reveled in their happiness and vicariously shared in it. I loved them both.

We were, in fact, a loving threesome, but I was next door with my pregnant wife and a marriage that was souring. We thought maybe our baby would pull us back together. However, Diane lost the baby in her fifth month of pregnancy. It would have been a girl. We were devastated and became very depressed, particularly Diane.

When Diane had recovered, she tried to get a job to keep busy. Weeks went by and nothing to her satisfaction came up. She felt house bound. I was so crippled we couldn't socialize with my old friends who still lived in town. Besides Josh, Michelle, and Derek, she had no friends. Even though they were true friends, Diane felt somewhat outside the foursome of Derek, Michelle, Josh, and myself. We four had always been so close.

At least twice that I can remember, maybe more often, when Diane had a problem I said, "Michelle would do this or that." Diane seethed quietly at the implication. She was a good woman, but without sex or outside activity in our lives, we had little commonality.

When summer rolled around, Diane got a job with the town recreation department. Hopefully, it would last into the fall or until she was pregnant again. By summer, sex started being a regular part of our lives again. For the most part, however, I guess I was no fun. I had lost my sparkle. I couldn't participate in most activities even though my knee was improving.

My first annual football contract review came around. Although I walked with a cane into the meeting there was no way I would be able to play football that season. Actually, I felt better with crutches, because when I used a cane, every now and then my knee clicked and it felt as if it were going to give out. I never actually fell, but I lacked the confidence to walk regularly without crutches. At the review meeting, I didn't want the team owners to see me using crutches so I used a cane.

At my salary review, they wanted to cut my pay 75% until I could play again. I talked them up to 50%, reminding them how Joe Namath wore braces on both knees for the last few years of his career. I told them I was sure I would be all right next year. I lied.

Come fall, I went back to American University with Derek as a full-time student. He was only part time. Without athletics to occupy so much of my time, I was able to get good grades for the first time since elementary school when Derek and I studied together. This was a great boost to my self esteem. Of course, I was older than most of the students which helped and I was married.

With the end of the town's fall recreational activities, they let Diane go. She went into a depression again. That, together with me spending hours at school and with my studies and hours with physical therapy at the gym, plus time with Mike, caused Diane to reach an all-time low.

"I think it's nice you spend time with Mike, but you spend more time with him than with me. He's not your child and I am your wife," she would tell me. Mike was such a happy, fun kid I hated the thought of giving up any of my time with him to spend with my somewhat dull wife.

The final straw came when one day I thoughtlessly said, "Well, Michelle sure as hell wouldn't do that."

The shit hit the fan. "You're in love with Michelle. I can't play second fiddle to her. I want a divorce."

I tried to explain, "Michelle's just a good friend. She's my best friend's wife. She's totally in love with Derek. You can see that. It's so obvious."

I found myself pleading, but inside not really believing. "You're my wife. You're the one I love. You're depressed right now, but you'll get over it. We'll have a family. Everything will work out."

"I don't believe it," Diane replied. "You paint a rosy picture, but I don't...I can't believe it. I want a divorce." She wouldn't make love that night and the next morning she packed up and headed for her parents' home eight hours away.

We tried to patch things up a few days later by phone. She wanted to give the marriage another try if I would move up by her parents. I actually agreed to give it a try, but as I drove north I was already feeling miserable. Leaving my house, my only home, my parents, my brother, college, and, of course, Derek and Michelle was a devastating concession to save a marriage I wasn't sure I wanted to save.

It took only two weeks before it became clear to both of us that it was over. A chapter in my life was closed. I crammed at college to make up what I had missed while away with Diane. My physiotherapy seemed to take a turn for the better. I could walk without a cane. Even Josh and I grew closer. He started talking some of the metaphysical stuff he and Derek talked about. I wasn't depressed about the divorce. It was over. Football next fall with a brace seemed a possibility. I was as happy as I had been in a long, long time.

For the next two years life proceeded rather smoothly for a change. My divorce was finalized the following spring. I continued with college in the off season and Derek, Josh, and I graduated together. Josh went to work for Derek and his father in their insurance agency. I kept myself in shape bicycling and working out in the gym. I couldn't jog with my knee.

I joined a singles club at the Y. My social life was minimal. I don't know whether to say I had matured and was less wild or whether the long recuperation with my knee, plus my divorce, had sobered me. But I was content to do less. Derek had once told me when I was in my wild sex period before I met Diane, that anybody could get mired in the physical plane if their life were wholly devoted to any aspect of the worldly life, be it sex, money, work, travel, drugs, whatever. We need to be balanced mentally, physically, and spiritually to accomplish our purpose in this life. At the time, I had no idea what he was talking about.

I played a lot with Mike. I was very fortunate in knowing I was always welcome next door. It was comforting and congenial. I believed that if I didn't go over daily I would be missed. That's how great it was. Derek was always my very best friend.

During the fifth and last year of my football contract I began to think more about the future. Did I want to continue playing football? Did I want to run the risk of a more permanent injury to my knee or even my other leg? Now that I had my college degree I could get a job coaching at a high school or maybe at a college.

I had also played basketball and baseball in high school and one year at college. Maybe a YMCA needed a physical director. I started making the rounds to the various high schools and colleges within commuting distance to Falls Church. Nothing surfaced. I was told it was one thing to play and another thing to coach and I had no experience in the latter. Besides, in small schools, coaches also had to teach and I was not qualified.

The owners were debating whether to renew my contract when I got a phone call from a high school I had visited. Their coach and physical director had a serious heart attack and they asked if I would be willing to substitute for a few months. I grabbed the opportunity. This still left me open for a possible football contract the following fall, and it would give me practical experience coaching and teaching.

As it turned out, the coach I replaced took early retirement and I was offered his job for the balance of the year. I guess I did okay. Before the end of the year the school offered me a permanent job. Professional football was history for me.

I felt good about it even with the cut in pay. Money wasn't everything and I had built up a nest egg. This was to be a new career, one that could last me until retirement, not just a short-term career that could result in a forced, unhappy, disabled retirement. I was then 26.

My life was now in a groove, not a rut, but a groove. I liked what I was doing. I had dropped the wild sex orientation of my youth. I dated occasionally. Derek and I did a lot of things together with Mike like we used to do when we were kids: fishing, camping, hiking, swimming, bicycling. Michelle often joined us. We even were into the family swim at the Y on Friday nights like when we were kids.

The next seven years flew by. I shared my house with another divorced teacher. Josh continued to live next door in the third floor apartment. He had moved there when I rented my house furnished to Grover Baldwin while he finished building his new home. Grover had been a close friend in high school.

Then came that afternoon in late fall. We were getting together to celebrate Michelle's pregnancy with their second child. Derek had not returned home from work yet. He was late and that was unusual for him. It was particularly strange since he knew of the celebration and was so jubilant about becoming a father again. I was already next door talking to Michelle. It would have been dusk except the thick rain clouds made it seem like night. A persistent rain had been falling all afternoon.

Then Michelle got the call from the police. Derek had been in a serious accident. We rushed to the hospital and he was still alive when we arrived, but he passed away within an hour. We held each other and wept. I didn't know what I could possibly do to ease Michelle's pain. And I was in pain myself. I had just lost my best friend whom I had known forever.

On his deathbed Derek wanted, actually told, Michelle and me to marry so the kids would have a loving family to grow up in. He knew I loved Michelle and that she loved me. Not like she adored him, but she loved me and needed me. Derek felt confident everything would work out. Michelle and I waited four months before we got married.

I don't know whether he was able to or not, but Derek said he would reincarnate in the unborn son Michelle was carrying. Knowing Derek, I believe it's possible. He said he would be a rebel and a reformer.

Young Derek was born without a hitch. From baby pictures he looked like his father. He was bright like his father. He didn't seem like a rebel, except he definitely had a mind of his own. He knew what he wanted, but he was a pleasant baby and child. He is now going on three and talks well.

When Derek died, he owned half interest in The Saul Insurance Agency which Michelle inherited. At the time of Derek's death, she was teaching again and in the middle of the school year. Her plan was to finish teaching that year, but not to teach again until young Derek was in school the full day.

At first, she thought of selling her half of the agency to Josh, but he didn't have any money. Roger Saul didn't want to buy it because he had reached retirement age. That left me. Josh and Roger Saul convinced me to quit coaching and come into the agency, which I did at the end of the school year. It has worked out well.

Last year Michelle and I had a baby girl of our own, Annie Bassett. This rounds out our family. We were pleased it was a girl, but we definitely do not want any more children. Mike's room was converted into a nursery for Annie. Mike moved upstairs into the apartment.

Josh moved next door to my house, but he continued to come back and forth, eating dinner with us most of the time, that is until he met, at the Unity singles' group, a wonderful young lady named Marianne Dalton. They have been married two years and have a little daughter. We are one close happy family. But, its hard not to miss Derek and wish he was still here with us.

Chapter Seven

Ken's Journal (April 7)

I just finished talking with Michelle at breakfast. It's been great having breakfast with her. Our banter is so invigorating I'm able to forget about my problems with Jenny. It's been a great time to talk about what's going on with the book or anything else we get started on. It's very easy to see why Derek loved Michelle. She's great.

This morning the conversation drifted back to Jan Hall again. Michelle gave me more background information. She explained how Jan Hall was a classmate whom Derek frequently invited to high school dances and school events, and occasionally to a movie or bowling. Derek never really had romantic feelings about her, nor she for him. They were just good friends.

Jan moved away, but after ten years came back to town to nurse her mother who was in the early stages of Alzheimer's. Her father had divorced her mother and moved away with another woman. Jan was furious with him and, by association, men in general. Jan had never married. While Jan was looking for a part-time job, she stopped at Derek's office. He didn't have a job for her, but they chatted and caught up on the lost years.

When Mike started school it was only half day. Michelle got a little restless and bored. She really wanted a baby-sitter and a housekeeper so she could resume her teaching career. Derek was not in favor of her doing this until Mike was in school full time.

The week after Derek met Jan, the high school called Michelle asking her to be a substitute for a French teacher who was going on maternity leave. So, Derek asked Jan if she would become their baby-sitter/housekeeper. She agreed and a friendly relationship developed between Jan and Michelle. The teacher on maternity leave never came back and Michelle, because she had Jan's help, was able to resume her teaching career. To Michelle, Jan became much more of a friend than an employee.

The night of the accident, Michelle was surprised Jan was with Derek as she wasn't expected at the celebration party since she usually had her mother to care for.

At that point in our discussion, an unexplainable flash crossed my mind. I asked Michelle if she knew for sure that Derek was driving at the time of the accident. She gave me an astonished look and then quickly shot down the possibility that Jan might have been driving. She's probably right. It was, after all, his car. She says she never heard anything from the police about who was driving, but never thought to ask and just assumed it was Derek.

It may not be significant, but why am I disturbed? Why do I want to check it out? Must be the journalist in me or maybe it's in an effort to understand how and why Derek passed away so young.

After breakfast, Michelle gave me the account she received from her brother Andre, who lives in Paris. I read it and think I'll leave it just as he wrote it. There are some funny little mistakes in his English, but the meaning is clear. Although Andre wasn't real close to Derek, his account tells a lot about Michelle.

I only met him once at the wedding, so I practically know nothing of him. I didn't know he was close to Derek. But, seems like there were a lot of people who were closer to Derek than I was.

Andre Duval's Account

Michelle writes that she is going to make a biography of her late husband, Derek Saul, which I think is great as they broke the mold, so to speak, after he was born.

Michelle feels that his biography ought to include where she comes from to better understand him. She also asks me to write in English. This will be a chore as I never write in English any more and rarely speak it. It has been 17 years since I moved back to France with Father. Please bear with me.

Michelle and I were always very close and were often treated as twins as she was only eleven months older than I. We didn't mind being treated as twins since we did think of life in terms of each other, particularly in our early years. We rarely squabbled and if we did, it didn't last.

When we were born, our father, Gaston Duval, worked for the French Embassy in Washington, D.C. Our older brother, Pierre, was born in France. He was two years older than Michelle. Michelle and I were born in the United States.

Our mother, Claudette, had a difficult time birthing Pierre. She got toxic and very high blood pressure. He came a bit early, but safely. My parents were advised that the next pregnancy could be normal, but also were advised to wait awhile. My parents were practicing Catholics and were not into birth control, so Michelle was conceived a little over a year later. Mother got much worse toxic again and Michelle came almost two months premature. It was very much touch and stop as to whether she would live, but she did, obviously, although she was puny.

My parents were strongly advised not to have any more children. My father was considering a testicle operation, but was waiting until it was certain Michelle would live.

Against the Catholic Church, they began to practice birth control. I don't know what technique, but it did not work. My mother got pregnant right away with me which she felt, according to Father, was punishment for trying to use contraception. No way would she have an abortion against the church even though the doctor strongly advised it.

Again she got more toxic earlier. Soon she was dying and was kept in the hospital under medicine. My father had two babies to take care of and Michelle was puny. Fortunately, the Embassy was sympathetic and allowed Father to arrive late a little and leave a little early. A neighbor mother came over daily after her kids went to school and stayed until they came home. They would then play at our house until Father got home. So Father tells me. I don't remember.

Mother got worse and at about seven months of pregnancy she died. I was born by cesarean on the spot. I only weighed one and a half kilo [about 3 1/2 lbs.]. I was, by good luck, quite healthy and after about a month, I weighed enough to come home.

Can you imagine my poor father? One son just three and running around like crazy and not understanding discipline, a puny daughter just one year old and me only one month and also puny. He was a saint to live without suicide. For more than ten years he lived like that. Every time he was not at work he was home with us. All my memory of those early years was he being loving and kind, but with gentle discipline. We were a happy family and did much things together.

I remember our favorite place was at a state park up the Potomac River where we would hike and swim and sometimes camp out in a big tent. We also visited important buildings and places in or near Washington.

When we grew older and Pierre and Michelle were in high school with lots of homework they each wanted a bedroom alone. So, Father, by himself, built a bedroom with bath off the kitchen for himself and left us with the three bedrooms and bath upstairs. Our house was on an older street in the town of McLean, Virginia, not far from Washington. Ours was a decent size lot with trees and quite a nice neighborhood.

We all did well in school and learned English without an accent, but, at home, father spoke only French because he knew that sometime he would be sent back to France and we must know French then. Father spoke good English, but with a little accent.

Father did not allow himself time to date women. We children were his entire life outside of work and that is why we were so close. It was good. We had our friends. Some were children of others in the Embassy and spoke French, but mostly our friends were from school and from our neighborhood and, of course, spoke only English.

Although my father raised us Catholic, I went to the Youth Fellowship of a Protestant church with some friends. It was a group of about 15 and we socialized a lot outside of church. We called ourselves "The Gang." Michelle didn't hang out with this group. Maybe a few times, but her girl friends were a year or so older than her and were dating college freshmen for the most part and Michelle soon did, too. She was probably the youngest of her group of school friends being born near the end of the year. Although I knew her friends just like she knew mine, I was not included in their social life, nor did I want to be. I had my own.

Michelle and I were always close, no secrets, lots of conversation on all subjects. Even little things like right now I would take time to tell her how the more I write this account of our upbringing the more easily it is to write in English. It's coming back, including the jargon.

When Michelle went off to college I was almost 17. I should mention that when Pierre turned 14, Father thought he was old enough to baby sit Michelle and me, and so he started socializing more. This was very good for Father. He was only 40, the same age I am now and I consider myself young still.

The summer before I entered my senior year in high school and Michelle started college, Father married a dominating, opinionated widow from the French Embassy. I think she must have pressured him unmercifully until he proposed or maybe she proposed. I often wondered if her first husband committed suicide. She made me wear a coat and tie to school. She didn't want me to go to the Youth Fellowship because it wasn't Catholic. She was afraid I might fall for a Protestant and marry one if I never met any nice Catholic girls. She smoked.

Ultimately, she pressured Father to transfer back to France so I could go to a good French college with nice Catholic girls. Protest though I did, I had no choice. I was still 17. Michelle was 18, which made her of legal age, plus she already had a scholarship for her second year in Middlebury College.

Fortunately, that marriage didn't last, but when it broke up, I was in my third year at the Universite de Sorbonne in Paris. I liked what I was studying. I had a new set of friends. I was adjusted and happy with life in France. I did, however, eventually marry a Protestant. Father also remarried a fine lady, but not until Michelle and I were married and on our own.

Late one fall, before I was married, Michelle telephoned. Father was not home, only me. Michelle was happy about that as I was easier to talk to. She was pregnant and was going to marry one of her high school students. I was shocked more than you can believe. It was good I broke the news to Father. She would have been killed in his explosion.

Father and I returned to the United States for the wedding. Although she was pregnant she didn't look it yet, and she was still teaching French in high school. Father paid for Pierre's plane fare to come to the wedding. He was working in San Francisco as I remember.

I got to meet Derek and it was love at first sight. Derek formally shook Father's hand as expected of him, but with me there was no formal handshake. He simply opened his arms enfolding me in the warmest hug possible and whispered in my ear, "I feel like I have known you forever." I'll never forget how my knees went weak. Although he was three years younger than me and only 18, I felt him an equal.

I was extremely happy for Michelle and knew instantly why she was so attracted to Derek. All thoughts about a tragic shotgun wedding to a high school kid four years younger than her flew out the window. I knew it was right. He had a quick, easy, warm smile. Infectious, you might say. He was cute, but masculine. He was small, about my height, one and two-thirds meters, with a solid, but slender build. Michelle says we looked alike, but I could never see that. I was happy for Derek also because I knew what a wonderful person my sister was.

My marriage gave me a good excuse to visit the United States again since Michelle and Derek couldn't attend. It gave me a chance to introduce my new bride, Pauline, to Michelle and Derek. Pauline did not speak English, but Derek's French was surprisingly passable.

I also got to meet Michael. He had been the best man at the wedding. I enjoyed Michael. I thought he was a neat guy and knew he had been Derek's best friend all his life, but the time we spent together was limited. I was much more interested in seeing Michelle, introducing her to Pauline, and getting to know Derek better.

About a year before Derek died, he and Michelle paid a visit to France to see Father and me and meet Father's new wife. It was a very enjoyable visit. From France they went on to Egypt first and then Tibet. Michelle had dual citizenship, but I don't know how they managed a visa to Tibet which was, by then, part of China.

One night, three years ago, I was getting ready for bed when the phone rang. It was Father. He came right out and said, "Derek is dead."

"Mon Dieu, mon Dieu!" [My God, my God!] was all I could say. I was so choked I couldn't reply.

"An auto accident," Father said as I hung up. I was too numb for the tears to flow. I just stood there with my hand still on the receiver.

Pauline walked in from the bathroom. "Who was that?" I couldn't answer. "What's happened?" she continued.

I took her in my arms and as the tears began to flow, I managed to say, "Derek's dead. An auto accident."

Later that day I called Michelle. I wish I could have been there and been able to hold her. We both cried. Then she told me of Derek's last request from his deathbed. He had said she knew that Michael loved her, wanted to marry her and he would make a wonderful husband and that she needed him. He had asked her to marry Michael before the baby is born. Derek had said if he could arrange it, he would try to reincarnate in the son she was carrying. I don't know how he knew it would be a boy.

I didn't even know yet that Michelle was pregnant. I did not think she would be able to bring herself to marry that soon. I did not know about reincarnation. I did not know why Derek would want his son to carry Michael's last name. Life has so many questions. All I could feel was that Michelle would do the right thing. I loved Michelle and had confidence in her judgment. I was very deeply saddened by the death of Derek because I knew how he meant the world to Michelle.

Everything worked out well for them and the baby was born healthy. I am sure that believing Derek would reincarnate in the baby made the transition easier for Michelle.

That's it. That's my story. I look forward to reading the book.

Ken's Journal (April 7, late)

Jenny, why are you always on my mind? I had thought my being away would give me a break—a chance to rest and recover—a chance to re-think. But I can't get you out of my mind. Maybe we're just meant for each other and should spend more time looking for each other's good points, rather than constantly fighting over our differences. You have so many good points, so many I have chosen to forget in recent years. But, I won't forget again. I only hope you haven't chosen to forget.

Part Two

Chapter Eight

Ken's Journal (April 8)

It's nearly midnight and I just realized I hadn't written a journal entry today. I've been so busy visiting with people and working on the book. The days are truly flying by.

I sent Jenny an e-mail last night. It was our first communication since I left. Maybe I should have waited a little longer to give us more time, but there's so much I want to share with her right now and I'm curious to know how she's doing and what she's doing, maybe even who she's seeing. I don't want to give her the impression that I don't trust her, because I do. I think I do. Well, I always have, but it's hard to know for sure after all the difficulties we've been through recently.

I heard Scott was back in town and I'm sure that was him who called several times. I wonder, now that he's had the kids and family he wanted with his second wife, if he's renewed his interest in Jenny. Maybe he realizes he made a mistake when he left her. Maybe she's curious to find out what would have been.

A week ago, I might have said fine with me. But, now I'm not willing to give up the woman I have loved so dearly for so long—certainly even before their marriage.

Ken's E-mail to Jenny (April 7)

Dear Jenny,

I miss you, Hon. I can't tell you how much.

I now believe our differences will resolve themselves. I would like to come back and begin working on that together.

Right now, however, it doesn't look like I'll be back soon. Putting this book together has become much more involved than I anticipated. I'm learning so many things I never knew, some of which I'll have to wait to tell you about later. I now seriously wish I had known my brother better when he was alive. His thinking on why things do or do not happen has strongly affected my understanding about life. He was truly a remarkable person.

To give you an example, Derek strongly believed in freedom of choice. Think about it a minute. How often have we considered the true consequences of freedom of choice? He believed we are where we are because we have created the circumstances that got us here. We are totally responsible. He refers to energy patterns we create by our thinking and actions and how what we think or do, creates the future. Thinking makes it so. He referred to this realm of being as the "etheric." Everything happens first in the etheric, or the fourth dimension. And our freedom of choice is the starting point.

For example, how I perceive what you say as unrealistic, or how you perceive what I do as selfish, and how neither of us will back down. All this has created our troubled etheric. I'm beginning to realize the extent to which I'm responsible for our difficulties. My negative attitudes may have a greater affect than I ever would have allowed myself to imagine.

At about this time, I know you're probably wondering who the hell is writing this. But I've really had my eyes opened to a number of things about myself, our relationship, and life in general over the past week. There's so much to tell you about. I can hardly wait!

Also Derek believed that God gave us free will so we could choose to be one with Him or not. God does not condemn us for bad choices for they aren't really good or bad choices or right or wrong as the church would have us believe. Our choices are just experiments. Hopefully, we'll discard those which don't work out well for all concerned but *when* we discard bad choices is also a matter of choice. We are always setting up energy patterns in the etheric which we have to experience, for how else will we know the effects of our erroneous or wonderful thinking. God does not punish us. We punish ourselves by having to experience what we have dished out and this can be pleasant or unpleasant. It's the first time I think I've ever really felt comfortable with a perception of God and religion.

I also believe I'm coming to realize that forgiveness is the only answer. Please forgive me, Jenny. I've been an asshole too often. I can't wait to talk to you.

I gotta go, but I'll call you soon.

I love you, Jenny. I always will.

Ken

Reply E-mail from Jenny

What you said sounds interesting, but do you really think things between us can change just like that? I do think we have a lot to talk about and it sounds like you are finally ready to talk about us, which is a start. But, I don't want us to look for a quick fix and then think everything is going to be all better.

It's going to take real work and a commitment to continue that work. Do you realize that? Actions speak louder than words. And why should I think that you aren't going to quickly fall back into a depressing outlook on things the same as you always do?

Jen

Ken's Journal (April 9)

I called Jenny after getting her e-mail last night and we actually talked for over an hour. I can't remember the last time we talked that long—on or off the phone. I know we still have a lot of issues to resolve, but I think we are making progress. At least, I hope so. I can understand her reluctance to believe anything has changed with me this quickly. But, that's just because she hasn't been here with me. I wish she could come down. I think tonight I will ask her to do exactly that.

Michelle gave me her account this morning. I have been anxious to read it and was wondering when she was finally going to finish. Every time I asked her if she had it, she would tell me she needed more time.

As she handed it to me, she gave me a hug and thanked me for all my help. I told her it's been my pleasure and that I was grateful for the chance to help and to get to know Derek. She said she only wished the two of us had been closer while he was still alive. She told me that even though I hadn't spent much time with him and we never became very close, Derek always spoke fondly of me. I wonder if she's just buttering me up.

I told her how sorry I was for not having been a better brother. She started to cry. Then I started to as well. I told her I wished there was a way to make it up somehow. She said that's what I was doing now in my own way. She's right.

Michelle then asked how things were going with Jenny. I told her all about the situation. She was sorry to hear things haven't been going well for quite some time, but thought it might eventually be good for our relationship if we were able to grow together from the experience. I hope she's right. I hope it's not too late. Although now I can truthfully say I believe it will work out. Derek would say that's positive thinking.

The only thing I didn't tell Michelle was that one of the reasons we're having these troubles, I think, is because Scott has re-entered the picture. I can't say for sure that there's anything still between them, but I have a feeling there might be. I hope he's just a confidant. Anyway, I'm not going to let him walk in and steal her away.

Michelle's Account

I had no home in the United States when I graduated from college and entered the working world, but I definitely did not want to go live in France with my father. The one summer I had spent there between my junior and senior years at college had convinced me of that.

Father had never urged me to go to college in France because I had a good scholarship at Middlebury College and he had not expected to move back to France when he did. He liked living in the United States and did not want to return to France, but his new wife, who is also French and worked with him at the French Embassy, insisted. Neither I nor Andre got along well with her. As a matter of fact, Father didn't either. A few years later they were divorced.

Upon graduating from college, I lived with a friend in McLean, Virginia, where I had grown up near Washington. I applied for a teaching position at a number of high schools in the suburban towns around Washington, DC, where I wanted to settle.

I spoke fluent Parisian French. I had majored in French at a college noted for its language department and had graduated with honors, but I didn't have experience which worried me and I looked young. I was only 22.

Despite my lack of experience, I had two offers and chose the high school in Falls Church, mostly because it was so close to McLean. I took a cute, small, one-bedroom apartment right across the street from the high school.

I was nervous my first day at school as I walked down the hall to my new home room. Some of the kids looked as old as I did. How was I going to gain their respect and keep them in line? I noticed two older boys walking together towards me. One was a tall, handsome boy who swaggered as he listened to his cute, shorter friend. The short one was jabbering away, but his eye caught me glancing at him. He stopped talking and watched me as I walked by. I looked away embarrassed. Once down the hall a little way, I glanced back. He was stopped and still looking at me. I was mortified. My first day in school and I felt sure he thought I was flirting.

Two days later, he walked into my third-year French class with a note from his faculty advisor requesting that I admit him, even though he was two days late registering. His name was Derek Saul.

He took a seat up front, but to the side near the window. He stared at me and I found it very difficult to keep from staring back. Even when he wasn't smiling, his eyes sparkled mischievously. Although I knew nothing about him, that smile endeared him to me. There was the right chemistry between us from the very start. He also somehow reminded me of my brother Andre, who was also short and cute and whom I loved dearly.

Derek volunteered frequently and spoke good French, much better than the other students. I was curious, so, one free period I went to the office and checked his record. He was a senior and had nothing but A's in every subject, but he had already taken my course.

The next day after class I asked him, "How come you are repeating this course?"

His reply was short and, as if caught in a lie, he blushed, "I arranged it."

"Why did you arrange it? You got an A last time."

"I told my faculty advisor you had an incredibly good accent and I was going to major in French in college," he answered.

"But you'd never heard my accent," I responded.

He had been caught in his lie. He blushed more. His eyes fell to the floor as he moved his toe across some dust, but in his embarrassment he still couldn't help but smile his adorable caught-in-a-lie smile as he said, "I just wanted to be in your class." For a quick second he lifted his eyes, looking directly into mine as if pleading for me not to kick him out. "Okay?"

How could I fall in love so quickly? But I had. Not wishing to give away my secret, I casually gave an approving, "Sure." Derek, with a smile of relief, spun around and was gone. I was already falling in love.

As a new teacher with five classes a day, I had a tremendous amount of work to do every night and on weekends. The teaching went well. Apparently the kids accepted the way I came across. Halfway through October the football coach came into my room during a free period when I was alone at my desk eating my lunch.

"I have a problem," he admitted. "My star player is not doing well in French II. His teacher, old Mr. Shea, told me if I couldn't stimulate him to keep awake in class and pass his mid-term exam, he'd have to flunk him. That would make him ineligible to play football for the rest of the season and this year that's particularly important because we could win the state championship in our division. Would you be willing to tutor him? Shea is about to retire and is anything but stimulating to anybody. I'm sure Michael would stay awake if you helped him."

I agreed to tutor him and the coach said Michael would drop by to set up a time convenient to both of us.

Was I ever surprised when Michael turned out to be that tall, handsome, athletic boy that I had seen with Derek the first day of school. None of our free periods coincided and I suggested he come up after school. He couldn't. He had football practice. I told him to come over to my apartment across the street after practice. That was a mistake. Let's just say that when he came over he was not solely interested in studying French. I was very nervous.

As a result, the next morning I arranged for Derek to tutor Michael. Because Derek was tutoring Michael, he came to my room regularly for advice and instructions. It also gave us a chance to chat. We had a free period at the same time and sometimes he would stay nearly half the period. He always had so much to say of interest and so much to offer.

After his tutoring ended, I told Derek I owed him a favor since he had helped me out tutoring Michael. I suggested he come over to my apartment for some tea and let me help him with his oral French. He was delighted.

In our first session, I explained how German was spoken from the back of the mouth, almost from the throat, and how English was spoken from the middle of the mouth. French, properly spoken, came more from the front of the mouth. We practiced.

In French I said, "Tu es comme mon frere, Andre." (You are like my brother, Andre.)

Derek replied, "Dites moi de votre frere, Andre." (Tell me of your brother, Andre.)

In simple French, I told him how our mother had died when Andre was born and that he was only eleven months younger than me. I told him how we were so very close, not only in age, but in temperament and interests, although now we were far apart and, unfortunately, not as close anymore.

We talked for a while sharing stories about each other. Then Derek slowly stood up, walked over, and stood behind me. He lovingly placed his hands on my shoulders and started massaging them. Then his hands moved up my neck and through my hair. He raised me up and, to my surprise, tenderly kissed me with a long, sensuous kiss.

Oral French sessions followed and, as one might expect, we became closer and closer. I looked forward to those times with such excitement that it became difficult to get through the day without thinking of him constantly.

Then came a particularly special day. As usual, tutoring gave way to tender moments of affection, but this time he led me into the bedroom saying, "Je t'aime. Je t'aime beaucoup." (I love you. I love you very much.)

I told him I had loved him since he first blushed while telling me that he just wanted to be in my class. He ran his hands up my neck and through my hair and began to kiss me on my neck. I began to melt.

It wouldn't have made any difference to me if we hadn't made love. I would have been happy just being close to Derek. But it was warm, compassionate love.

Afterwards, as we lay entangled in each other's arms and legs, Derek said with tender devotion, "Michelle, I want to spend the rest of my life with you. I want to marry you. Would you marry me?"

I found it impossible to believe he had actually proposed. He was so young. I immediately wanted to say yes, but would it be right? I finally told him I wanted to say yes, but that I would have to wait or my conscience would bother me.

As these thoughts raced through my head, Derek started pleading his case, "I know I'm young, but you're only a few years older. I know we'll be happy. My father will employ me. I can go to college at night, maybe a few day classes. We don't have to have children right away. We're made for each other, Michelle. I know. I've known it from the moment I saw you in the hall the first day of school. Marry me, Michelle."

"You think you know me, but you only partially know me. There are some things about me you don't know yet," I said, trying to stall for time to gather my emotions.

"I don't need to know," Derek interrupted. "I'm not marrying your past. Don't try to persuade me not to marry you. I love you as you are. I know you are the one. Please say you'll marry me."

He was so serious. I realized he wasn't smiling. "Smile first," I said.

He smiled radiantly, squeezed me until I almost broke in two. "Thank you, my love, thank you. I'll do everything to make you happy."

Teasing, I said, "I didn't say I would marry you. I just said smile."

"But that meant yes," he said with confidence.

"Maybe."

"What do you mean maybe?" he said, letting go of me and looking into my eyes. "You teaser!" he said smiling. "Say yes or I'll die."

"Well, I wouldn't want you to die now. Yes, I'll marry you, Derek. I will. I might be crazy, but I couldn't imagine saying no."

So, that's the way it was. We were so in love it seemed impossible. But, were we fooling ourselves? Would it last? I knew I wanted to marry Derek. I didn't want him to lose interest or find some other woman. But, I worried. What would his parents and my father think? Could I stand the criticism that was bound to come? Well, at least we could wait while I figured. The wedding wouldn't have to be next month. Maybe next year when he was in college.

Derek didn't tell his parents right away. I sensed he was a little apprehensive about the consequences. What would his parents say? He was convinced everything would work out for the best. Derek was always sure things would work out for the best and for him it did. Derek was positive that doubt is what keeps things from working out.

As the days went by, we learned each others preferences. We bicycled and picnicked on weekends. Many evenings I had homework to do and Derek would sit in a corner and read a book or two. He was a voracious reader.

In mid-November I missed my period. I went to the doctor for an examination. The weekend before Thanksgiving, I told Derek I was pregnant. "You're kidding me, aren't you?" was his reply.

"No," I said. "Dr. Halverson said so."

Derek held me in his arms and whispered, "It's too late to say we should have taken precautions, so, we might as well rejoice." Derek's smile was as radiant as I had ever seen it.

It was a Friday night. We stayed up late discussing all sorts of possible plans for a wedding and afterwards Derek called up his parents about eleven o'clock to tell them not to worry, but he was spending the night at my house. That surely set their minds at ease!

The next night, he invited me over to his parents' house for dinner. Obviously, things were moving along rather quickly. I was so nervous, you can't imagine. I went out and bought myself a new demure, but chic dress. When Derek came to pick me up, he said I was overdressed. I wore it anyway. The Sauls were hospitable, but I could only imagine what was going through their minds. Maggie, who was home for Thanksgiving, wasn't quite as hospitable that first meeting, but we soon became very close. Roger Saul in his account described well that evening, so I won't go into the details.

Then I had to tell my father. I dreaded calling him. How could I fully explain. If only he could meet Derek. Maybe I could send a picture. No, that would take too long and wouldn't show what kind of person Derek was anyway. We only had a month until the wedding. Could I do it in a letter? No, it was too important.

I wished I could write Andre and have him do the job. Andre would understand. I even imagined Andre reading my letter and saying to Father, "Oh, by the way, Michelle is getting married next month and would like you to come. Incidentally, she's pregnant."

I could just see Father falling over with a heart attack. Of course, I had to call. There was no other choice.

Andre answered the phone. I was so glad it was Andre! Father was not home. By the way, Father was single again, having divorced that horrible woman the previous year.

"Andre, don't be judgmental," I started out. "I need your support. I particularly need you to separate me from Father's anger. I'm so happy I could explode, but there are circumstances that could make it seem an unwise decision if you were not in my place."

"Slow down, slow down. What are you talking about?" Andre interrupted.

"I'm engaged."

"That's wonderful! When is it to take place?" Andre said approvingly.

"Right after Christmas," I said.

"This year or next?"

"This year. He's the most wonderful person you'll ever meet. You'll see at the wedding. You have to come to the wedding. You will won't you?" I was so panicky I was lucky I was talking to Andre.

"Why so soon? How long have you known this guy? You aren't pregnant are you?" Andre said, getting right to the point.

"I've known him since school started and yes, I am pregnant." I replied, shuddering at what the reaction would be.

"Is he another teacher? How old is he? Has he been married before?"

What wouldn't Andre think of next. I was so glad it wasn't Father!

"He's never been married. He's not a teacher. He's a student and he's almost 18. He'll be 18 before the wedding," I told him.

"Mon Dieu, mon Dieu." (My God. My God.) And then there was a silence. "You're right," he continued, "there are circumstances that would make it seem unwise." He paused and then asked, "What else?"

"Nothing really. He graduates from high school in June. He is gorgeous. He is brilliant, head of his class and an athlete. He has a job in his father's insurance agency." I paused to gather my thoughts and then continued, "What else? Oh, yes, he reminds me of you. He is so thoughtful like you. You'll love him."

"First of all," Andre started out, "wild horses couldn't keep me away from your wedding. I have to meet this stud and I'll kill him if he is less than you say. Secondly, I'll break the news to Father gently so you won't have to. Thirdly, I'll tell him you want him to call you and ask him not to ruin your happiness by exploding. I'll tell him it's too late to get angry. The die is cast. Just to give you his love."

"I love you, Andre. I do. I do. You're making me so happy I want to cry. Thank you. Thank you. Thank you."

"I have to hang up. Father is coming in the door. Bye, and God bless," he said and hung up before I could say good-bye. Father did call me. His call was not enthusiastic, but tolerable.

After Derek's announcement to his parents, he moved into my apartment. We started making the details for a small wedding right after Christmas when Maggie would be home from college to be my maid of honor. Both the wedding and the reception were held at the country club where Roger Saul was a member.

Although I was raised Catholic, I wasn't a practicing Catholic any more and Derek was always questioning the honesty of organized religions and thought it hypocritical to have a church wedding. We were to be married by a judge who was a friend of the Sauls and one of their insurance clients.

Roger Saul wrote to my father, stating he would like to help with the cost of the wedding. This was a surprise to my father who wasn't aware of the American custom of the father of the bride paying for the wedding. Father called me when he received Roger's letter and I explained the custom and they ended up splitting the bills.

Andre came over with Father several days before the wedding for Christmas and a series of family get-togethers and parties with their old friends who still lived in the area. Father paid my older brother Pierre's airfare so he could join us. He was working in San Francisco. Father was reserved about Derek, whom he called "the immature kid." He did warm up eventually and sincerely wished us well.

We were married on Saturday, December 28. We had very little money. Our cash was to go toward the baby and rebuilding the apartment on the third floor of the Sauls' home. So, our honeymoon was in New York for New Year's Eve in Times Square. We had planned to go sight-seeing, take in a couple of shows, and come home on New Year's Day. However, we received several checks for wedding presents so extended our honeymoon five days and made a lovely tour of snowy New England with our last night spent with Maggie in Boston. Ken briefly flew down for our wedding, but because he was traveling for his paper, couldn't stay long. Fortunately, he was able to join us for dinner at Maggie's. It worked out nicely since we didn't have classes until the following week.

By the fourth month, it was obvious I was pregnant. I carried it all out in front. By then everybody in school knew I was married to one of my students and guessed I had to have gotten pregnant before our marriage. I caught a lot of flak and cold shoulders, but I was happy and if they couldn't share in my joy, to hell with them.

By May, I couldn't wait for school to end. When school did end, I couldn't wait for the baby to arrive, which finally happened August 8th without any complications. Derek named him Michael after his best friend. I tried to object, but Derek said, "He's a close friend of yours, too. We'll call him Mike." I agreed with mixed emotions.

Mike was a healthy, active baby and always hungry. He didn't sleep through the night for two months. Derek didn't care because I nursed him. However, Derek did take a lot of chores off my shoulders, including cooking the evening meal. While we washed dishes together we talked and joked. I should probably say while we talked and joked we washed dishes. It was a wonderful time of sharing.

I loved and admired Derek. He filled my heart with joy, with his loving expressions, his thoughtfulness, his smile, and his beautiful heart. I was continually saying to myself, and to Derek, how fortunate I was. It was an incredibly busy time, but we got through it. Actually, we used to talk about how life seemed to be speeding up for everybody and wished that the world could slow down enough to enjoy some of the simple things in life a little more.

I remember one particular conversation we had. We were sitting outside in the backyard on a beautiful, warm summer night. Derek was sitting in a rocker and holding Mike in his arms as he gently rocked back and forth. I could tell he had something on his mind and asked him what he was thinking about.

"We are all caught up in the same impatient trend of thinking," Derek began. "We want change to occur quickly. We don't want to work at it, nor do we want to compromise or debate our thinking peacefully. We want our way and want it right now."

"I know. Isn't it a shame people are in such a hurry all the time," I said. "They don't take the time to enjoy these kinds of moments like right now."

"Yeah, it sure is a shame. You know, I was thinking, first we had the train, then the automobile, then airplanes, telephones, radios, and computers. They have all speeded up our thinking habits. It, unfortunately, follows that we are less rational in our desire for speed, in getting our own way right now. We forget patience and forgiveness. Look at commuter traffic. Everyone exceeds the speed limit and there are those who dart in and out recklessly to get there faster. Look at the lotteries and the get-rich-quick mentality. Speedy results without persistent effort. Add to that the belief that if a little is good, more is better and you have our inflammable society. We're greedy. What can we expect? We teach by example. The terrorists want speedy results, too. They want their own way now."

"People forget it's the journey that is rewarding, not the results. The joy is in the journey," I added.

"Exactly. Many of the wealthy who already have considerably more than they will ever need are out trying to get still more, building up greater treasures on earth. When is enough, enough? Fortunately, some are also very generous, some even humble, but changing peoples' attitudes is rarely speedy. Growing old is mandatory, growing up is optional. We resist change. Change is threatening. Many, maybe most, don't yet want to share. Mark my words, something will happen, probably sooner than later, that will make sharing a way of life, like in the Arctic with the Eskimos where each winter can be a catastrophe. They share as a way of survival."

"We think our way of survival usually involves avoiding sharing," I remarked.

"How true," Derek said, gazing down into Mike's eyes. "Few people realize that as you sow, so shall you reap. The more sharing you do, the more the universe will share with you. I just wonder what it's going to be like for this little guy."

"That concerns me. What is it going to take to change?" I said, gazing up into the star-filled sky.

Derek joined me in admiring the night sky, took a deep breath, and then continued, "Some people grin and bear it. Others smile and change it. But, so far, it seems that only a catastrophe will cause men to band together. So, when catastrophes comes, be thankful for another possible learning experience and hope we actually learn from it. We, and that includes groups, races, and nations, attract catastrophes subconsciously by our attitudes and beliefs. God's most effective way of communicating with us is by letting us experience what we've created. Secondly, it's by our feelings and, lastly, by words, or inspiration, or warning via people, books, or intuition. But, He will not take away our free will, nor our consciousness, to realize the good or bad of our choices."

"That's the key, though. We have to learn from our choices. Many people don't. Many people don't even try," I said as Derek stood up and strolled around the yard with Mike in his arms.

He turned towards me and then continued with his thought, "Atrocities result from someone experimenting with God-given free will. It's all right to experiment, but our suffering in this life or the next will be as severe as what we inflict, because what we plant, we must harvest. That is spiritual law and we can not break spiritual law. We can only observe its outworking. Grace comes by forgiving ourselves. God is always forgiving. Accepting God's forgiveness is grace and is up to us individually. The big problem is that we are often unaware of the vibrations we have set in motion, so, we don't know enough to forgive ourselves and, therefore, must experience the effects…or we suffer from guilt and can't forgive ourselves. It's too bad we can't look at ourselves as God does."

"Yes, it is. I never considered how much power our minds actually have. But, it's definitely far more than I ever dreamed," I added as I walked over to steal Mike from Derek's arms.

Derek continued, "We experiment to learn. How else can we learn? Groups, even nations, must experiment and choose. When we decide to discard unfortunate choices, it is still freedom of choice. So, all that is happening around the world is happening for the long-term good. Denial is not a river in Egypt, as they say."

Derek and I were both dead set against maintaining a strong military. We are training men to kill without guilt. By innuendo, this is passed on to civilians, as well as retained by veterans. Violent TV and movies help to train our minds. Preparing for war will attract war or warlike problems, because like attracts like—another spiritual law.

The summer before Derek died we prevailed upon Josh and Michael to look after Mike while we made our first extensive trip on our own. It was the first time we had both taken time away from Mike. We divided our month roughly in thirds, starting off by visiting my father and Andre in Paris, then to Egypt, and lastly to Tibet. We spent a couple of days in Kathmandu, Nepal, as that was the point of entry into Tibet. It was a wonderful trip and one we had wanted to do for a decade. Derek was the one particularly interested in Egypt and Tibet, because that's where certain ancient spiritual thinking and practices originated.

We had the opportunity to join a group for an hour's meditation in the King's Chamber in the Great Pyramid. Derek did not have a great experience there. His comment was, "It doesn't help to be in a great edifice, whether it be a pyramid, temple, or church to contact the mind of God. We have to turn within, closing our eyes to the outside world. God is everywhere, including within us, and within ourselves is the only place we can consciously meet Him. Being in a noted place can often serve as a distraction," as it was for him in the Great Pyramid.

Derek observed that many of the more recent pyramids and other ancient structures were in worse shape than the Great Pyramid, which still looks sound even though the outer coating of polished limestone was removed 1200 years ago to build parts of Cairo. Derek's thought was that Pharaoh Cheops might not have built the Great Pyramid, but restored its deteriorating exterior. Thus, the bulk of the Great Pyramid would be much older than Cheops (2600 BC). Derek wondered where the samples used in dating the age of the Great Pyramid were taken from and if some were taken from the original core of the pyramid.

In Tibet, we were fascinated with the stark, extremely beautiful, mountainous topography, the monasteries, and the people. It was hard to think of Tibet as part of China for, culturally, it is not Chinese. In theory, communism is supposed to be a sharing philosophy, but the way the Chinese destroyed monasteries and killed people in Tibet reflected only cruel despotism.

During the cultural revolution of the 1950s and 60s, when 90% of the 3000 or so monasteries were destroyed, thousands of monks were either murdered or sent home. One out of seven Tibetans were killed, leaving about six million, which is a very sparse population for a country about the size of California, Arizona, Oregon, and Nevada combined. Primarily, those killed were the educated and/or those opposed to the Chinese takeover. The Chinese ordered the monks from worship to work. A few monasteries were being rebuilt when we were there. In them were many statues of various Buddhas and past Dalai Lamas, which were very colorful and ornate, but not lifelike. The temples themselves were colorful on the outside and inside. On the inside they were usually intricately painted with many scenes of their history and religious life. They were so detailed and exquisite it was amazing enough monks had the talent to do it all.

The devotion of the common man seemed genuine. Even in their extreme poverty, they left gifts of money at the statues to be used for the upkeep of the monastery. The fees we paid to enter the monasteries went to the Chinese government. The Tibetans seemed, in our eyes, to be accepting their plight with the Chinese conquerors without gross bitterness and obvious hate, which is what the present Dalai Lama in exile is teaching. There are many small photographs of him in the monasteries, probably not allowed by the Chinese, but overlooked. He is not forgotten, even though he's been in exile since 1959. Again, not knowing the language, we couldn't speak with the people to learn how they really felt.

I know I may be rambling here a bit, but this is something Derek and I felt so strongly about and I have continued to follow it very closely. It was a great learning experience for us. He concluded it was the devotion to God in all religions that is most important, not the form, but the actual devotion, the love.

He criticized himself for not earlier having applied this same understanding to the many fundamentalist religions where devotion abounds, and yet he had been critical because of what or how they taught. He believed these fundamentalists, however, would also do well to open themselves to the possibility that truth exists outside their narrow beliefs. But it was their devotion that impressed Derek.

Derek spoofed the idea of ministers and priests wearing dresses when they preached. Of course, the clergy call them robes, but Derek thought it was not a good idea. It separates the clergy from the parishioners and elevates the ministers and priests' egos, to make them think they are better than the unschooled people.

"Are they willing to learn and perhaps change?" Derek once remarked. "All great truths begin as blasphemies."

Derek and I were not social butterflies. We had a small group of friends, but our primary focus was our family, which included Michael and Josh, of course, and Mom and Dad Saul and Michael's and Josh's parents. We developed friends with some of the parents of our son's friends and sometimes would have outings with them. A few of Derek's and my teenage friends still lived nearby.

In good weather Michael would frequently have us over for a barbecue. He loved to barbecue. Josh would occasionally have us to his apartment upstairs for dinner. He was a lousy cook, but I guess he felt obligated to have us up because we had him down so often. Josh was good company though, and it is a good thing as he was around so much, even if he was the quiet one.

Both Derek and I liked to have our heads massaged. Sometimes we would be reading in the evening and I would look up and Derek would be staring at me with his glorious smile. Just staring, and when I would catch him he would often come over and sit on the floor, putting his head on my lap so I could massage his head. He might say, "I'll give you a year to stop," or "I want you to know I'll still love you even if you do stop tonight."

Sometimes when he would come home from work I'd be preparing dinner. He would saddle up to me, put his arm around my waist, pull me close, and kiss me. "I love you," he would whisper in my ear. Derek was so sweet to me and always thoughtful in little ways. It was impossible not to love Derek. What more can I say? He wrote a poem once, proclaiming his love to me.

Dearest Michelle

Oh, spring, that beautiful season when flowers bloom
And spread the rapture of their fragrance through the air;
When happy song birds sing to their elusive mates
Who nonchalantly flitter through the trees
As if to avoid their destinies, their fates.

How do we know? How dare we ascribe to them
Their thoughts when we do not understand
Why we do what we do when our natures call us
To respond to the urges of our flesh,
To the machinations of our minds?

My darling, dearest wife, the only one I love
And want forever by my side, the only one who fills
My heart with the springtime songs of birds,
And the fragrant perfume of blooming flowers.
Take my life, my being, my love to be forever yours.

My dearest, darling wife, you are the joy of my smile,
The only song, the only fragrance that fills my soul.
Even if your graceful moves about our home
Were to pass away with age, you'd still be there
Untarnished by the passing of the years.

Your clever mind and sweetly chosen words
Will always charm my heart and fill again
That heart, that soul, with love supreme.
My darling wife, I love you beyond all reason.
I knew it the moment when first our eyes did meet.

I had to give myself away to you and since you
Also loved, I've held you tightly all these years.
Oh, my true, sweet love, I feel so blessed!
May I never for a moment of this earthly life be deprived
Of the springtime song and fragrance of your soul.

Derek and I had an active love life and it was a "love" life. We didn't have to worry about birth control as we wanted a baby. It took a dozen years before it happened. Then just briefly after we knew I was pregnant, Derek died from the auto accident.

That fateful night of Derek's death, we had planned a celebration because the doctor's tests had confirmed I was pregnant. I had telephoned Derek at his office and told him the good news. He was overjoyed to put it mildly. I could hear him yell proudly to his father that I was pregnant. I was on cloud nine myself. So what if I didn't teach for five years until the baby was in school. Derek's income was more than sufficient. My joy was unbounded. I did not invite Jan Hall to the celebration because she had her mother to care for. I suspect Derek encouraged her to join us at the last minute.

Michael's coaching at high school ended early so he was already there. Josh had also arrived home from work and he said he thought Derek would be right behind.

It was gently raining and Derek was late. Not late enough for me to worry, but later than I expected in view of the celebration. Then the phone rang. It was the police. "Are you Mrs. Saul?"

"Yes," I replied.

"This is Police Headquarters. One of our troopers has just radioed us that your husband has been involved in a serious auto accident. The other car skidded on the wet pavement during a turn and hit your husband broadside."

"Is he hurt?"

"The trooper at the scene seemed to think so. He's unconscious. An ambulance is coming and he will be taken directly to the hospital."

I was more numb than panicked. I phoned Mom and Dad Saul. Though they weren't home, I left a message on their machine.

Michael drove. We raced to the hospital. We were told to wait in the waiting room. After what seemed like an eternity, a surgeon dressed in a white gown came into the waiting room.

"Mrs. Saul?" he asked.

"Yes?"

"I'm Dr. Gabler. Your husband has had extensive internal trauma. We almost lost him on the operating table."

With tears beginning to stream down my cheeks I stammered, "How is he now?"

"I think we stopped the bleeding, but the heart muscle was torn. He has stabilized, but is extremely critical."

"Can we see him?" I pleaded.

"You may go in...for a minute. He's sleeping," Dr. Gabler replied.

We were led to the intensive care room. Derek was alone. We could see some contusions on Derek's face, but his head was not bandaged and in a way he looked fine, just resting. His head was turned slightly away as we entered. I took his hand. Michael pushed a chair up for me.

"Derek, stay with me. I love you so much. You have to fight, Derek...please!" I said as I laid my head to Derek's good shoulder and started to sob. Derek's head slowly turned towards me and his eyes partly opened. I detected his movement and straightened.

"Hi, my love," he whispered. Then looking at Michael, he continued, "Hi, Michael. I'm glad you could make it."

"Derek, you're going to be all right," I assured him. "Everything's going to be all right."

Derek smiled softly and then winced as he moved his hand to touch my cheek. "Listen carefully," Derek started. "I haven't much time. I have been to the other side and I must return. I have important work to do that I can't do in this body. To be sure, the crash was an accident from an earthly point of view, but from a cosmic point of view it wasn't an accident. My spirit is being called over without a debilitating illness."

"No, Derek, no! You must fight! I don't want to hear this kind of talk." I urged him as I struggled to keep from crying, but tears continued to roll down my cheek. Derek wiped them away with his finger.

"Don't cry, my love…I no longer have a choice. Even before this incarnation I was preparing for what is forthcoming. This incarnation was like a vacation and a learning experience, putting into practice what I am to disseminate next time."

"Please, Derek, stop…."

Derek continued, "My next incarnation will be hard work. I will be a rebel fighting the powers that be in religions throughout the world. Religious leaders have for millenniums been teaching many misinterpretations of truth and the erroneous thinking of many well-meaning men. Religious leaders will fear and hate me as they did Jesus."

"Derek, don't leave me. I love you, Derek, I need you. Let someone else carry out this work," I pleaded.

"I love you, too, Michelle, but you don't need me anymore. You will have Michael. He loves you and you love him."

"What are you talking about? I want you, Derek. I want you!" I said loudly, starting to cry again.

"A soul doesn't enter, can't enter a body that is not ready or is no longer able to support it," Derek explained. "Your fetus may have life, but it can't support a soul until about the time of birth. I will do all I can to reincarnate in the son you are carrying. Are you prepared for a rebel?"

"Yes, if it's you. But please stop talking like this. I want you to live as you are now. Please stop this talk." I replied, getting louder and more desperate.

"I understand, but that time has passed." he continued, "Now I want you and Michael to marry right away, before the baby is born. You need Michael. And he wants you. I want you to call the baby

Derek Saul Bassett. That name will give me the internal energy to carry out my work."

"What if it's a girl?" Michael interjected.

"Don't worry, it's a boy," he assured us. "I want you to tell Josh to start teaching me right away, even before he believes I can understand anything, long before I can talk. He's been taking notes on our discussions. People don't really teach. They just awaken what is already in, or available to, our subconscious."

"Derek, why do you have to leave? Please tell me you're going to stay right here with me," I desperately pleaded with him.

"I will always be with you, my love, but I do have to leave," he replied. "Do either of you have any questions before I go?"

We were in shock. Neither Michael nor I could think of anything. I thought I must be dreaming a terrible nightmare.

He went on in a weakening, muffled voice, "Please don't grieve. It would hinder me on the other side." He smiled, "Oh, yes, one more thing, tell Josh to go to the singles group at Unity. There's a young lady there who wants to meet him. Then let them live next door."

He squeezed my hand, closed his eyes, and sighed, "I must go. I love you both." He smiled his lovely smile and stopped breathing.

Oh, how I wanted to believe! I desperately wanted to believe Derek would reincarnate in the child I was carrying. I prayed he would be back. I must admit, however, I frequently wondered if Derek was fooling me by saying he would reincarnate in the baby to make me grieve less and to marry Michael. After a few months, I began to feel that marrying Michael was the right thing to do, even though I hurt so much from the loss of Derek. Derek was so clever. Did he lie to save me grief?

Four months after Derek's death, Michael and I were married. Four months after that a son was born.

He has been a good baby, and smart. We named him Derek Saul Bassett as Derek requested. The baby looks very much like baby pictures of his father.

I have adjusted to life without Derek, but it is still very hard. Not a day goes by that I don't think about him. Every time I look into the faces of our children, particularly little Derek, I can't help but see him again.

Ken's Journal (April 10)

It's been one hell of a day!

After my discussion with Michelle yesterday, I was curious to find out for sure who was driving the night of the accident. I checked with the police yesterday afternoon and, at first, they said they couldn't find the information in the report. But they checked further and called me back to let me know that it was, in fact, Jan who was driving that night!

I was not very surprised. That flash of insight yesterday. Where did it come from?

Now, however, I am confused. I was expecting to confirm it was Derek, but instead end up making this discovery that's going to be difficult to explain to the family.

I asked the police for more details on the exact nature of the accident, but they didn't have much. Apparently, it was a blind intersection and the person pulling out may not have had enough time to see them and tried to turn going into a skid on the wet pavement. The officer said it was possible that Jan was speeding at the time. The intersection is known to be dangerous, particularly if someone is approaching it too fast and the pavement is wet, which it was.

Now I'm not sure what to think. Could Jan have been responsible for Derek's death? Why was she driving anyway? I'm not sure I want to share this with the family. I'm not sure it's necessary. I think I'll wait.

I called Jenny again tonight and told her of my idea for her to come down for a few days. I filled her in a little on all that's going on, but it's simply too much for over the phone—especially after this latest revelation.

She reminded me that it's tax season and so, as much as she would love to join us, she just can't. She said maybe in a month or two we could both come back down here. I'm not sure she's really that busy, or she simply doesn't want to come down. But I'm going to try to wrap things up here in the next few days and finish the rest back home. It's seems like it's been much longer than it actually has. And there's still so much work to be done.

Michelle and I were talking this morning about how Alton Benson had not responded to her letter. It's not as though we really expected to receive one from him as he was Derek's Sunday school teacher at the time Derek quit and, obviously, they did not part ways in the friendliest of manners—considering Derek had called him an antichrist. Still, we thought it necessary for the book to see if we could get a response. It was, after all, a turning point in Derek's life.

We decided there was no reason why I couldn't give him a call. Besides, I figured we had to hear from at least one person that had something negative to say about Derek. The following is the short phone conversation as best I can remember.

Phone Conversation with Alton Benson

Alton: Hello.

Ken: Hello.

Alton: Who is this?

Ken: This is Ken Saul. I am the older brother of Derek Saul.

Alton: What do you want?

Ken: When Derek was alive, he mentioned that you made an important contribution to his life. His wife Michelle sent you, and several others, a letter awhile back asking....

Alton: I got the letter all right. I didn't answer because I didn't have anything good to say. He was a bright kid, all right, but he wasn't always right, even if he did think so and he always did. He tried to change the gospels to suit himself.

Ken: Did you ever argue?

Alton: All the time. He wasted more of my time than any five students I ever had. He called me an antichrist, so, I kicked him out.

Ken: What was that argument about?

Alton: Well, that was awhile ago, but I think I told him he was going to hell if he didn't believe what the Bible says. He said he wasn't going to hell because God would forgive him. He said he didn't believe in hell because God forgives everybody.

Ken: And what did you say?

Alton: I told him the truth. All sinners go to hell. And he said I apparently disagreed with Jesus and, therefore, I must be the antichrist. I told him to get out and stay out until he could apologize. I was so furious I saw red. Imagine him calling me the antichrist. There is no better Christian than me.

Ken: Did he ever come back?

Alton: He came back and apologized, but he never came back to class. He was always rattling off, but rarely knew what he was talking about.
I'm sorry he died and I hope he repented and didn't go to hell. That's about all I can say.
I have to go so....

Ken: Okay, well, thanks for your time.

I had hoped to get a little more out of Alton, but it was still interesting to hear his side of the incident. He still remembered it rather well after all these years, which indicates to me that it left a significant impression. I doubt he was ever called an antichrist another time in his life. Or maybe he has. Who knows?

It's a pity Derek and I never really had any serious conversations or talked about any of his ideas. I guess, as everybody has been saying, he never really shared his personal ideas unless he was asked, and, the few times we were together, I never asked. I have to say it would have been great to sit around sometimes and talk, but that chance is gone.

Actually, as I think about it, I almost never inquire about anybody's thoughts or feelings. Specifically, I'm thinking about Jenny and wondering when was the last time I asked her about her life and showed real interest. It's no wonder she may be talking to Scott to fill that void.

I find it interesting that I'm not angry with Scott. I'm angry with myself. I'm fearful I've scuttled my own boat. Fear is that little dark room where negatives are developed. I tell myself that everything in the universe is subject to change...and everything is on schedule. I will win Jenny back. What a man can conceive and believe, he can achieve. I'm beginning to sound like one of those motivational speakers, but I believe it's all true.

I'm definitely going back home as soon as possible and will finish this work there. Even if Jenny wants more time apart to figure things out, I need to talk to her now so she can see and hear how much she means to me.

I have to wonder how Derek would have handled my situation. He never had to worry about another person coming between him and Michelle. It was always just them right from the start. I should have contacted Jenny much sooner after I heard about her divorce, but I was resentful. Looking back, it is ridiculous to hold a grudge and waste so much time that we could have had together.

Chapter Nine

Ken's Journal (April 12)

Michelle came up with a good idea today. She checked with the high school and found out the name of Janet Hall's brother, James S. Hall, Jr. He's actually living in Lawrence, Massachusetts—probably only an hour or so from where Jenny and I live. I was thinking I could visit him when I get home, but when I phoned him, he was very uncooperative. He said it would be pointless to drive out to see him as he had nothing to offer. Sounded like he might have had something to hide. He said Jan had her own life and he had his. They weren't close. He felt relieved and appreciative when she moved to Falls Church to take care of their mother.

He said it was also pointless to see their mother, as she had so deteriorated that she sometimes didn't recognize him and he saw her twice a week at the nursing home on the way home from work. I didn't ask him the name of the nursing home because I was afraid he would tell the staff to not let me see her. I called several nursing homes near Lawrence and she is living, if you can call it that, at the Heritage Nursing Home.

I didn't expect I would have to put my investigative journalism skills to work when I took on this project, but I suppose there is always truth below the surface of any subject you address. The funny thing is that a few weeks ago I wouldn't have cared if I found out that Derek wasn't driving at the time of the accident and I wouldn't have cared who was driving.

(April 13)

I'm finding it very interesting that nearly everyone who has submitted an account regarding Derek has wanted to meet and talk with me personally. It's as though they want to make sure I understand what they have written. Many of them seem to think that, since I didn't know my brother well, they need to explain everything to me, which is probably true to some extent. It certainly helps to put a face to a name and meeting everyone has made it much easier to visualize what Derek's life was like.

Today I received a call from Derek's former professor of Religion. He asked if I, or actually Michelle, had already had a chance to read his account. When he heard I was in town helping to edit, he was eager to meet and talk. He talked as if he almost knew me, as if I was a long lost friend that he couldn't wait to see again. He said Derek had talked about me quite a few times which surprised me greatly. Maybe he was prevaricating.

I suggested we meet over at the cafe on Third Street since I was really craving a good Reuben and they serve the best in town. I thought he was going to order something, too, but he just sat and talked while I proceeded to stuff my face. I felt bad, but I think he was far more interested in sharing stories about Derek to even notice I was eating and he wasn't. He said he used to go there with Derek sometimes and the two of them would sit there for hours and order nothing but a glass of iced tea because they were so busy talking.

He told me a number of times that I should not be ashamed to print anything that was written in his account because he wasn't. He never told me exactly what he was talking about, but he kept insisting not to worry, because he wanted everything to be told. Obviously, I'm very curious to read it now.

It sounds like he was Derek's closest friend, aside from Michael and Josh. I felt very comfortable talking with him and we both agreed to get together sometime again when I'm in town, which I thought was really nice. A very sharp man...it would have been nice for the three of us (Derek, Phillip, and me) to have a glass of iced tea together while discussing politics, spirituality, and life in general.

Phillip's Account

One fall day, a young man appeared in the lecture hall seconds before my class on "The History of Religious Thought." He was dressed in a nicely tailored sport shirt, slacks, and polished leather shoes. He sat in the front row near the door.

"My, my," I thought to myself, "who's he trying to impress...and why?"

It was a hot, early fall day. Everybody else was dressed in jeans or shorts and a tee shirt. He continued to show up well-dressed like this. I knew his name was Derek Saul, but who the hell was he I wondered. As soon as class was over, he was the first one out the door.

It was my habit to give a quiz every other Friday. My first quiz was one question: "Why are you taking this course?" Derek's answer was fine, but short and obviously not designed to butter me up. He said something like "I am very much interested in the growth of spiritual thinking." I remember he did not use the word "religious" as was in the title of the course.

My second quiz was two weeks later. Derek again was the first to finish. As he came up to my desk to hand in his paper, I got a closer look at him. He had no lines or wrinkles or any sign he was any older than the rest of the students. Twenty, at most, I thought, though probably 19 as he was a second-year student. As he put his paper on my desk, I noticed he was wearing a wedding ring. "Poor fellow," I thought. "Married and still a kid." I wondered how long it would last. My curiosity about him was aroused further.

He spoke as he handed me his paper. For the first time I heard his voice. It was a quiet, appealing voice spoken with self-assurance, maturity, and poise.

"I'd like to talk with you. Could I take you out for lunch Monday?" he asked.

"I don't think it is a good policy for a professor to accept lunch from one of his students," I replied in a friendly way because I really wanted to have lunch with this curious enigma, but not at his expense.

"Oh, you can pay for your lunch if you want to. I just want to talk a bit." Derek quickly replied. Then he broke down all my defenses when he flashed his beautiful smile and added, "You can even pay for my lunch if you want."

I had to smile, too. "That's very generous of you, Derek. Since you put it that way, I can't very well refuse. What time and where?"

"If you don't have an eleven o'clock class, could we do it right after class? I have to get back to work." he replied. That explained his dress code, I thought.

"Eleven is fine," I agreed. "What kind of work do you do?"

Glancing at his watch, "I'm late. I gotta go. I'll tell you Monday. Okay?" he said giving me a friendly tap on my upper arm as he turned to go, still smiling, and obviously pleased I had accepted.

That quick, gentle tap on my arm made my heart flutter. It was a friendly tap of understanding or agreement like I might give to another professor, but one I wouldn't expect from a student. He was also the first student to ever ask me out to lunch.

I knew he couldn't know I was gay. I had kept that very quiet. Those who know, tell me I don't act or look gay, but…"No, it couldn't be," I said out loud, talking to myself. "I'm twice his age…. Still, he is cute. A living doll! No, it could never be…but…some guys like older men. We're more mature…or something. No, not Derek. Anyway, he's married I reminded myself. Still…."

After class on Monday, Derek stood by the door while I answered a few questions from other students. We walked down the hall and out into the bright sunshine. "Shall we go to the cafeteria?" I asked.

"Let's go to Wendy's," Derek suggested. "I used to work at a Wendy's. They always have a good salad bar and it's cheap."

So, off to Wendy's we went and after we served ourselves at the salad bar, we sat at a corner table next to the window, but out of the sun. I had been noticing how muscular he was for a short guy.

"How do you keep in shape?" I asked casually.

"I used to wrestle and do gymnastics. Now I only have time to wrestle with my son," he replied.

"And how old is your son?" I inquired.

"Fourteen months." Derek replied. Then, with that adorable smile, he added, "When we wrestle, I always win."

What a charmer! I wanted to hug him and never let go. I could fall for this one quickly! But he's one of my students!

After a chuckle, I responded, "You don't look old enough. How old are you?"

"Nineteen," he replied.

I paused momentarily as I quickly went through the mathematics. He must have been seventeen when….

Derek interrupted my thinking, "That's right."

"What's right?"

"Your mathematics. I was seventeen."

"And…."

"And my wife is 23," Derek said, interrupting my thinking again. "And you should know that I don't give a shit what people think. We are very, very much in love."

He had read my mind. He had closed his eyes as he spoke his final sentence. This time I felt I could read his mind. He was transported home and was holding his wife lovingly in his arms. It was clear that just feeling he was in the same room with her was all he needed to experience the glow of their love. I was convinced he was not in the least bit gay.

His hand was on the table. I reached over and gave him an approving tap. "You told me Friday you'd tell me what kind of work you do," I reminded him.

"I work in my father's insurance agency. He lets me sneak out to take classes. He encourages me actually. So, I make some night calls on clients to make up. I'm not carrying a full course load. Anyway, what I wanted to talk to you about was…." He paused. "Where to begin?" he said musing.

With his mind made up, he started, "Jesus is quoted as saying, 'I and my Father are one.' And 'I of myself do nothing. It is the Father in me that does the good works.' Also, 'All that I do, you can do and more.' And also 'God is spirit and must be worshipped in spirit and in truth.' It's the 'in truth' part that is at the root of my searching. My belief is that Jesus was really saying that he, the real him, is spirit since we are supposedly created in the image of God. Therefore, his body must be merely his vehicle for getting around in this three-dimensional world. That's the only way he could say, 'If you've seen me, you've seen the Father' or 'I and my Father are one.'"

"Perhaps. One could make that interpretation," I said, putting my fork down and settling back into my chair. I hadn't expected such a serious conversation, but I was intrigued by his ideas.

"So, what is the purpose of life?" Derek continued. "One point of view is that we are here to learn to give up our egos, our earthly desires and fears which establish duality, instead of oneness, and, therefore, separate us from God. Another point of view stems from Jesus allegedly saying, 'Be you therefore perfect even as your Father in Heaven is perfect.' From this point of view, we do not set aside our egos, but live and think so that our wills become one with the will of the Father, and thus we follow the commandment of love that Jesus taught. What do you think?"

Never having thought of those subtle differences before, I was somewhat taken aback. Unsure of my response, I turned it back to him. "Why do you ask? Why should my opinion be of any consequence to you? Isn't it better you develop your own understanding of truth?"

"Wow!" He paused, "Wow!" His irresistible smile flushed across his face. "I should have realized that. You're a genius. Thanks."

He had attributed much more significance to my answer than it deserved, but I didn't tell him so. I wanted to have more time with him.

"How would you answer your own question?" I asked.

"I'm really not sure. That's why I asked you, but you are right. I must be the one to make up my own mind. If something doesn't ring true to me, I must have the integrity to throw it away or I'll be just like the people that I'm being critical of, people who accept others' beliefs without discovering their own," Derek admitted.

"However, each person's individual discovery process can be sparked by other people or from books," I pointed out. "What started you thinking about all this anyway, Derek?"

"Well," he said dropping his eyes towards the floor, "I supposed it started when I was 12 and in Sunday School. I called my teacher, who was one of these well-meaning religious men, an antichrist and he kicked me out."

"Why did you call him that for heaven's sake?" I asked.

Derek sighed as if he didn't really want to get into it, then he continued, "He and I were always arguing. For him, everything was black or white, which I considered to be unreasonable. Then one Sunday he told me I was going to hell because I didn't believe what the church taught. I told him that, according to Jesus, God wasn't going to send me to hell. Jesus says we should forgive our brother 'seventy times seven' times and surely God will forgive us more. Then I added as an afterthought, that since he disagreed with Jesus Christ, he must be an antichrist. He told me to get out." Derek glanced at his watch, "I gotta get out, too. Have to get back to work. Can we do this again?"

"As often as you can spare the time," I assured him.

"How about next Monday?" he asked.

And so it became a tradition. Lunch on Mondays. I watched as he sped off. I was on cloud eleven, which is two higher than cloud nine in case your math is as slow as mine. I was sure nothing would develop between us beyond friendship, but it was wonderful to be near him.

It will be impossible to synopsize our many conversations. Some were mundane. Some were highly metaphysical. Sometimes, we skipped lunch and played racquetball. Sometimes, we rode our bicycles and carried a picnic lunch. After Derek graduated, our luncheons were less frequent, perhaps once every month or two.

Derek was obsessed with truth. He was a 20th-century Diogenes. He wanted to know cosmic or universal truth and was convinced that a lot of what was being taught in churches contained only partial truth, only man's concept of truth.

I remember one particular conversation regarding heaven and hell. It was during one of our picnic lunches and something had sparked Derek's thinking, as often was the case.

He began, "We have the freedom of choice and the consciousness to observe the results of our choices. Right choices lead us to that state of consciousness called heaven and wrong choices lead to hell, but it is all in our consciousness, the way we perceive the results of our choices. Of course, we still must harvest the seeds we have sown, unless we can recognize our error and accept God's forgiveness, which is grace."

"Is that what you consider grace?" I asked.

"Yes, I think it is very simple. Grace is always there if we just accept it, but forgiving ourselves is our stumbling block, particularly if we don't realize we need to forgive ourselves. I feel God's grace is always ours if we can forgive ourselves and accept God's forgiveness, which is His grace. God never sees what we do as right or wrong, good or evil. What we do is either a fortunate or unfortunate use of our freedom of choice, a learning experience. Hopefully, we'll discard the unfortunate choices when we see their unfortunate fruit. As heaven and hell are states of consciousness, so are guilt and grace states of consciousness. So, it is the state of our consciousness which makes grace possible, our forgiving of self."

"I see," I replied, as I tried to digest what he said. To me, his understanding of grace was so simple and accurate it astounded me, primarily because so many theologians say grace is a gift of God and cannot be earned.

"I don't believe anything can simply be given," he continued as he searched through the picnic basket, took out an apple and began to wash it off. "Take baptism for example. I believe that it is only a symbolic gesture and unless the person being baptized personally has a strong belief in its efficacy, it will be meaningless. It certainly is not a determining factor as to whether one gets to heaven, whatever that is."

"Yet since some believe it is a determining factor, they do believe in its efficacy and perhaps, therefore, an otherwise meaningless ceremony becomes meaningful," I replied "But you're right, unfortunately, many believe such symbolic gestures are all that's required. I know many such people personally."

Derek smiled at me, took a bite of the apple and then jumped on to a new train of thought, "Another thing, many Christians believe Jesus' death propitiated the sins of all men for all times. 'He shed his blood that we might be saved.' It is true Jesus shed his blood that we might be saved, but not by simply saying 'Yes, I believe.' We were saved by being showed the right way to live and think. Jesus said, 'I am the way, the truth, and the life and no one comes to the Father but by me,' that is by following 'my example as I have lived and showed you the way to live.'"

"And so you believe that we are all to follow his example?" I asked, "And be crucified?"

"Well, in order to demonstrate his way, Jesus had to oppose what the synagogue of his day was teaching. Jesus called its leaders hypocrites. He pointed out their errors. He so riled them to make them feel seriously threatened and he was attracting their followers. Jesus was fully acquainted with the law of what you sow you must reap, but he was willing to pay the price and continued preaching his truth, the doctrine of love and forgiveness. He would not even speak in his defense at his trial which, if he had, might have set him free. This is why Jesus had to die. He had sowed the seeds of attack and, therefore, had to reap the harvest of being attacked, which turned out to be crucifixion."

"That's an interesting perspective. I never quite looked at it that way before," I remarked

"I think it just comes down to whether one will believe what is true to him/her, or whether one will simply believe what they are told to believe," he concluded.

I noticed Derek was always quick to say that what he believes is not necessarily truth and that each person must decide for himself.

As I search through my memory, I am recalling another serious conversation we had. Of course, one of many.

I asked Derek whether he believed humans to be inherently good or bad and I remember he wasted no time in formulating his response.

"I believe there is more good in the worst of us than bad," he said. "Actually I believe there is no bad in people; only that some people, who are experimenting with their God-given freedom of choice, have chosen unhappily. Looking at life this way, it would be much easier to accept misfortune and forgive. Forgiving is what is most important! As we forgive, so also shall we be forgiven. It's the law. So, it would follow that what we experience on earth is a mixture of pleasant and unpleasant, heaven or hell, since we ourselves are a mixture. The best vitamin for making friends is B-1."

"I don't think anybody would argue that," I said with a laugh.

"We now have too many religions based on fear, untruth, and disrespect for each other, even hostility. And I'm saying religions, not just Christian denominations. That is why understanding truth is so important. I have already discarded a lot of myth, ignorance, and superstition. For an example of error, look back about five-hundred years ago when the Pope excommunicated Copernicus for insisting that the earth circled around the sun and then placed Galileo under house arrest for life because he agreed with him."

"Nobody is saying that religious institutions have been without fault, Derek. Should such mistakes in judgment be enough to undermine all the good that these institutions are seeking to achieve?" I asked him.

"No, but perhaps that is only the beginning and many of the other truths they speak are equally misguided. For instance, consider Jesus' virgin birth. Certainly, the people of his village didn't believe in Jesus' virgin birth. To them, Jesus lived under the considerable stigma of being a bastard. Mary was lucky she wasn't stoned, wouldn't you say?"

"Well, it's true such an event wouldn't normally be very believable or easily accepted. But...."

"Maybe being a bastard in the eyes of the local people was the cause for Jesus' later saying 'a prophet is not without honor except in his own country and in his own house.' Was Jesus an embarrassment to his own family because he prophesied, which meant preached in those times, and the local people didn't accept him as a prophet, preacher?"

"Clearly, he was not accepted by some, but that does not mean everyone felt that way," I added.

Derek gazed out the window. He went to take a bite of food, but put it down as he gathered his thoughts. We rarely had time for eating when we got together. We were always too busy exchanging ideas.

Derek began again, "I also wonder why only two of the four gospels, Matthew and Luke, mention a miraculous virgin birth? The two gospels of Thomas and Mary, found in sealed jars in the desert in the 1940s, Paul's letters, and the other letters in the Bible, never mention a virgin birth. How come? Wasn't a virgin birth important enough to be mentioned in every gospel?"

"One would think so," I said.

"Or was it possibly added later to two gospels to take away the stigma of him being a bastard? Or, maybe it was added to make his birth conform to the prophecy in Isaiah that a Messiah would be born of a 'virgin,' which in those days meant simply 'a young woman'—as mentioned in Joel 1:8 where a virgin grieved her husband's death."

"You've certainly thought a lot of this out, haven't you," I said to him with a smile.

"Actually, I thought about some other possibilities as well."

"Really? Don't hold back on me now, Derek. I want to hear it all," I replied and leaned back in my chair, inviting him to begin.

"Are you sure? These are not ideas that most people are eager to hear about," he warned me.

"Yes, of course."

"Well, I recently read a book called *Abduction* by Dr. John Mack, MD and another book by Budd Hopkins on the same subject. Mack is a practicing psychiatrist and professor at the Harvard Medical School who has developed a reputation for using hypnosis to handle cases of psychological trauma caused by UFO abductions."

"I've heard of him," I said.

"The abductees Mack had hypnotized could remember many details of their abduction experiences under hypnosis. The details seemed to Mack to be blocked from conscious recall by the extraterrestrials. However, I contend that the ETs have the ability to change physical matter, including our bodies and clothes, to a less dense medium so it could pass through walls and ceilings as the abductees describe when under hypnosis. The brain of this less dense body, which I call the 'etheric body,' functions only on the subconscious level. Thus, the conscious mind does not have the memory of these abduction experiences, but the subconscious mind, accessed through hypnosis, does. In many abduction cases the ETs are collecting sperm and eggs, fertilizing them and putting the fertilized eggs in an abducted female to develop. About three months later, she is abducted again, the fetus removed and put into a clear fluid in a cylinder to complete its development. It seems possible that this process might be to find a more perfect physical, earthly body into which the advanced intellect of an extraterrestrial soul could incarnate. Perhaps the purpose of this advanced being might be to guide humanity out of the quagmire into which it is buried, much like Jesus did 2000 years ago."

"I can see what you mean about people not being very open to these kinds of ideas. They are, shall we say, unconventional," I said, looking around the room as though we should be careful about who might be listening.

Derek went into further detail using an example of a plane going through a cloud without even noticing it.

"The cloud is visible having meets and bounds. If a UFO were of a cloud consistency shaped like a UFO we could see it, but we wouldn't feel it even if we passed through it. This would explain why UFOs can fly into water or mountains as have been observed and not be damaged and why abductees when changed to that consistency can float through walls and closed windows and drift up and into a space craft as they report under hypnosis."

"All this has been reported under hypnosis?" I asked.

"Yes. Once in this less dense body, or 'UFO consistency' etheric body, the abductees report they could see with their eyes, but would communicate by telepathy. They could also see other abductees in the UFO. They could be operated on or have eggs or sperm taken from their body to be used in experiments. Later the babies thus created could be changed back to the dense physical body we live in here on Earth as can the ETs themselves."

"Can all this be true?" I asked as I began to wonder very seriously.

"We all know that H_2O can be solid ice, liquid water, invisible water vapor, or visible steam or clouds," Derek noted. "Why can't the ETs use a technology, based on their minds, to do an analogous change? Just because we can't, doesn't mean they can't."

"Are you asking me seriously? I think I would need some time to get back to you on that one," I said jokingly. "Actually, no, I don't see why it wouldn't be possible, now that you mention it."

"If an ET and his spaceship were in a solid, earthly state, then it could be destroyed like in the famous 1947 Roswell, New Mexico, crash where even ET bodies were found and the government, in a state of fear and panic, quite successfully undertook a cover-up. If they were in their higher vibration, they wouldn't have been damaged. There is an excellent book disclosing the facts of this 50-year cover-up written by Col. Phillip Corso (Ret.) called *The Day After Roswell*. Starting in the '60s, Corso was a participant in the cover-up and now is a revealer of it all."

"Sounds fascinating," I said

"In a still higher vibration," Derek went on, "they wouldn't have been seen or been able to be picked up on radar or could have disappeared...poof. I wonder if ETs would need to eat or breathe in that vibration? Or could eat and breathe? They could live on Mars which has little water and air. The abductees, including their bodies and clothes, can be lowered into our earthly vibration and returned to their beds, or wherever they started from, and then be restored back to their solid physical bodies."

"Those are some pretty far-out concepts. It really is extremely fascinating," I said. "Although I suspect many people don't want to hear about such things. It's certainly not the norm for lunchtime conversation."

"I suppose this idea would have to fall in the same category," he said as he gathered himself to continue. "If Mary, the mother of Jesus, was such a high soul to be able to serve as the mother of the perfect physical and mental being of Jesus, could she not have been chosen by extraterrestrials 2000 years ago? Could this extraterrestrial experimentation have resulted in Jesus? Maybe the Holy Spirit, which supposedly fertilized Mary, was indeed an extraterrestrial. And, could the star of Bethlehem have been a UFO? A UFO can stand still in one place and look like a star, but a lawful star cannot. God is lawful and would not break the law to make a star stand still. Or was the star story just another myth?"

"I don't know. You'll have to give me time to digest that one," I told him.

"Maybe the purpose of life for the ETs is different than ours," Derek went on. "Our purpose is to eventually recognize our oneness with God while living within the limitations of a physical body, most likely after many incarnations. Jesus said, 'I and my Father are one,' and also 'All I do, you can do and more,' the implication being that we also are one with God, but don't yet realize it. There is only one self and we all share in it. We are created in God's image. Therefore, we also are spirit, but temporarily encumbered by a body, our vehicle. The ET agenda is different because, not only can the ETs change their bodies from a solid state like ours to an etheric body, but they communicate telepathically and thus have no secrets. In effect, they could have one mind, so their agenda could be to become one with God together. Another issue on this concept of one mind for ETs is leadership or decision making. Do some of the ETs have to surrender their free choice in order for any project to proceed? Whose decision is final? Or, instead of trying to create a perfect mind and body like Jesus, maybe they are cloning bodies without souls to be servants. Who knows?"

"That's certainly interesting. Two different ways of trying to achieve a similar goal. I have the feeling you wonder which way is more effective." I said, sure that he had already made the comparison.

"Yes, I do. I wonder which would be harder to do and, therefore, whether they or we might be more highly evolved. We could be more highly evolved because we have taken on an almost impossible soul task for our species to become one with God individually. Certainly, they are more advanced technologically, but that may well be as poor a measure of spiritual advancement as the amount of wealth one accumulates here on earth."

"And we already know the latter doesn't mean a thing when it comes to spirituality. But, tell me, how did you become so interested in aliens?" I asked.

"I've had some experiences, read some books and I've also done some study on Area 51 in Nevada. Did you know they have UFO wreckage and captured ships there for back-engineering, along with captured ETs, dead and maybe alive? Too many videos have been taken and too many people have seen UFOs rising from Area 51 for me to question their existence. The people employed there are under serious threat if they talk openly, which some have done anyway."

"Have you ever seen any UFOs?" I asked.

"Yes," he replied to my surprise. "The first time was when a group of about 20 of us from all over the country met in Crestone, Colorado, with Dr. Stephen Greer of Afton, Virginia, who is the founder and head of the Center for the Study of Extraterrestrial Intelligence. One night we were out watching the heavens. We had seen several satellites move rapidly across the sky and then a brighter white light moved similarly. Greer spoke in a loud voice so we could all hear and have the same thought at the same time, 'If you are not a satellite, please let us know by turning sharply or blinking out,' and immediately it blinked out. Another evening we saw a bright red light appear above a mountain ridge to the east which is towards the Air Force Base near Colorado Springs. We watched it slowly move a short way and disappear as quickly as it had appeared. There were no clouds."

"That's pretty amazing."

"One time we were visiting friends who lived on a hill nearby, but away from the lights of Washington. Michelle was with me. They had seen several UFOs previously from their yard at night. So, we went outside and were amazed to see three. Two were standing still. They were bright white lights which sometimes also blinked red and sometimes turquoise. A third one came in from the north, passed fairly close to one of them and turned east toward town. I followed it, then I quickly turned back to look at the other two, which were still there. When I turned back, the third one had disappeared in a matter of seconds. Again there were no clouds."

"I've never had such an experience. I wish I had. Have you had any others?"

"Yes, another time I was heading home from a meeting at night and I had a very powerful urge—so powerful I followed it. What I was receiving was telling me to pull into the school yard coming up, get out, and look for a UFO. So I did. This was the only time I had ever received a strong impulse like that. There in the sky was a bright white light standing still. It occasionally also blinked red, but the white light never went out. Shortly, about 20 degrees away, another started doing the same. I got so excited I drove to our friends house, but they weren't home and it was all over. On another occasion, I was traveling towards town at night with my son, Mike, and I found myself telling him to look for a shooting star. We bent forward, looking out of the windshield, and there came one right in front of us. However, when it approached about 20 degrees above the horizon, it went at right angles and soon was blocked by the trees. We tried to follow it, but never saw it again. I have also seen a cigar-shaped object hovering over a nuclear power plant under construction about three miles away. I couldn't see any details. It just looked black and motionless."

"Why you?" I asked.

"I have no idea," he replied. "None." Then he went on to speculate, "The two times I picked up telepathically on where to go or what to look for seemed to me to be their way of saying hello, but why me, I don't know."

As you can see, Derek and I rarely had a boring conversation. It was always fascinating. He certainly had one of the most inquisitive minds I've ever known. Derek contended that in becoming non-thinking followers, people form a pattern of behavior that leads them to become a bundle of conditioned responses, similar to Pavlov's dogs. What might seem like a good habit is, nevertheless, a conditioned response. We still have given away our free will, but it is for the good of humanity. So, he wondered if it could always be bad to give away our free will, or if it is a good conditioned response, does it make us closer to being one with the Father.

He mentioned how many of the wealthy have the habit of thinking that if a little is good, then a lot is better and they go on accumulating, or trying to do so, well beyond their needs. Wouldn't it be better to adopt a habit of thinking that the excess could do far more good if shared with the less fortunate or used to reduce the national debt? Maybe a bonus system could be worked out when people give to reduce the national debt.

I recall Derek saying that such a plan would have to be voluntary, not legislated, or the negative vibes created would be destructive and good would not occur in the long run.

So, the change in the habit of thinking for the wealthy, and not just the very wealthy, would be to share. There is only one self and we all share in it. Therefore, what I do for another I am really doing for myself, because all is oneness, oneness, oneness. Likewise, what I do for another, I do for my God because "Inasmuch as you do it unto the least of these your brethren, you do it unto your God."

Another time in a discussion about Stephen Hawking, who is considered by many to be the greatest theoretical physicist since Einstein, Derek remarked on what Hawking said about the "big bang" theory of creation. Hawking, who wrote the book, *A Brief History of Time*, said that if there were enough matter in space, the gravitational attraction of these bits of matter to other bits of matter would eventually slow down the expansion of the universe to a stop and then reverse the process, starting the "big crunch." The Universe would contract upon itself until its energy was so compacted as to cause another "big bang."

Hawking said it is currently believed by scientists that there isn't enough matter to slow down the expansion. Derek said that if the ancient Hindu vedas are correct, the "breath of Brahman" is 35 billion years, meaning one exhalation (the big bang), plus one inhalation (the big crunch), takes place every 35 billion years. We are about halfway right now. Derek's thinking was that the big crunch does not need to be a total crunch, but only enough of a crunch to compress matter, or energy, to reach a critical mass to start another big bang. This would undoubtedly leave a lot of relics in space from the last big bang.

Derek also said Hawking didn't discuss the power of the mind. For instance, Uri Geller can bend keys with his mind. Greta Woodrew in her book, *The Slide of Light*, describes how she has bent spoons without touching them. Sathya Sai Baba, the avatar in India, can materialize rings and trinkets out of thin air for devotees as talismans. He says he does it by thinking.

We know that brain waves can be measured, so they must be energy, and energy impinging upon matter, which is all energy, does cause change.

Since my many discussions with Derek, I have become quite interested in all of these matters. I also read Dr. Deepak Chopra and found there are many instances of healings by the laying on of hands, or spontaneous remissions of cancers and other illnesses by the changing of one's ways of thinking.

On the negative side we find many examples of psychosomatic illnesses that are caused by our negative thinking. Also economic distress or accidents, which aren't really accidents, but are what we have attracted to ourselves by our thinking. These are examples of the power of man's thinking which has changed matter, or the course of events.

Hawking doesn't discuss the many UFO sightings and how they get here from outer space, which would have to be at speeds greater than light, which Hawking considers to be a physical limit. Hawking doesn't discuss how UFOs blink out or turn at right angles at great speeds. Or travel at incredible speeds quietly. Or enter water as if it were air. All of which have been observed more than once, including by members of my family.

After I became so interested in all this, I began discussing it with my family and both my father and my cousin admitted to having seen such phenomenon. They have been fascinated by it themselves, but were reluctant to say anything. I wish Derek was still here to join in our conversations now.

Derek believed UFOs and ETs travels at the speed of thought after changing spaceships and bodies into "thought particles," or etheric matter. The UFO technology is, undoubtedly, millions of years ahead of us. Carl Sagan, the astronomer, is alleged to have said, "I don't believe in UFOs because they can't get here from there," as if our technology were already perfected.

Derek wondered why extraterrestrial people would ever want to expose themselves to our wretched, uncivilized, cruel, vicious, and violent society anymore than we would like to dwell in a nest of rattlesnakes while studying them. Yet we are curious about rattlesnakes and want to learn by observing.

Derek said he never saw a drawing of an ET showing a smile. I have found the same. I wonder if they can smile. Have they lost their desire for vivacious, joyful, carefree living? Or lost their emotions, compassion, and joy while they have developed their technological brain? Are they looking to us as teachers in this regard? Can we help them?

Their technology is so advanced; why don't they just land on the White House lawn and make their presence and mission overt? And what is their mission? Perhaps we will never know, but I have become very curious to find out.

Derek was very spiritual, but he was, obviously, anti-organized religion. Derek felt that stuffy people make stuffy churches and they drive away many of the good at heart who can't afford to dress well and are not well educated. Also, he believed that requiring the celibacy of priests, ministers, monks, or even members is unnatural and, therefore, creates an unnatural organization. Yet Derek was quick to admit that the sex emphasis today was too rampant, like in Rome before its fall.

Derek once asked, "Does God prod us to do certain things? Are we inspired by God to act, think, or feel a certain way at a certain time?"

"What do you think?" I asked, reversing the questioning as I liked to do.

"I asked first," Derek said with his big smile.

"But I'm the professor," I retorted. "Socrates taught by asking questions. So, what do you think?"

"I don't think God acts outside of universal law and He is that law, as well as love, truth, energy, and much more. Love is the glue that binds the universe together. I believe there is a lot of law we still have no idea about, other dimensions of consciousness, for instance. Why are we attracted to something or certain people? Are we attracted so we can learn lessons? Are we attracted to have a fun time? Am I a pawn in God's great plan? Or am I predisposed because of my thinking or actions?"

"As you sow, so shall you reap. Isn't that one of your favorite quotes?" I asked.

Derek smiled and went on. "Is it law that if we ask, it shall be given to us? Seek and we shall find. Knock and it shall be opened unto us? Or was something missed in an early translation or inserted by some optimistic scribe?"

"If we have doubts, aren't we limiting or ruining our ability to receive? By doubting, haven't we already canceled our asking? If we have sufficient faith can't we move mountains?"

"I wonder," Derek replied. "It would be nice, but I can't help wondering if there is another state of consciousness we must enter into before we can have that kind of knowing. Do we need to participate in the mind of God somehow? Jesus said, 'You are Gods.'"

"In the making," I added.

"He didn't say that," Derek countered. "He was quoting the Psalms. Sathya Sai Baba has said the same thing. He was asked, 'How can you say you are God?' Sai Baba replied, 'That's only half of it,' and then he added, 'The other half is so are you. The only difference is that I know it and you don't.' If Sathya Sai Baba can materialize things out of thin air like rings, statues, or amulets, what state of consciousness is he in? If Milarepa, the great 12th-century Tibetan yogi, could be in several places at the same time, what state of consciousness was he in?"

"Good question. Have you seen Sai Baba do this?" I asked.

"I held a ring he materialized for former astronaut Dr. Brian O'Leary which he was wearing at a talk he was giving. I've held another ring Sai Baba materialized as a parting gift to a humble woman who had lived 18 years in his ashram in India. It was nice, but much less ostentatious than O'Leary's. I've seen, smelled, and tasted some of the sacred vibuti ash Sai Baba had materialized. It has a wonderful fragrance and taste."

"It looks as though you are smelling it and tasting it as we speak," I told him.

"Yes, I am."

Derek said he had read an account of Sai Baba bringing an American man back to life after he had been dead several days. The man returned to the United States and lived a short time and then died. Sai Baba is quoted as saying it was easier for the wife to have it happen that way.

I have heard that Sai Baba healed someone and later became ill himself. It is almost as if he, by healing that person, left their negative energy floating. In order to negate those negative vibes, he took on an illness himself. When the negative energy was dissipated, he healed himself and immediately was well.

Another time Derek told me of an experience he had with Jesus. He and Michelle were spending an evening at the house of friends. The wife was very spiritual and quite clairvoyant. After her kids were in bed she went into sort of an alpha state and opened herself to psychic impressions. She said Jesus was behind her and the door was too small for him, which she said meant "Why are you limiting me?" Derek said that at that time he was limiting Jesus to just being a good teacher.

Then the wife said Jesus was coming around in front of her. Jesus said "Remember, I have walked these paths before you," which was particularly meaningful to Derek at that time.

I asked Derek if he ever talked about these experiences with anyone else.

He said, "Only Josh. Josh is the only person, except you, whom I know is really on the spiritual path. We talk a lot. Occasionally, I talk with Michelle and my son because I feel it important to let them know where I come from spiritually. Michelle is very enlightened without trying."

Derek continued, "I don't talk about anything spiritual with people unless they bring it up because I believe people are who they are because that's where they belong in accordance with their needs and development."

In one of our discussions I was defending another professor who had been arrested for soliciting an undercover police officer for gay sex. The professor claimed he was approached by the undercover policeman. When my friend accused the policeman of approaching him, the policeman merely said, "You'll have your day in court."

My friend knew if he fought the charge he would get tons of negative publicity and might even lose his job or never get promoted and all the world would think he was gay. In court it would be his word against the policeman's word and even if the case were thrown out, the negative publicity would still be there.

It was a clear case of entrapment by the officer, which is illegal. I made a point of how gays and particularly bisexual married men can have their jobs, their productive livelihood, their married lives ruined forever by entrapment by a non-thinking, insensitive undercover cop.

Derek knew I had never married and my use of the words "my friend" and my emotional objections to my friend's predicament prompted him to ask straightforwardly, "Are you gay?"

I was in a state of panic. Even though Derek had never showed any tendency to be homophobic or judgmental, would my acknowledgment affect our relationship? Could I avoid the question? I wanted to tell him, but should I? Surely Derek wouldn't talk about it to others. After a pause I looked him squarely in the eyes and simply said, "Yes."

"You hide it very well," he said and then continued, "I would never have guessed, nor does it matter to me. As I have said before, we are all where we are because this is where we need to be. Do you try to hide it? Are you ashamed?" he asked sympathetically.

"Maybe," I replied, "but more fearful of the consequences if I came out of the closet. Although I like being accepted in both the gay and the straight worlds, I would greatly prefer to be straight. I've prayed and prayed that this cross might be lifted from me, but I've experienced no relief. Why? Why? I ask myself. For years I hated myself for being gay. Now I have accepted it and come to respect myself for the good I am doing."

Derek's answer was simple, "That's good to hear. Perhaps your homosexuality is related to a previous life. You could have been a female in your last incarnation and the desire for males is a carryover, for instance, or maybe you were cruel to or just strongly negative about gays in a past life and need to face the energy patterns you sowed then. Maybe you must learn patience or humility this time. You could have been pompous and arrogant in a previous life and this time you have an outlook you want to change, but can't. I wouldn't worry about why if I were you. You are handling it well. You are leading a productive, serving life. You are a great person. I think the world of you; always have and always will."

"I have thought of many possible reasons why one person is gay and another is not, including some of those, believe it or not," I told him. "But, regardless of the reason, I believe that if there is love and compassion and not just compulsive promiscuity, homosexuality is no worse, nor any better, than heterosexuality, or bisexuality for that matter. Wherever there is love there is God, for God is love. Whether one is gay or straight, should not be used for power or hidden agendas, nor for ego-gratification or dominion. Sex should be for the purest joy and the highest ecstasy, given and shared."

Then came Derek's great smile. It was filled with compassion and acceptance. He reached over and squeezed my hand to let me know all was fine. I must say I felt relieved he knew. I had nothing to hide anymore. Our friendship was as solid as ever. I was overjoyed!

Derek added, "Praying repeatedly is preparing you for your next incarnation. You will most likely be straight because what we desire and concentrate on becomes as law. However, if mind is the builder and the physical is the result, to pray for something is to admit a lack and what are we creating? The lack we admit to. Never pray for a lack to be filled. Pray a prayer of thanksgiving that the lack has been filled and sit back and wait for the fulfillment, never doubting. 'Ask knowing you shall receive and you shall receive.' 'Knock, knowing it will be opened, and it shall be opened unto you.'"

Derek asked me if I had any psychic glimpses into my past lives that might explain my sexual proclivity. I told him of a dream I once had that took place in the 1700s when I was a thin, bony, austere Puritan minister with the stove pipe hat and turned-around collar. I was a Bible scholar and looked down on my parishioners. When they deviated from the "Good Book," I put them in stocks in the town square to humiliate them into being good. I was particularly severe on adulterers and sex offenders. I had a very small penis and felt inferior in that regard, but felt superior in my religiosity and intellect. In those days men didn't wear jockey shorts and I could see the well-endowed men bouncing around in their pants as they walked. I was jealous of them and particularly severe with such men since they must be evil I thought. I was stern. There was no joy in my life.

"Did the whole dream take place in that one time period?" Derek asked. "If it did, it could be a good indication of a past life recall."

I told him it had.

"How did your homosexuality first manifest in this life?" he asked.

I told him how, at about seven years of age, I discovered masturbation on my own and did it often. I had no idea what the penis was for except to urinate. I felt sorry for my sister because she had nothing to show but a slit. My masturbation imagery was always men, never boys, because men had the big penises which I wanted.

A couple of years later, but still before I had learned of the reproduction function of the penis, I was swimming at an out-of-the-way beach near my grandfather's cottage with a high school youth. He goosed me. Later he took me down the beach to an out-of-the-way spot and we took off our bathing suits and played with each other's erections with our hands and orally. He said the guys at high school did this often. This experience solidified my sexual thinking and masturbational imagery and I have never been able to shake it. Through the years it grew.

I think if child molesters realized the devastating effect their molestations have on the children they molest, they would be much less inclined to molest.

Derek pointed out I had no choice in my sexual orientation in this life. I was destined because of a past life and experiences early in this life and, apparently, this is what I needed to experience this time.

He pointed out that even if I didn't believe in reincarnation, as he did, the early experiences of this life would have been enough to explain my sexual orientation. It helped when he said I should feel no guilt, although he was quick to add that lust and promiscuous behavior without love and compassion could set up energy patterns that would have to be faced in the future.

Derek pointed out how many churches think gays have the choice to be gay or not and cruelly treat them as criminals. "Better they should treat them as cripples," Derek said, "and give them that same compassion and forgiveness." That way those self-righteous church people wouldn't be setting up negative energy patterns they will have to face later.

Derek one day questioned the story of the dove descending on Jesus when he was baptized by John the Baptist. "How could John see the dove and hear the voice of God say, 'This is my son in whom I am well pleased' and then later, when in prison, doubt and send a messenger to Jesus to ask, 'Are you he, the Messiah, or is he yet to come?' The baptism was before Jesus had chosen his disciples. Who was there to witness the dove and the heavens parting who later participated in the writing of a gospel? Surely Jesus wouldn't have told them."

Derek often questioned many passages from the Bible and we would sit around and debate them for hours.

It surprised me when Derek asked if I thought God had free will, probably because I had never even thought of the question before. Could He intervene in the affairs of men? Change things for those who prayed fervently?

With anyone else I would have instinctively answered, "Of course. God is all powerful," but Derek always had an unpredictable twist up his sleeve. His mind was so creative. I raced to think of something brilliant and insightful. After a long pause, I answered, "Of course. God is all powerful. Why, what do you think?"

"Well," said Derek looking down at the table as if he had written it there, "I am wondering if God has allowed himself to have free will. If God is law, besides being love, life, energy, truth, and so forth, would He go outside the law, which He is, to grant a favor? Could He? Or would He be defying Himself if He did? Would He be denying Himself? Can He deny Himself? Under what circumstances would He allow Himself to do this, if He would allow Himself? And if He would allow Himself to do so, wouldn't His decision be arbitrary, outside the law? And if His choices were unpredictable, wouldn't it lead to chaos in the cosmos since we would then never know what is law?"

I asked, "How do you know it would be necessary for him to go outside the law? Who, besides Him, is able to say what law is? What about the miracles like changing water to wine or your Sai Baba friend creating stuff out of thin air? Is that outside the laws created by Him?"

"I would venture to say those things are laws we don't understand yet," Derek replied. "Probably people attuning to the mind of God, plus their free will, create the miracles. If we use our free will and the energy of God given us, is it outside the law? It would certainly be outside the law if God did it by Himself without our participation."

"What about the miracles at Lourdes?" I asked.

"I should be asking you these things. You are the professor," Derek said staring off into space as if the answer were out there somewhere. "I suppose that some entity, not God, somebody with great faith established a healing energy there. Then after several healings, the energy was perpetuated by those who believed. There again it would be a combination of the God within us, that God force, and our free will to use that God force, His energy."

Derek didn't stop there. Still staring off into space he continued, "The antichrist is that same energy used negatively. The antichrist does not manifest as a person, but if we attune to negative thought forms, which the anti-God is, and use our free will in that direction, we have attuned to the antichrist, a thought form. And that is what will be manifested through us. Negative results." As he frequently did, Derek added, "I don't proclaim this to be truth. It's just an opinion."

"And a very fascinating one at that. So what is your conclusion about free will? I asked.

"I do not think God can step outside of the law, because He is that law, but we, using the spirit, the power, He gave us, that part of Himself in us, can create because we still have the free will He gave us to be one with him or not. That's why we can mess up in our activities and our creations." Derek added. "Does not the microcosm know the macrocosm and vice versa? God, the macrocosm, can only work benevolently on earth through willing souls. Looking at God as a being, a body in space, can only hinder one's understanding of God. We simply have to get away from that 'father,' that human form to start knowing that spirit which is God. God is Wholly Spirit."

I suggested, "Every thought good or bad, evil or beneficent, pleasant or unpleasant should also be considered a prayer."

"That's exactly what I'm getting at," Derek replied with enthusiasm. "Every thought, every emotion, every attitude sends out vibes as does a prayer and has the same power of a prayer. We are always directing energy, the God force, given to us to work or play with, to create. In the physical world it takes more time than in the etheric, or spirit world, where we don't have low-density bodies, but our minds start things happening here nevertheless. Prayer is our way of organizing our thinking. God already knows. It is we who don't. It is we who must organize our thinking."

"I wish more people believed in the power of prayer. Or, if not religious prayer specifically, at least in the power of their thoughts and wishes," I mentioned.

Derek nodded his head and sat there for a moment before a story flashed into his mind. He looked straight into my eyes as he recalled it. "I read in a book about a Catholic mother superior and the writer who became very good friends and learned to communicate telepathically with each other. When the mother superior died the writer discovered they could still communicate telepathically. The mother superior in the spirit world described an example of life on her side. If she wanted a garden it was there as soon as she thought about it. A perfect garden in the etheric. If she worried about weeds, there appeared weeds to worry about. What you and I worry about in the physical world we are attracting to us, we are attracting into creation. Feeling guilty is attracting what we feel guilty about."

"Rather ironic," I said. "Which is probably why most people would refuse to believe it even if they felt it to be true."

"If we see negative qualities in ourselves and consciously or subconsciously condemn them, we are adding energy to those negative qualities, making them worse. What we are doing is concentrating on a negative quality and seeing it existing which means we are not seeing it not existing. If we see a way to change those negative qualities for the better, then we are making energy available for the change. We would then be seeing a negative quality done away with. Just try forgiveness of self. Accept God's forgiveness—his Grace. Sai Baba says when tempted, give him your temptations and you will be free of them."

"To see the power of our thoughts and desires, is to accept responsibility for them as well." I said. "I imagine that's a scary thing to do for many. I know I have trouble with it myself."

"It may be scary for some, but I believe it is important to appreciate. If we see a negative quality in another person and choose to mention it to the person, then that energy is compounded. This is why the spoken word is so powerful. We should always look for the good in others and frequently mention it. This compounds the good in that person. Compliments are beneficial."

"I think most people would have to agree with that," I added.

"In my opinion," Derek continued, "we have to invite God to work through us. God will never force Himself onto us. We must invite Him. To do this we must attune to God, consciously and unconsciously, and let him express. We may never know why or what we are really doing. Hence the good results are not ours. They are law taking place through us and we would be wrong taking credit. We can't break God's laws. We can only observe their outworking."

Derek often said, "What we see in others is a reflection of what is in us." Regardless of my sexual orientation, Derek told me at a later time, "I see you as a loving, bright, caring, giving, wonderful person."

I was quick to remind him, "That must mean, according to you, you are a loving, bright, caring, giving, wonderful person."

He gazed at the floor and blushed smiling his wonderful, shy smile, "You're embarrassing me."

I adored Derek!

Shortly after finishing my course, Derek invited me over for dinner so I could meet Michelle and their son. I was very pleased to see firsthand the marvelous family life they had. Knowing Derek, I presumed it had to be this way.

One morning, years later, I brought my bowl of cereal and coffee to my breakfast table and went to the front door to get the local newspaper. All was fresh and clean from the rain the night before. I glanced at the paper as I walked. I noticed a smaller headline near the bottom of the front page about a fatal accident. Sitting down I wondered if it was anyone I knew. I took a sip of coffee as I started to read. "Derek Saul, a local insurance agent, died last night as a result of an automobile accident on the wet...."

I couldn't read any more. My eyes blurred. "No, not Derek, no. It can't be. Please not Derek." I was comatose. I cried. I called in sick. I couldn't teach that day or the next.

However, in my heart, and in the hearts of many, Derek still lives.

Life is a process. It is not a destination, I remind myself.

I thank God for having known Derek!

Chapter Ten

Ken's Journal (April 15)

I've been trying to get everything organized before heading back up north tomorrow. I won't be able to meet some other people whom I was looking forward to meeting, but I intend to get back down soon to make the rounds again.

Things are getting complicated with the revising, editing, and compiling of this book. So many details and chapters are being tossed at me all at once. I find myself being quite critical of what I am doing. I feel rushed. I hope I am still sticking to the original purpose of creating an inspirational book that anyone can relate to. As I read the accounts coming in, I, too, have come to know my younger brother was really extraordinary. Inside I feel a pressure to relay his story.

I called Jenny tonight and she seemed a little more eager to see me this time. When I mentioned it previously, she was rather reserved—as if to say it won't work. I have to admit I was wondering if it could have been because she was seeing him. I trust her and sincerely doubt she would do anything without giving me a clearer indication than she has. At least I hope so. Anyway, it was a relief to hear her a little more enthusiastic about my return. She said she initially was hoping to have a little more time to catch up on work before I got back.

I talked about the two of us getting away for a weekend vacation...someplace where it can be just the two of us, and no phone. She was receptive to the idea, so I've already become busy considering various itineraries. When we finally get the time together, I won't know where to begin. I'm sure she will notice a different attitude. I hope I can maintain a positive attitude similar to Derek's, but any change is good.

I don't think Derek had to face some of the problems that I have had to face. And I don't think that he saw many of the things I have seen in my time, which I believe is one reason why it was easier for him to remain positive. Although he did have to raise a child and support a family as a teenager...while still going to college. I suppose he did have trials of his own.

(April 17)

I'm home now. Got back last night. It's so good to see Jenny again. She looks great. I can tell she's being very cautious about the new me. When I went down to Falls Church, I think she was sure our marriage was over. So was I, but now I believe she's probably figuring she'll give us another chance. I hope so.

Actually, after I half-joked about how good it was to see she was still here, she said, "You don't think I would give up on you that quickly, do you?" Truthfully, I thought she might. And she probably would have been justified. I've practically ignored her over the past year, rather than argue all the time.

I finally got her to take a day off. The tax deadline had passed, but she was still finding a lot of reasons to keep going. Some of her clients had to take an extension because they didn't get their act together on time. I told her that was their problem and she needed time off. Being ever dutiful, she said she would clean up some important things in the next few days and then we could take off. We have got to find more time together. It's too hard to be close to someone when you really only see them an hour a night.

(April 19)

Today I was surprised to see that all of Derek's coaches replied to Michelle's letter. Michelle had put all the replies together and mailed them up to me. I wonder if my high school baseball coach even remembers me.

All Derek's coaches made similar remarks about being happy with Derek. A few had unique comments that I will be sure to get in the book. One letter even came from the little league coach of Derek's sons. It was interesting to hear him saying similar things about Derek as an adult and how he continued to have an impact on others.

Now I'm only hoping I have time to finish this project. The Globe called today. They heard I was back in town, although I have no idea how. They figured I would be eager to get back to work. I told them otherwise.

Still, they want to send me to the Near East to cover the Palestinian, Israeli, Arabic tensions. I told them I was finishing a book and would need more time, but they said a month off should be long enough and they want me leaving in two weeks.

Any other time I'd be glad to, but with everything going on between Jenny and me and with the book, now is not a good time.

Account by Bud King, wrestling coach

I already knew Derek before he showed up for wrestling because he and my younger son had been on the YMCA gymnastics team together. I knew he was coordinated and agile, but small at 125 pounds...maybe.

There was a friendly quality about Derek, not just to me, but to all the team members, even the older boys. He was always joking and horsing around. He had a great smile and pulled some of the world's worst puns which he made up.

Derek was always on time for practice and worked hard. When he was wrestling, it was total concentration. Derek learned a lot about wrestling by intensely studying the others. When watching other wrestlers, his body would be twitching as if he were going through the match himself.

His teammates would enjoy practicing with Derek because he would confide in them what they should be doing. He was, in effect, coaching them—which made my job easier. One of his favorite sayings was, "Don't think so hard, it gives you away. When an inspiration comes, act fast before your opponent catches on." Derek could do this.

In other ways, sometimes, he didn't make my job easier. Derek annoyed me repeatedly during the last two years he wrestled. After he finished a match, which he usually won, he often went over to his opponent and told him why he lost. Derek would tell him he could have won if he had done this or that. Or that he had hesitated too long, thinking about his next move and his body language gave him away. Things like that.

I told him to knock it off, to let his coach tell him. Derek would tell me his coach doesn't wrestle with him, so his coach doesn't know. Or that the guy has talent and with a few hints he could be good.

"But he's your opponent," I would try to explain.

"Aw, come on," Derek would say, "don't be like that." With such a beautiful attitude I had to stop telling him to knock it off, even though I hated to see him training my opposition.

By his junior year, he had put on more heft and wrestled in the 145-pound weight class and won the state championship, which is unusual for a junior.

Even other coaches felt he would win the championship again his senior year, but he got married instead and dropped wrestling, which surprised everyone. I tried to persuade him to do both, but he was adamant. He had to finish an apartment on the third floor of his parent's home before the baby arrived. I would never have guessed Derek would have a shot-gun wedding.

His wife took a lot of guff from the faculty because she was his French teacher, four years older than him. She was accused of seducing him. Derek was popular with the girls, but wasn't the promiscuous type. In time we could see how happy they were. His untimely death was a tremendous shock to us all. I don't usually like to say that I have a favorite, but of all the guys I've coached, Derek would be the one.

From the account by Guy Patterson, gymnastic coach

Derek had been a diver for the Y swim team. He understood the uses of his body, so, was a natural when it came to gymnastics. He understood what I was trying to get across. Even though he horsed around a lot, there was a seriousness about his practice.

I once heard him say to another teammate, "Nothing happens to us in the physical without first happening in the mind. Mind is the builder. You gotta really concentrate before you start." Derek was always there to give guys helpful suggestions. He was a team leader.

I once mentioned to Derek how I liked the way he smiled even when he messed up and he replied, "A smile is one way to let God shine through us. Guys who don't smile are walling out their happiness. A smile is contagious and we should start an epidemic."

He never let an injury, or a bad routine, stop him from smiling and remaining positive. That was what made Derek so special in my eyes.

From the account by Brent Caird, Derek's Scoutmaster

Derek Saul and Michael Bassett were members of my Boy Scout Troop for only two years, 7th and 8th grade, but they were outstanding scouts. In high school they were too busy.

Derek was quick and bright and small. It did not take him long to learn his material and pass his tests. Most of the kids in the Troop were quite serious about the program, but Derek and Michael were into fun and games, which, honestly, got me pretty annoyed sometimes. They were always wise cracking and thinking up new ways of doing things. Derek was a little frustrating at times being a bit disruptive, although I admit a lot of his suggestions were clever and innovative.

I don't think Derek and Michael ever missed a hike or a camp out. They knew what to do and the easiest way to do it. Their fathers had taught them well. I hope Derek was able to pass it on to his children before his untimely death.

Account by Rusty Bianchini, football coach

When Derek walked in the gym his freshman year to join those coming out for football, I took one look at that little squirt and shook my head. "He'll be killed," I thought to myself. His voice was still changing and he probably didn't weigh 125 pounds soaking wet.

After the exercises, I took Derek aside. I didn't want to hurt his enthusiastic feelings, but at the same time I didn't want him around. I did not want the responsibility of him getting killed. I looked into those enthusiastic eyes and just couldn't tell him to get lost because he was too small.

I figured a kid with that kind of zest and zeal would have to make a good team manager. I found myself asking him to be my freshman manager. I told him that way I knew he would be an asset to the team and wouldn't get ruined by those big thugs out there.

Without blinking an eye or losing his smile, he quickly replied, "I'd like that." I know he had realized that it was that or nothing.

Derek turned out to be such a good freshman manager that I kept him on as manager of the varsity team for the next three years. In those four years there were countless times I was convinced Derek could read my mind. He would have already done something I was about to ask him to do and you can't ask for any better than that.

Account by Bruce Novak, Little League coach

When Mike and Andre Saul were playing on the Little League team, I was coach. Their father, Derek, was almost always at the games. Eventually, I asked him if he would give me a hand running things which he did right up until he passed away.

There really isn't much to tell. There wasn't much practice as our league was a fun thing and our games were, for the most part, our practice. But whenever I needed Derek, he was there. He got along famously with the kids.

What impressed me most about Derek was his willingness and the fact that I didn't have to tell him what to do. If he saw something that had to be done he just did it. I remember once when Eddie Brett didn't show up, Derek hopped in his car and went and got him. I hadn't even noticed Eddie wasn't there.

If we needed cash for something and were short a few bucks, Derek seemed to know it before I did and would come up with what we needed.

I don't have much else to say except Derek was conscientious and a joy to work with. I was extremely grieved at his passing. He was a good man. He was a great person.

Ken's Journal (April 21)

I received a letter from Alton Benson yesterday in response to my phone call of a few days ago. Michelle told me he might be sending something, because he called her and asked for my address. He said he had some clarifications to his religious position in case anyone ever read Michelle's book and wanted to know the "truth."

I had to laugh, thinking that after all these years, he's still trying to win that argument with Derek. Maybe not, but it's still sticking with him, that's for sure.

Letter from Alton Benson

Dear Ken Saul,

After our talk the other day I thought I'd better write you the truth about the differences between Derek's and my thinking so that if you ever get published your readers will at least learn the true teachings of Jesus and not the errors of Derek.

The most significant difference is that Derek doesn't believe the Bible is the inspired word of God as I do. Even the various translations are either all God or none of it is. Men have tried to prove through the years that the Bible is in error in some ways and that it isn't what it claims to be. Yet, I don't recall the name of any man that has proved any of it to be in error.

I believe that God also has the power to preserve the integrity of the Bible and present His revelation of Himself to man as He sees fit. If it is not from God, on what criteria would you base your determinations of what is of God and what isn't? My beliefs are based on my conviction that the Holy Spirit of God inspired and instructed the writers of the books of the Bible and, thus, it is God who is the author.

Derek contended hell is in the mind. Hell is, if you take the Bible literally as mentioned by Jesus in the gospels at least ten times, a place of torment and punishment and through John in Revelations as the place of punishment of the wicked after judgment. Those who have never heard of Jesus or the Law will be judged by God on the basis of their conscience.

However, if you have heard of Jesus and his offer of salvation on Judgment Day, I believe you will be accountable for that. If Jesus was only a good man martyred, and not the Son of God, or God, himself, in the flesh, paying the price for our sins, why worship or follow his teachings? Yet, if God is perfect and absolutely Holy and sin separates us from Him, then there was and is a real need for atonement. Not only by saying yes, and believing, but by repentance and turning from our sinful natures are we saved.

I am totally convinced that every word of the Bible is inspired by God and that its contents are 100% true and I am willing to tell others that I believe it. In Christianity you are compelled by Jesus to tell others. "Go therefore and makes disciples of all nations, baptizing in the name of the Father and the son and the Holy Spirit."

This is why I'm writing you. When you accept Jesus as Savior and Lord you give up control of your life to His guidance and God expresses through you. The Christian Bible states very clearly that spiritual salvation and everlasting life can be achieved only through recognizing Jesus Christ as our Savior. We essentially must be "reborn" Christians.
Sincerely,
Alton Benson

Ken's Journal (April 23)

I faxed a copy of Alton's letter to Michelle to see what she would think. She obviously thought quite a bit, because she answered right back. I hadn't really noticed it before, but obviously she and Derek shared a lot of the same perspectives and you can certainly hear it in her reply.

I think it's very important that a couple share their views on life. Jenny and I used to be more like that, but in recent years we rarely share our views on anything. I'm sure she would make the case that she has tried, but I was never receptive. I don't know why I haven't been interested in listening to her. I guess it all gets back to being overly self-absorbed.

I let Jenny start reading the accounts from everybody. I want her to read them and I want us to talk about them on our mini-vacation. I could sit down and tell her about everything that has happened over the past month, but this way she'll be able to read and know exactly where I was coming from while down South. Of course, she can also see how my feelings towards our relationship have changed. I could tell her the same, but it still seems easier for some things to be said on paper. I'm really looking forward to our short trip.

Anyway, Michelle's reply had the most fire I think I've ever seen from her. Maybe I just haven't known her well enough. It's so strange to never really have known the people in my own family.

E-mail from Michelle

Ken,

I know what Derek would have said if he had read that letter. I can hear him now. Actually, a lot of Alton's remarks hit me strongly and I feel the need to reply to him. I know I won't though. What would be the point? He's convinced he is right.

But with regards to the last two sentences of Alton's letter, the Bible does not state, clearly or otherwise, that recognizing Jesus Christ as Savior is the only path to salvation. If it were true, it would certainly exclude the majority of humanity from salvation. This surely must be seen as an exaggerated, over-exclusive, and unloving claim made, not by Jesus himself, but by St. Paul, the over-zealous Christian-hater turned over-zealous Christian promoter, who never met Jesus or even heard him speak.

The path to salvation does not consist of the recognition of any teacher or guru now, or in the past, but in the recognition that each one of us is an expression of the Divine, and has the ability to demonstrate that divinity in all its fullness.

"I and my Father are one," and "All I do, you can do and more," as Derek always quoted from the Bible. I believe that if the entire Bible were the inspired word of God, then it must follow that all interpretations must also be inspired so we all would know what was inspired and think alike, which obviously we don't. So what good would an "inspired Bible" be if every reader is not inspired alike to have the correct interpretation? And if every reader is inspired, then how come there are differences in our interpretations? Or are only certain church leaders inspired?

Michelle

Chapter Eleven

Ken's Journal (April 24)

Jenny and I finally managed to escape for a couple of days. We drove to Kennebunkport and stayed at a nice B&B. No cooking, no gardening, no housework, no phone calls. It was a joy and the perfect environment to explain Derek and his thinking, and to make love. Things went so well, I truly believe Jenny and I are overcoming our impasse. I don't just hope so, I believe it. Positive thinking, without doubt. (Thanks, little brother)

I got some insight into Derek's professional life today when I returned to find that Michelle had forwarded accounts from his former colleagues.

I never took much interest in Dad's business. I chose to go a different way. I never thought that Dad might have interpreted my lack of interest in the business as a lack of interest in him. Next time I see him I want to talk to him to make sure he doesn't feel that way. I think it was wonderful Derek could help out with the business and carry it on the way he did. Like everything else, he did it in his own special way.

Regina Schofield's Account

I was employed at the Saul Insurance Agency longer than Roger Saul. It will be 45 years next July. I was first employed as a secretary by Derek's grandfather, who was the founder of the Saul Agency. Roger, Derek's father, was still in college when I was hired. As the agency grew, I was promoted to office manager over a staff of six. Now we have twelve, including two salesmen who really report to Mr. Saul.

So, I knew Derek since he was born, his sister also. I also knew Derek's grandfather and grandmother, his mother and, of course, his father best of all.

Once a week, often with her kids, I would see Mrs. Saul, or Emily as she told me to call her, when she would come in for her check for groceries and household things. She called it her "pay check" for putting up with Roger. Putting up with Roger, I know, wasn't a chore. He was a very considerate and kind man and not at all prone to temper tantrums.

I do remember one time, however, when he lost his temper with me. We had hired a new secretary and after a couple of months and a zillion mistakes he came out with an important letter she had typed with three misspellings and something else wrong. He was livid. He told me to fire her.

"She will never learn fast enough," he said.

I didn't want to fire her. She may not have been the brightest secretary, but we were friends. I suggested to Mr. Saul that it would be a better learning experience for her if he fired her and explained why.

"Maybe so," he muttered as he went back into his office. Moments later he was back and angry. "Damn it to hell, Regina, you fire her. That's what I pay you for!" And he stomped back into his office.

When Derek was older and Maggie was in school, he often walked in with Emily. He always had a big smile for me and was curious about what I had on my desk. He would tiptoe to peek over the edge, often reaching for something. Sometimes I used to let him sit on my lap at my electric typewriter and we would go over the letters. He already knew most letters as he had been watching Sesame Street on TV.

He was a cute kid, into everything. If his father was in, he would go into his office and bother him. Not really bother, but you had to keep your eyes on him. His active little hands were indeed active and he was curious. I used to keep a small supply of those caramel cubes wrapped in cellophane. Firstly, they were hard to open and, secondly, hard to chew. It kept him occupied.

When Derek was old enough to go to school, Emily would come in when he was at school, and I didn't see much of Derek for quite a few years. When he was in middle school and old enough to ride his bicycle around town, he would occasionally drop in to see his father. Occasionally, he would have Michael with him. They were always friendly.

"Got any of those caramels?" they would always ask.

When Derek started high school, he would come in to use one of our electric typewriters. They were better than the old manual one at home. When we switched to computers he got one of our electric typewriters for himself, but he then came in to use our computers.

There was no question about Derek being bright. I would have said he was a genius. His father used to brag about him getting all A's on his report card. When he sat down at the computer to do a paper, his concentration was so intense I could not get his attention. So, I gave up trying and saved my small talk until he was finished.

Derek wasn't all mental though. He was into athletics also. First diving and gymnastics at the YMCA, then wrestling at high school. He was always busy.

Then came the day in his last year in high school when he announced his engagement to Michelle. You could have knocked me over with a feather. I couldn't believe it. I didn't even know who she was. I had never heard of him dating anyone, let alone getting serious with someone. I found it hard to believe.

When Mr. Saul told me the news, I said "You've got to be kidding." Then in the same breath he told me Derek wasn't going to college, and was going to come to work with us and learn the business.

What a waste, I thought! That guy could be a college professor. Of course, I was delighted to have him in the office, but I didn't think it was right. I think Mr. Saul should have put his foot down and made him go to college even if he was married. He could afford it.

Within two months came the news that Michelle was pregnant. I couldn't believe how soon that happened and again thought it was such a shame. Then I realized why the marriage was so soon. She was already pregnant when they got married, and that was another shock I found hard to believe.

When I first met Michelle at the wedding, I was prepared to hate her for robbing the cradle and getting pregnant, but I liked her. Although I had some difficulty convincing myself that I wasn't being fooled. As time passed, I came to genuinely like her.

Derek took several of our insurance company's home-study courses. He spent his spring vacation in the insurance company's branch office with the underwriters learning their end of the business. He went over our filing and accounting systems with me and then office procedures. His mind was like a sponge. He graduated from high school in June.

A healthy baby boy arrived in July. Derek was so proud he was ecstatic. By then he had finished building a third-floor apartment in his father's house and had moved in. Also he was working full time in the office mainly delivering policy renewals, meeting the insured, and getting increases where needed, sometimes a new policy. He was doing better than okay. He was doing well. I was proud of him and he wasn't even my son.

In early September he got his high school transcript and letters of recommendation from the principal, the football coach, and the wrestling coach and proceeded, without an appointment, to the admissions office of American University in Washington.

This is what he told me he said to the admissions officer, "I presume it is against your policy to admit students on the spot for a semester that starts the next day, but I am here to plead with you to make an exception."

He laid out his transcript, letters of recommendation, and told them of his marriage, the baby, and his job and why he had not applied earlier. The director of admissions read them all and called in a couple of others from his staff to interview Derek. Then Derek was asked to wait in the hall while they talked in private. Shortly, Derek was invited back. And the director of admissions extended his hand saying, "We're happy to admit you."

I always loved that story. Derek said he was so emotionally overcome, his eyes began to water and he choked up so he couldn't even say thank you. He ignored the extended hand and gave the director a hug. The next day he started school with two courses.

There is very little to say about the day-to-day events in the office. Things went smoothly for the most part. Derek got along well with the staff and our clients. A lot of our clients knew him because our town has that small-town feeling even though we are very close to Washington. Derek had a good reputation from high school, so when he called on the parents of his classmates he was well received. Besides his name was Saul, which definitely helped, and he was personable and spoke convincingly, despite his extreme youth. People wanted to believe in him.

The greatest tragedy in my life, aside from the loss of my parents, was Derek's untimely death. Josh Bassett, who worked for us and lived in the third-floor apartment in Derek's home, called me at home late that fateful night and tearfully broke the news.

He sobbed as he told me he wouldn't be able to come into the office for awhile and he wanted me to handle things. I did not want to come in either, but someone had to. All I did the next morning, after telling the staff the news, was to change the announcement on the answering machine and put a notice on the door that due to Derek's death the office would be closed until after the funeral. The funeral was mobbed.

There was no getting back to normal without Derek. He had been taking an increased work load, giving his father more time to enjoy life. Mr. Saul was 65 and anticipating retirement. His first reaction was to sell the agency and get out, but Michelle had inherited Derek's half and needed the income and wasn't emotionally able to think about what to do for awhile.

My mind was working overtime as to what the prospects might be for the agency's future, because my future also was in the balance. Josh was a possible buyer. He was almost in the family, but he wasn't the manager type, had no money, nor credit. Without Derek, Josh's spirit was crushed. They were such tight friends and, besides, Josh was a quiet, introspective, solitary soul. I'm not sure he would have wanted the agency if it had been given to him.

John Parker was the logical buyer in my opinion. He had worked for us for a number of years before starting his own agency. He had wanted to buy into the agency before he left, but Mr. Saul wouldn't sell then, wanting to keep it a family agency. He still brokered commercial lines with us. He and Derek had worked closely on several brokered commercial accounts.

Mr. Saul wouldn't do anything yet. He and Josh increased their work loads and many things went undone. It was no longer a cheerful office, but business continued. We adjusted.

Then I learned Michelle was pregnant. How sad, I thought, that the baby would never see his wonderful father. But, at least, Derek knew before he died that he was going to be a father again.

One day, about three months later, Josh called a staff meeting. He explained that Derek on his deathbed had pleaded with Michelle and Michael to marry soon, before the baby was born. Derek had told Michael, who had driven Michelle to the hospital, that she needed him. He told Michelle that Michael loved her, worshipped her, and would be a wonderful father to her son. Josh then told us they were going to be married in a small private wedding the next month and we all were invited.

Mr. Saul stepped up and announced that at the end of the school year, Michael was leaving his coaching job at school and was coming to work with The Saul Agency.

"That way he can keep us from robbing his wife," said Mr. Saul, adding a humorous touch to the announcement.

I knew that Michael was no Derek. Nobody could be, but I was willing to see how things worked out. I was not unhappy at the prospects. To say the least, I was surprised, because it was nothing like what I had predicted.

Michelle's second son was born eight months after Derek's death and was named Derek Saul Bassett. I must confess I wish they had named him Derek Saul, Jr., but that was not my decision. In the almost three years now that Michael has been with the agency, things have continued to go well. Michael has learned the business and fits right in.

Last year Mr. Saul retired and sold his half interest to, of all people, John Parker. Why he didn't sell to Michael and Josh I will never know. I was never privy to the decision making. John is a good man as I said before. Maybe Mr. Saul thought that, since John knew many of our clients, he could pirate them away with his experience and Michael's lack of experience.

With Mr. Saul and Derek gone, the Saul name was gone, too. Maybe he figured John Parker would be the experienced manager the agency needed as I was about to retire. I'll never know for sure, but for the past year all has worked well and there has been enough income to go around. I will retire on my 65th birthday next June.

I still miss Derek.

John Parker's Account

When I first came to work for Roger Saul, I was pushing thirty and had been a special agent for one of Roger's insurance companies. I wanted a change from constantly traveling from one agency to another, drumming up business and solving the problems of each particular agency. In the long run, these very agents who were relying on my greater knowledge of their business were building an agency and an investment that could far exceed my future pay and retirement benefits.

So, when Roger offered me a job, I grabbed it hoping that some day I might get to buy in. It was an older, medium-sized agency founded by Roger's father in a good location and with a good potential for growth.

I first met Derek when he came into the office with his mother. He must have been in fourth or fifth grade. By the time he was in middle school he was riding his bicycle everywhere and would more frequently drop in to see his father about something or other and then be off just as quickly. He always seemed to be on the go, and had great energy. We scarcely said more than, "Hi, Derek," and "Hi, John."

By the time Derek was in high school, I would ask him about the things he was doing and we had a number of short, casual conversations. He would sometimes drop in to use our computers for an assignment. He certainly was an active person, into everything it seemed. From time to time, his father would brag about Derek. So, I felt I knew him fairly well. He was thoroughly likable.

His marriage to Michelle and her pregnancy came as a big surprise to me. It just didn't seem like Derek. I couldn't help but think he was just too young and wondered if it would work out. It was then he started coming in the office daily and asking me a lot of questions as he was taking home-study insurance courses.

At that time he was all work. He was intent on learning the business and passing his licensing exams. He would study so hard I am sure he never knew what was going on around him.

People would come and people would go, phones would ring, but nothing would bother him. Sometimes clients who knew Derek through his father would say something to Derek and he would never hear them. I found myself having to explain to people that he was not ignoring them or being impolite, but he just didn't know they were there. I've never seen a person with his powers of concentration, which probably explained his good grades in school. He could just wall out all distractions. People would actually leave admiring him more. I would think to myself with a smile, "There you go again, helping your competition."

However, I never minded helping my competition when it was Derek. There was that something about him. Perhaps it was the energy of doing the right thing with joy and enthusiasm that was contagious. He was the kind of young man every mother would like to hug, while every father would be wishing his son were like him. It was impossible not to like Derek.

I don't know anything about Derek and Roger's pay arrangement, but he surely was worth every cent he may have been paid. He passed his license exams with flying colors before he graduated from high school. He immediately started delivering renewal policies and talking over values and increases our clients needed. He knew his premium rates and could tell the clients their costs.

At first his father or I would go over these renewal policies with him giving him suggestions, but in less than a month he was doing this on his own. Occasionally, he would ask our advise. Sometimes he would ask to watch me go over one of my commercial accounts. However, for the time being he kept to residential accounts.

Frequently, he would be busy all day delivering policies and renewals on Saturdays. Roger and I almost never worked weekends and eventually Derek didn't either, but at the start he was gung ho, which paid off for him and the agency. He would precede his visits with a phone call. A good practice which I was overlooking.

Derek would also do cold-turkey solicitations on the parents of his classmates and his former teachers. These calls proved profitable for him. Everyone seemed to know about Derek's marriage and forthcoming parenthood and then later his new son. He already had their sympathies and attention.

Although teenage pregnancies were frowned upon in Falls Church, there were enough of them that it did not mean ostracism and to have a teenage father work like hell taking the responsibility for his mistake was a feather in Derek's cap. Of course, Derek's winsome personality and appearance helped him greatly. It didn't hurt that his name was Saul working for The Saul Agency.

To say Derek was organized was a fact. I was curious as to how organized he really was and asked once to see his datebook, which he always kept with him. It wasn't all work. He had allowed himself time to recreate. I remember noting the first work day of every month was "lunch with Mom." Frequently, "fishing with Michael," or "racquetball with Phillip" would be scheduled or so and so for dinner and so forth, but he was always busy with a seemingly inexhaustible supply of energy.

As time went by, Derek developed commercial accounts of his own and occasionally Roger would turn one over to him probably because it required too much of his time. After a year or two, instead of delivering renewal policies, he took to calling. I heard it so often that I still remember his approach clearly.

"I was about to mail you your renewal and I noticed you are only insured for so much," he would start. "Don't you think you should have a little more? Maybe $30,000. You couldn't replace it for what you have on there now." Then having called on the clients in person once or twice, they knew each other and a phone call was enough. I actually started copying Derek's technique with his phone calls. I knew it was the right way, but I had just been too lazy.

After Derek had been with the agency five years, his father gave him 25% of the agency, with another 5% a year up to 50%. By this time Derek had bought his father's house. As I have said, Derek was always busy.

I felt it was time to take steps if I was ever to own part of the agency. I offered to buy a third interest. Roger wouldn't sell. He explained how his father had started the business, how he had joined him, and now his son had joined him. He was hoping that a grandson would later join them. For the time being, he wanted to keep the agency a family business.

I understood, but was a little surprised because I felt like a part of the family. Roger reminded me that he had set up a good retirement plan for me and my pay was as good or better than other salesmen in other agencies. Although I stayed on for the better part of a year, I really wanted my own agency.

When I did announce this, Derek took me aside. Mind you now, Derek was only 24. His wisdom and understanding made me think he was nearly my age. I remember the conversation very clearly.

"John, I know Dad's thoughts and he is the controlling partner," he said. "But I don't agree with him. I think there is enough for all of us. You're a good man and a substantial asset to our agency."

"I appreciate that Derek," I said, not sure of where he was heading.

"Although right now we own the policies of your clients, I feel sure a large number of them, particularly the personal lines, came to us because you serviced them or they were your friends or relatives. I feel sure they hold their allegiance to you, not the agency, and when their renewals come due, you will be able to get most of them to switch over to your new agency."

"I would like to think so," I said. "But I wouldn't want to...."

"If you agree to my plan, I think I can get Dad to agree. He doesn't know what I am proposing. I suggest on your personal accounts, not business accounts, that we write them a letter stating you are a good man and want to start your own agency. We wish you good luck and as a token of our appreciation for years of fine service we are turning their personal accounts over to you upon renewal of the policies, unless your clients were to notify us they don't want to switch away from us."

"And you really think your Dad would be agreeable to such a plan?" I asked doubtfully.

"Sure. Why not? And as to your commercial accounts, I would guess that you were able to land many or most of these accounts because you represented our agency. I bet that I could retain at least half of these accounts. My suggestion is that we continue to write these policies on renewal, you continue to service them, and that we continue to pay you the same 50% of the commissions as we do now. In effect, we would be co-agents."

"Sounds good, but...."

"Or, if you wish, you could write the renewals and service them and you pay us 50% of the commissions and I agree not to try to compete to retain that business. I do not think this latter system will work to your advantage because a portion of these commercial accounts will remain loyal to The Saul Agency and will not want to switch to a small, newly formed, one-man agency, even though you serviced them for years for us."

"That's probably true, but I just don't know if your…."

"Don't worry, I'll talk to Dad shortly about it and then we can iron out the details," Derek quickly responded and then walked off as if everything had been taken care of.

I thought about it for a day and agreed Derek's plan would work best for me and them. Derek convinced his father and that is what happened. There were many times both Derek and I would call on a customer when a major problem arose. It worked out splendidly. I must say I have always enjoyed working with Derek and have never regretted my decision.

The news of Derek's untimely death came as a severe blow to me. My heartfelt compassion went out to Michelle, their son, and his parents. What a loss!

I was a bit shocked when Michelle married Michael so soon. I agreed that the two should marry. It was logical, but why so soon? Why before the baby was born? Later I learned it was Derek's deathbed wish.

Last year Roger Saul retired. He sold me his half-interest in the Saul Insurance Agency because I was an experienced insurance agent for over 20 years and owned half interest in some of their commercial accounts. Michelle had inherited Derek's half-interest in the agency and Michael was running it for her.

He is doing fine, but is still inexperienced. Josh has almost always handled personal accounts and is not experienced with the larger commercial accounts, many of which I had serviced and owned half-interest in since I left the agency years ago. I get along well with the Bassett brothers and everything is working out well.

I owe a lot to Derek and I am grateful to have known him. Not just for his help in starting my own agency, but for the opportunity to have felt his love and energy for life.

Part Three

Chapter Twelve

Ken's E-mail to Michelle (April 25)

Michelle,

I want to fill you in on the details of my visit to Mrs. Hall, Jan's mother. After all the investigations to track her down, I finally got over to the nursing home to see her today.

It was eerie trying to get her mind to work and not have her realize she was divulging information she might not have divulged if she were in her right mind. I felt guilty digging up stuff and causing her to remember things she might, otherwise, like to forget. Being accustomed to having my little recorder along for interviews, I recorded the conversation and will relay the important parts here.

"Good morning, Mrs. Hall. I'm Ken Saul, the brother of Derek. You remember Derek, don't you? He hired your lovely daughter, Jan, to baby-sit his son while his wife, Michelle, taught at the high school."

"Oh, yes. I remember Derek. He was in the car when Jan was killed, wasn't he?" she replied, encouraging me that her memory might not be so bad. She wasn't completely out of it, as her son had implied. Mrs. Hall was dressed snugly in her warm bathrobe and sat in a wheelchair in the hall outside her room. Her head, as I approached, was drooped with her chin in her chest as if asleep. She raised her head as I spoke and weakly smiled.

"Wasn't it a shame? I feel so sorry for you, losing your daughter," I started. "Losing my brother gave me much grief also. That's why I am here, to express my condolences. I know it's been three years now, but I heard you were staying here and I don't live far away. How do you like it here? Do they treat you well?"

"I don't really like it, but it's better than living with my son, who was never around when I needed him. He had to work. In Falls Church, at least Jan was there all morning and for dinner. Oh, how I miss Jan." She started to cry.

"I'm sorry I brought up such a painful subject."

"Oh, don't feel bad. Don't go. I enjoy talking with someone who knew Jan."

"Jan was such a loving person. Michelle said that many times," I told her, pretending that I actually knew Jan.

"Jan loved Michelle and the boys. She didn't see much of Derek because he was always at work, but she liked Derek, too. He used to date her in high school. He was a very good man, but Michelle was her favorite of all people." Then she paused before saying, "Jan liked women better than men anyway."

"Was she a lesbian? I'm sorry. I shouldn't have asked that. It just slipped out. It's none of my business. A person can be a lesbian or gay and still be a wonderful person."

"It's all right. Truth is truth. Yes, I guess she was a lesbian. That's why she had to get out of the Army. They kicked her out. They couldn't see that she was really a wonderful person." Mrs. Hall started crying again. I felt like a shit.

"Would it help to talk about it with someone who understands?" I asked, feeling awkward to be prying, but curious to find out more.

"They said Jan met one of the wives of a sheik. She was stationed in Saudi Arabia, you know? Someone must have found out. We never, never talked about it."

A long pause followed as I wasn't sure how to respond, but then she added, "I understand it took an act of Congress to get her out of Saudi Arabia alive, but we never, never talked about it."

I knew right away that this was the episode I had read about years ago in a newspaper. One of the guys in the office had shoved it in my face, "Is this what all the girls are like in your old hometown?" he said.

Now I know why Hall, Jr. was so uncooperative. I asked Mrs. Hall if she remembered anything about the night of the accident. She said, "Nothing much. The doorbell rang and Jan left with someone saying she would be back early. I presumed she left with Derek because she was in his car when it crashed, but I never saw the person who rang the doorbell. Oh, yes, about the time of the accident, Jan asked me if I had my son's telephone number. Why would I ever want his number unless Jan weren't around? But it turned out I did need it. I thought that was pretty strange."

My conversation with Mrs. Hall dwindled now that I had learned what I wanted and I started to leave. I thanked her and was about out the door when Mrs. Hall said, "Derek was considering buying a new car and Jan was considering buying his old one, the one in the accident."

"I didn't know that," I said. I immediately thought that this might be the reason she was driving. She was test driving Derek's car.

I told her it had been nice talking to her and that I had to be going.

I was relieved to finally uncover what it was I couldn't remember about Jan. It's strange I never made the connection before. No big deal I guess. But it is interesting, don't you think?

Ken

Ken's Journal (April 26)

After I met with Mrs. Hall yesterday, I drove directly to the microfilm records of The Globe. On the way I got to thinking about some things I had never considered at the time of the accident. Some things I didn't want to mention in my e-mail to Michelle either.

Could Jan have been in love with Michelle? They spent so much time together and, given her sexual persuasion, it seems quite possible that she could have been attracted to Michelle. Maybe she had even made advances towards Michelle. And been rejected. Maybe Derek stood in the way.

Suddenly I remembered what Mrs. Hall had said just before I left. Why would Jan have asked her mother if she had her brother's telephone number before she went out that night? My mind was really racing and still is. I can't help but wonder if maybe Jan could have played a role in the accident? Was she depressed enough to have wanted to cause the accident? Could she have wanted Derek out of the way?

At the office it took a while, but I found the article. It was essentially the same as Mrs. Hall had said. I remembered that a few weeks later in the office the guy who made the comment about the article to me, had said something else. He had shoved another article about Jan in my face and told me, "That hometown lesbian friend of yours, I hear she's working for the Kettle of Fish Bar in Cambridge. You know, that gay/lesbian bar. You oughta check it out. You're 40 now, old boy. It's about time you got married."

His teasing pissed me off. I remember saying, "Fuck you!" Of course, I never checked it out. But, now I had a reason to and so I left the office and headed for the bar.

The bar owner remembered Jan and said she was a good worker. Then he added with a sneaky, gossip-like expression, "She didn't go to Virginia to take care of her mother. She was forced out of town, or should I say, strongly advised to leave."

"What do you mean?" I asked.

"She was raped by a husband who came home and caught Jan in bed with his wife. It didn't make the newspapers. She wanted to place rape charges against the husband, but her lawyer strongly recommended she leave town instead. Her mother's ill health was a convenient excuse."

I talked with him some more, but didn't get anything else out of him. I stayed to have a beer and then decided to get back home. It turned out to be a very interesting day, but the more I found out the more questions I have about Jan's relationship to Michelle and Derek.

I couldn't imagined how hectic it would be trying to get all the work done for the book before I have to leave on my newspaper assignment. And now Josh's account arrived today and it's huge! Michelle e-mailed me the other day to warn me it was coming by snail-mail. She told me it was much too long and was probably filled with his nightly conversations with Derek. She didn't even start to read it, and she doesn't know what I'm going to do with it. Neither do I. Although she suggested that we might consider a separate book containing his spiritual conversations with Derek.

Next time I get down there I want to sit down with Josh and talk about what we might do. Knowing how close he and Derek were, I get the feeling he could write much more. I would also like to get to know Josh better. Since he was so much younger, I rarely bothered in the distant past to talk to him. But he's always been very close to the rest of the family. It's going to take a while to separate Josh's conversations with Derek from his experiences with Derek.

(April 27)

I read a portion of Josh's account this afternoon. I am stunned. I don't know what to think. Michael and Michelle have been lying to me all along...to everyone. It is possible Josh is making up the whole story, but I sincerely doubt it. He has nothing to hide.

I am angry, very angry. I can't believe this. I can't believe Michelle and Michael would go to such effort through all these years to hide the truth.

I feel like quitting and throwing it all back in their laps. But I ask myself, what would Derek have done? The answer is obvious, he would have forgiven them. I know I am not seeing things as they are. I'm seeing things as I am.

I sent an e-mail to Michelle right after I read part of Josh's account.

Jenny is actually excited to be heading down there with me, although she's a little anxious about the confrontation that may be ahead. I agree I would like to be taking her down there under better circumstances and I wish we had more time.

Ken's E-mail to Michelle

Michelle,

I started reading Josh's chapter. I am trying to hold back my anger. *You, me, and Michael have got to talk!*

Clear your calendar. I am flying down tomorrow for the weekend. I'll bring Jenny. Please tell Mom to expect us.
Ken
P.S. Don't call me. We have to talk face to face. This is too important to discuss on the phone.

Ken's Journal (April 28)

We flew to Washington, rented a car, and arrived in Falls Church about 11:30 in the morning. Michael and Michelle were waiting for us. They didn't smile when we got here. Neither did I. It was clear they were dying to find out what caused me to make the trip down.

They didn't want to mess around with small talk. Michelle asked what this was all about. Before answering, I took everybody to the back porch where Mike wouldn't be able to hear us.

"Okay, now tell us what's going on," Michelle said sternly.

"Do you mind if I record this?" I asked, getting my tape recorder out of my brief case.

"Why the hell do you want to record it? Tell me what you're up to," Michael demanded. I have to say I've never seen Michael so belligerent. He stood up and came over towards me. "No, you can't record anything," he said, reaching for the tape recorder.

"Relax, Michael. I am going to record it, but I'm not going to do a damn thing with the tape that all of us don't agree to. Now, sit down and let's talk."

He calmed down a bit and I began, "I believe Josh. He has nothing to hide." I paused as I determined what to say next. I can't describe the questioning looks that splashed over their faces as they wondered what the hell it was I knew. Turning towards Michael, I asked, "Are you Mike's father?"

Michael, in shock, looked at Michelle. Her eyes told him to say yes and he sheepishly answered, "Yes."

With firmness I replied, "You know you can't hide that from the book. If you do, I don't want to be a part of it."

There was a long silence as the two of them looked at each other, considering the possible repercussions.

I continued, "As Derek told us, God expects us to make errors, poor choices and we must live with the fruits of our choices. And we must forgive ourselves.... I'm sure Derek forgave you. It's your free choice whether you forgive yourselves or not. Hiding is not forgiving."

"I disagree," Michelle replied "It can be more hurtful to those involved if some things are exposed. What good would it have done for the world to have known Derek was not Mike's father? Would life have been easier for Mike, or Derek's parents, or even me or Derek? Derek knew and he saw nothing to forgive. He thought it was a blessing. It meant he got the chance to marry me right then. I didn't know he knew until moments before he died when he confessed to knowing all along. Michael at 17 wanted an abortion. I didn't. I don't believe in abortions."

"Now can you see why I wanted to come down to talk about this?" I said. "I didn't think I could understand why you kept it secret, but I guess I had never looked at it from your point of view. I was just pissed off at you two for hiding the truth from me."

Then Jenny jumped into the conversation. Her words were filled with truth and they hit me hard.

"Ken, this is the same way you've been treating me. You never look at things from my point of view."

"You're right." I paused. "You're absolutely right." There was nothing else I could say and I gave Jenny a long hug. Everyone was a little stunned and not sure what to say. Michelle finally broke the silence.

"Ken, I'm so glad you've come to know your brother better and what his life was all about. And I hope that continues. I'm also glad we've come to know you better. Even though Derek passed away three years ago, he is still having a big impact on our lives and bringing us all together."

I had always appreciated Michelle's intelligence. She was a beautiful, down-to-earth person, but she was also bright and good-natured. It was no wonder Derek had been so swept away by her.

"We have no other secrets Ken," Michelle said. "Why don't you quiet down now and we'll explain?"

I said, "Obviously I want to hear all, but before you begin, let me get one finding I made out in the open."

Then I brought up the fact that Jan was driving at the time of the accident. Michelle was shocked. She gasped and put her hand to her mouth. She stared a moment while we all waited. Then she asked of what significance it was.

For the first time I really stopped to think about it, and couldn't come up with an answer for her. I probably should have let it go at that, but I couldn't. "Doesn't it upset you that Derek could still be here if it weren't for Jan?" I persisted.

Without a blink, Michelle responded, "Not at all. From the greater perspective what happened was supposed to happen. Nothing happens by chance."

"But did you notice in my conversation with Mrs. Hall that on that night, before Jan left with Derek, she asked her mother if she had her son's phone number?"

"Yes. So..."

"Well, why would she ask such a thing?" I said, getting more worked up. "What if she planned the whole thing?"

"What thing?"

"The accident."

"I don't know. So, what if she did?" Michelle responded, appearing completely undisturbed by the implication. "Perhaps she asked about the phone number simply because she thought she might be home late. Or maybe she intuitively knew that something was about to happen and she needed to be sure her mother would be all right before she left. Anyway, what does it matter now?"

"Well...I...I don't really know," I finally said, stumped for a suitable response and amazed at Michelle's ability to grasp the cosmic picture.

I quickly realized I was stuck in the small picture once again. Rather than being caught up in what I viewed as negative aspects of Jan's character, I should have been reminding myself that everything happens for a reason, a purpose—related to the development of each individual's soul.

Then, as if she knew what other doubts were on my mind, Michelle continued. "And if you're thinking there was ever anything between Jan and me, let me assure you there was not. Jan had great respect for my relationship with Derek," Michelle explained.

"I never really..."

"Jan was a truly wonderful person if anyone ever took the time to get to know her."

The rest of the afternoon was spent discussing what really happened and the various alternatives for the book. In the end, Michael and I agreed that the full story of Derek would be best told if it was known how loving and forgiving he was and how accepting he was that everything was working out the way it should...for the best. How he never doubted. How his faith was so extraordinary. We decided that Michelle and Michael would write an additional account filling in the details they previously left out, that the truth had to be known. However, let me give you Josh's account next.

Chapter Thirteen

Josh's Account (the abbreviated version)

Derek and I had a lifelong, beautiful friendship. To say I loved Derek has to be an understatement.

I lived next door to him or in his third floor apartment all of my life. After college, I worked for him and his father in their insurance agency.

I was two years younger than Derek, who was the same age as my brother Michael. Michael was Derek's best friend in their younger years, but in our later years we shared that honor, though in different ways. That is, Derek and I had a special interest in the spiritual, the metaphysical. He was almost like a guru, but fortunately that word is not needed to explain how things were between us.

By the time I got to high school, Michael was heavy into athletics and girls. Michael was an outstanding athlete and handsome. I admired him and was proud of him, but was also somewhat envious. I was thin, almost scrawny. It was then, however, that Derek and I became real close. I guess you could say I was an intellectual; Michael wasn't. Derek was both an athlete and an intellectual.

Derek and Michael didn't drift apart during their high school years, but saw less of each other for several years until Michael was married and injured his knee in professional football. By then Michael had bought our parent's home next door and I continued to live there and looked after things when he was away playing football. Then came the time a high school friend of Michael's wanted to rent his house for a few months while he finished building his own. It was then I moved into the apartment that Derek had fixed up for Michelle and himself when they first got married. I never moved back until I married Marianne.

After his football career and marriage ended, Michael started coaching and teaching at a local high school. It was then that the three of us guys were really close, but this closeness included Michelle.

I was almost always invited to join them when they got together for dinners or such, which was usually at least twice a week. More often than not Michelle did the cooking, but every couple of weeks Michael or I would entertain. When Derek and Michelle went out, I usually ended up baby sitting.

Mike usually held center stage as babies and small kids are prone to do until they are sent off to bed. I was the quiet one, kind of shy and lackluster you could say, but we were a happy and devoted bunch, an extended family.

Most evenings after work I would stay at home. I enjoyed being by myself, yet also being part of the family downstairs and playing with the kids. But like many grandparents who love their grandchildren, I also enjoyed being able to get away to my own space. I read a lot, and watched TV and videos. After a while I started writing. Short stories at first. I took a course in creative writing with The Writers' Workshop. Most of all I enjoyed my private conversations with Derek after Michelle retired.

I didn't date much, hardly at all. Occasionally, I would take one of the unmarried secretaries out to dinner or to a movie or concert, but she was a few years older than me. We never considered marriage. On several occasions, someone fixed me up with a date which was nice, but nothing permanent happened. I was never promiscuous like Michael. In fact, I was very shy with women and although the thought of intercourse was appealing, I panicked when an opportunity seemed close.

I told Derek a dream I had once. Derek believed a dream was our higher self talking to us, but most often we do not recognize the symbology in the dream. Our dreams may not mean much to us on the surface, but should be studied.

In my dream I was about to go off and do something sexual, which I felt I should not do. Jesus appeared and asked if he could join me. I said, "No. You are the Christ!" And that was the end of the dream. Derek said that either my higher self or Jesus himself appeared in my dream and the dream was telling me that any time you can't take the Christ with you, don't go.

Michael was well into his promiscuous phase of life as a high school senior and the football team captain. He even wore his sleeveless tee shirts cut up high to expose his midriff and shoulders and tight shorts showing off his muscular legs until the principal told him his dress was not appropriate. He knew what women liked and knew what he liked…women.

I admit I was resentful I didn't inherit his perfect physique, blond hair, and good looks. He used to rinse his hair with lemon juice because someone had told him it would keep it blonde. Right now it's sandy colored.

(Note to Michelle: I know you may not want to share with others what I am about to say. But maybe you will and maybe it's time you did. I will leave that up to you, but as you asked me to talk about my experiences with Derek, it's something I feel I must include. I feel I would be dishonest if I didn't tell my full story, but whether you tell it in the book is up to you.)

I watched Michael closely as the years went on and wondered how he managed to not intervene in Derek and Michelle's marriage. He had been so promiscuous starting in high school and up until his marriage that I had to admire his circumspect behavior.

I could see Michael was so obviously in love with Michelle that it had broken up his marriage. I know it could only be his love for Derek and his respect for Michelle's adoration of Derek that made it possible for him to vicariously enjoy their relationship as if watching a movie and never being tempted to intervene. I don't think he was jealous. I think he was happy for them…with them. I don't know how I would have felt and acted if I were Michael. I greatly admired Michael for being a great soul.

I was the only one who knew Michael was the biological father of Mike. It was me who told Derek after I had overheard parts of a phone conversation that Michael had with Michelle.

To make a long story short, Michael had seduced Michelle when she invited him over to her house to tutor him in French after school, because he was flunking French. If he flunked any course, he couldn't play football and he was our star player. Of course, seducing women was easy for him, having the perfect physique and being handsome and likable to boot. He'd done it many times, I'm sure.

But Michelle immediately knew that she had made a mistake and so she refused to tutor him anymore. It turned out, however, she was pregnant. Apparently Michelle didn't believe in abortions and Michael didn't want to get married. The night she found out she was pregnant,

Michael went over to her apartment to discuss things. When he got home that night, he called her up to discuss his ideas about Derek.

Michael had his own phone in his room. Our parents were out. My bedroom door was open and I wasn't there. He was unaware that I was sitting on the toilet in the bathroom between our two bedrooms. The door to his room was closed. I heard him dialing. In almost a whisper I heard him say, "Michelle." His hushed tone of voice was not like him. My curiosity was aroused and I listened all the more intently.

I could not hear most of the conversation. Then it became apparent they were having a disagreement. Michael's voice got louder. "You would not be setting him up. Derek loves you. He would not mind raising my child."

His voice became quiet again and I could no longer hear him for awhile. I sat there wondering if I was really hearing what I thought I was. Then his voice turned louder as he got excited again.

"I know we both made a stupid mistake. At least see him alone. If he doesn't want to marry you, I will. That's how sure I am he wants you." There was a long pause, as Michelle was clearly giving him an earful and then he said, "Okay, just think about it. Good-bye."

I was in a state of shock. All I could think of was how could my brother set up his best friend. I grabbed a sweater and started for next door. Fortunately, Michael's door was closed. I sneaked down the carpeted stairs skipping the third stair which squeaked. Derek was in his room reading. I took him for a walk to get him out of his house.

"Michelle's pregnant with Michael's child," I told him, wasting no time getting to the point.

"How do you know this?" he said, clearly shocked.

"I overheard Michael talking to her on the phone."

"What did he say?"

"Well, he was agreeing with her that they both made a mistake and they were trying to figure out what to do. I'm sure he wants her to get an abortion."

"And she won't have one. Is he going to marry her?" Derek asked intuitively.

"You know, Michael. What are the chances he would be ready to settle down now? No, he doesn't want to marry her. He wants you to marry her."

Derek didn't say anything. He stopped walking and just stared at me with a very serious look that told me to continue.

"He told her you love her and that you will surely marry her. He said he was so sure you will marry her that if you don't, he will."

"What did she say? Did she go along with this?" Derek asked.
"It didn't sound like it. He pleaded with her to think about it."
"Does she want to marry him?"
"I couldn't tell. When he suggested he would marry her if you don't there was a long pause and when Michael continued I couldn't hear what he was saying. You're psychic. You tell me what she said."

Derek took a deep breath, put both hands in his pockets, and replied, "I think she wants to marry me, but feels guilty about trapping me."

After a short pause, he started walking again and then came to an abrupt halt, stopping to look me directly in the eye.

"I want you to promise me you will never, never, never tell anybody about their conversation and this conversation between us," he began. "I do want to marry Michelle, but if she thinks I'm marrying her because she is pregnant she will think I am marrying her out of sympathy or pity, and that would be the worst way to start out a marriage. I want to marry her because I love *her*. And not for any other reason. She's wonderful. She's beautiful. She's intelligent. Our chemistry is perfect. I love her and I think she loves me. I'm sure she does. And I don't mind raising Michael's child. Anyway, he's not mature enough to be a father and husband. I think I am."

"How can you think like this? How come you're not furious with Michael?" I asked, dumbfounded by his complete lack of anger at being set up.

"I guess it started back when I was in Little League," he explained, "It was tag day and we were all dressed up in our uniforms and stationed up and down the main streets with a can in our hands. Anybody who dropped a coin in got a tag. Two men came by dressed in suits carrying briefcases. The first one said, 'You've got a great organization. Not only is it fun for you guys, but it's teaching you a great lesson—cooperation. A team without cooperation isn't a team. And life without cooperation can be a horror.' When the second guy came along he said, 'I might as well get one of these tags now or you S.O.B.'s will be pestering me the rest of the day."

Derek turned to check my reaction and seeing that I was not following him, he continued. "Both men seemed alike. They both did the same thing, but for very different reasons. I got to thinking about it. It's not what we do or say, but *why* we do or say it that counts. We are the *why* of what we do and say. We are our motivations. The real us should be measured by our motivation, not by our jobs or cars or houses or neighborhoods or education, or the amount of money we make.

"I see what you're saying," I replied. "But still he's trapping you. He's dumping his problems on somebody else and you're letting him."

"But he's not trapping me. Michael knows what I want. Michelle argues with him about not wanting to trap me. Both motivations are good. She and Michael may have made a mistake, but they are not the first to do so. It's more important that the two of them do not worsen the mistake by forcing a marriage that was not meant to be. It's important for the child to be born into a healthy, loving environment."

I have never told our secret to anyone. One time Derek and I were up late talking and I asked him if Michelle knew that he knew. Derek said she didn't. I asked if he was ever going to tell her. He said he didn't think so. He didn't see what good it would do. I never brought up the subject again.

It was usually after everyone else had retired that Derek and I would have our discussions. They weren't all metaphysical, but he was always giving a cosmic twist to everything, very reasonable yet from a universal point of view. Sometimes we would talk way into the night.

For instance, Derek once said the only advantage of a war is that the people on each side were bonded together in a closeness of cooperation and purpose. The greatest disadvantage to war is not the needless killing and destruction, but the lasting effects of hate, fear, distrust, and revenge that persists for generations. Souls can reincarnate, buildings can be rebuilt, but the devastation to character that occurs with the lack of forgiveness goes on and on.

Derek never needed much sleep. He told me to take notes, not during our discussions but afterwards, as some day I might be called upon to be someone's special teacher. I don't know if he could see into the future, but on his deathbed he not only told Michelle and Michael to get married, but told them I should start teaching Michelle's new baby right away as even babies pick up things we adults are not aware of. We knew Michelle was pregnant. On his deathbed Derek said he was going to try to reincarnate in that unborn baby whom they should name Derek.

Derek said we don't really teach. We awaken, or bring into consciousness, knowledge which is already there in the subconscious and usually hard to access. Sometimes our subconscious can access another person's subconscious to get certain information. Consciously, we are not usually aware when it happens. People call it being telepathic or psychic. So, I have been talking metaphysics to young Derek right from the start. I often feel foolish. Very often. So foolish that I would not be doing this except for the fact that Derek was so right on with all his thinking.

Derek was a great soul. When we had our many conversations, he seemed in touch with some authority. He knew that he knew. I cannot begin to say how much I miss him. His untimely death pulverized the very essence of my being. If it were not that he said he would reincarnate in the body of baby Derek, I think I would still be mourning. I want to believe he's there. Actually, I guess I do believe it.

I don't know how he knew, but on his deathbed Derek also told Michelle and Michael to tell me to go to the Unity church's singles group where I would meet a special woman. I went and as soon as I saw Marianne Dalton, I knew and she knew. We are now married, have a baby daughter, and live next door in Michael's house which he has agreed to sell to us.

"Living in the now" is a frequently used expression. Nothing happens next; this is it. The implication is that the past and the future can't be lived in.

Derek explained it differently. Suppose you have a friend who one day says unkind and untrue things about you and pisses you off so that you discount the friendship and actually start hating the son-of-a-bitch. Thus, you have set up energy patterns of hate and some time in the future you will have to face those energy patterns of hate, for 'as you sow, so also shall you reap.' These energy patterns are still in the etheric, as Derek would call it, because they are not yet in the physical.

Later a mutual friend comes along and explains what a stressful time the former friend was going through with his wife and a child and how his estranged mother had died, leaving him with considerable responsibilities. He just wasn't himself when he made his remarks. So, you willingly forgive him in the "now."

Your forgiveness is now *and* in the etheric. However, by forgiving, you have obliterated your hateful energy patterns in the etheric. You have, thus, changed the past in the etheric. You have also changed the future in the etheric because you no longer have to reap those hateful energy patterns which you had sowed. They are gone. So the future has been changed by changing the past in the etheric. Anything can be changed by changing your mind, that is, by changing how you look at or interpret things or by changing motivation, emotions, desires, or fears. Derek called the etheric the fourth dimension, and the three-dimensional world we live in he called its shadow.

All things in the physical are created first in the mind. Nothing in the mind is cast in concrete because we can fortunately always change our minds, but mind is the builder, the physical is the result. The mind is both the etheric and the mental. All our bodies and all objects and thoughts are also the etheric. All the world and what is therein has a counterpart in the etheric. That's why some advanced souls say this world is illusion and the etheric is the real world. This physical world was derived from the etheric. Derek would not argue with people because that creates turbulence in the etheric.

Most people don't understand the etheric. They think it is merely the mental, but it's not. Everything starts in the etheric before manifesting in the physical, but our thinking, actions, and choices create energy patterns that change the etheric constantly, which in turn changes our physical, which could mean disease or poverty or just as easily a blessing and pleasure. All that is attracted to us comes from the etheric, the fourth dimension.

To better understand the mental, physical, and the etheric, think of two circles which partially overlap. One circle is the physical world; the other is the etheric world. Where they overlap is the mental. The mental is part of both the physical and etheric worlds. The etheric is the most important thing I learned from Derek and what I am now trying to explain to baby Derek. And one should always remember…you are unique…just like everybody else.

Although, I'm not so sure he cares at the moment.

Ken's Journal (April 29)

Recalling yesterday's conversation with Michael and Michelle, I was thinking how interesting it was. Everybody thought that Derek was rushing into a marriage simply because he got Michelle pregnant and had no other choice. Instead, he actually had a number of choices at the time and the one he made says a lot about him. I think most people would have been tremendously angry at the news that their best friend had accidentally impregnated the person he loves. I know I would. But Derek was different. Clearly, he did think the world of Michelle right from the start.

It also makes me think about how many times I still get so wrapped up in my selfish, emotional interests. When things don't go the way I want or the way I envision them going, I can still get easily frustrated and resentful towards anybody who may have played a role in disturbing my well-laid plans. It's been a long time now that I've been clinging to my ego and it's been affecting my relationships.

Obviously, I'm thinking of Jenny at the moment. It should be no surprise that I have been receiving back exactly what I've been dishing out. And I'm sure Derek would have been quick to tell me the same.

Last night Jenny and I got into a serious discussion about where we are headed. It's clear she definitely was ready to move on, until she began to see I might be changing. I asked her how she had used the time apart. She said she kept busy with work and did not have a lot of time to think about us. I asked her how she used the free time she did have. She could tell I was in search of some information and said, "Why do you need to know? Why should it concern you?"

I told her I wasn't worried, I was just curious, but she knew what I was getting at and assured me that she had not seen him while I was away. My suspicious side is still reluctant to believe her, but I will. I must trust her. And anyway, it doesn't matter now. It's time to look ahead.

Michael's Second Account (This time with the real details!)

In my senior year I was captain of the football team and I was not doing well in French II. My French teacher, old Mr. Shea, warned Rusty, the football coach, that if I didn't pass my mid-term exam he would flunk me and make me ineligible to play football for the rest of the season. Rusty didn't want to take the chance, so he talked Michelle into tutoring me. Knowing me, he was sure she would keep my attention.

When I went to Michelle's classroom to make my appointment for her to tutor me, she suggested I come to her classroom right after school since none of our free periods coincided. I told her I had football practice and asked her if she was tied up after practice. She paused and then made a fatal mistake no experienced cute, young teacher would make...at least not with me. She told me her apartment was right across the street and I could come over after practice.

I was there freshly showered...and horny. We sat at her kitchen table next to each other, she on my right. I had my textbook to my left and my open notebook in front of me. Michelle stood up to point out something in the text she wanted me to work on. I moved my shoulder slightly away from her so she would come closer since the text was on the other side. When she bent closer, I slowly moved my shoulder back against her and rotated it against her body while I let my hand fall limply to my crouch. She went into the other room while I translated some sentences. After I had written out what she wanted me to, I went into the living room to tell her I was finished.

Michelle put down the newspaper and came back to the kitchen table and sat in her chair. I pushed the notebook in front of her, but remained standing next to her as she read my work. I didn't want to appear too forward and scare her, so I gently, with hardly any pressure, touched my hip to her shoulder. When she found an error, I bent over to see better, rotating slightly so my crouch was to her shoulder and put my hand on the back of her chair with my thumb against her back. When I stood up, I commented on how soft her hair was and ran my fingers up her neck and through her hair. When she didn't object, I stood directly behind her and massaged her shoulders and neck. She didn't object and I knew it would only be a matter of time.

And it was. But, unfortunately, I had scared her. Afterwards, she had great remorse. She felt the anguish of guilt. At that age I was always horny. Sex was always on my mind. Fantasy often gave way to my physical desires. After I had seduced her, I wanted to again and again.

The next day she talked Derek into tutoring me. Derek was excited about tutoring me because it gave him the opportunity to see Michelle. He had noticed her in the hall the first day of school and said right there that she was the woman he wanted to marry.

Derek and Michelle used to talk about how to tutor me at school during a free period they both had. A close bond developed between them and continued to grow. For Michelle, this bond to Derek started, no doubt, in admiration of his quick mind, but Derek was also good looking. He exuded the good vibes that everybody enjoyed. Then to win more brownie points, that son-of-a-bitch asked Michelle to speak to him in French. There was no way I could compete. It was during these few weeks that they fell hopelessly in love. And I mean hopelessly. Unfortunately, I did, too.

I passed my French mid-term exam and so I got to play in the big game, which we won. There were several scouts from different colleges scouting me at that game. One by one they talked to me about a football scholarship. I was at an all-time high. That is until I got a phone call that evening from Michelle saying she was pregnant.

I went directly to her apartment. I wanted to know how she knew so quickly and how she knew I was the father. She had missed her period a week earlier and she was very regular. So, after a week she got a test which confirmed her suspicions. She said I had to be the father because she had not been intimate with anyone else. She bristled at my suggestion. To say the least, Michelle was distraught. And so was I.

I told her I had just had not one, but several offers of football scholarships to different colleges, and that I intended to go on to professional football. I was only 17 and not ready to get married and settle down with a family.

I told her I would somehow pay for an abortion. She said she did not believe in abortions and would not get one. Obviously, I was afraid she was expecting us to get married. But, she wasn't. She wanted my support, but she wouldn't get married just because a brief affair produced a child, which was essentially the case.

We argued. I told her I didn't know how much support I could give her. I was not ready to be a husband and father. I reiterated my offer about an abortion. We parted with the understanding we would both think about it. Frankly, I don't think either of us knew what we wanted, or what would be best. We were in shock.

That night on the way home I thought about how Derek was so interested in her and how he would probably like to be in my situation. I couldn't believe what I got myself in to. I felt so stupid. I was very angry at my lust, but felt there had to be a way to resolve the situation.

I called Michelle and told her I had a solution.

"The first time Derek saw you in the hall the first day of school he said you were the girl he wanted to marry," I told her.

"What are you saying? You want me to marry Derek?"

"You would not be setting him up. Derek loves you. He would not mind raising my child."

"I can't believe you! You think you can solve things like that and make decisions for other people. I made a stupid mistake and now I have to deal with it. I'm not going to put my problems on somebody else. Particularly not Derek. And you shouldn't want to put your problems on him either."

"I know we both made a stupid mistake," I told her. "But at least see him alone. If he doesn't want to marry you, I will. That's how sure I am he wants you."

"I told you I am not interested in marrying you now. We hardly know each other. I expect your support for the child, but I'm not going to compound this problem by going into a marriage with somebody I know nothing about, except that he likes sex."

"Okay, I understand if you don't want to marry me. I want you to know I want to support you with the child. I don't know how, but as Derek would say, 'Think positively.' I just came up with the idea considering how I've seen you and Derek get along so fabulously and thought maybe it would work out better for everyone. Just think about it. Okay?"

There was a silence. I waited. Finally Michelle said, "No, I can't. No matter what you say, it would be tricking him. He's not even 18. I'm 22. He's got so much promise. I'd be robbing him of his youth and early manhood, his career opportunities. I love Derek. I love his character. I love his personality. I love his mind and sense of humor, his energy. He is the kind of man I want to marry, but I don't want to do it under these circumstances. I just can't. I won't."

"Look at it this way," I tried to convince her, "you both love each other. You want each other. Isn't that what really matters, your happiness? Just being together. I've known Derek since birth. He's resourceful. He'll go on to college. He'll have a successful career."

Michelle listened. I could almost hear her wheels going round.

During the next week, Derek and Michelle got together as usual during their free period at school, even though he was no longer tutoring me. I could tell Michelle was opening up to him more seriously. Derek wouldn't stop talking to me about how well things were going between them and how he was sure she was the one. It was hard to listen sometimes, but I was only hoping things would work out for the best.

Then one night it was confirmed. Michelle called me and said, "Derek has proposed, but I haven't said yes."

I could tell she really wanted to make sure I hadn't said anything to him. I thought she might have told him the situation, but she couldn't.

"He wouldn't let me," she said. "He says he's not interested in my past, even if there were mistakes. He says he wants to marry me because he loves me as I am."

We probably should have said something to him at the time anyway, but it just didn't happen. Then a few nights later I called her to see how things were going.

"Fine," she said coldly as if it weren't really any of my business. Then in a different tone she continued, "You know, I really do love Derek. He's such a wonderful person."

"So you'll marry him?" I asked.

"I'd love to marry him, but I just don't know. It just doesn't seem right. He should know, but I can't tell him. And now things have become a little more complicated."

"What do you mean?"

"Well, we...."

"You slept together? You did, didn't you? That's great. When?"

"It doesn't matter when. It just matters that it happened and now I really don't know what to do. He proposed again."

"So, that's wonderful. What are you worried about?"

"Oh, maybe just that when I tell him the truth I will ruin the best thing that ever happened to me. Never say anything to him; I will handle it. Okay?"

I never said anything to Derek and it turned out that neither did she. After awhile, we just didn't even think about it anymore. They were so in love. Things seemed great. I was happy for them, but torn between many emotions.

At the time, I thought it was my close friendship with Derek, but in retrospect I was falling in love myself and she was carrying my child. I was jealous. Even though I knew it was the right thing, I was jealous...at least very envious. No, I was jealous.

I know Derek went over to Michelle's every afternoon and weekends, too. I know his parents thought he was being tutored in oral French, but I'll leave that part of the story for Michelle to tell. I only wish I was there when they broke the news to his folks. Wow!

In school none of the faculty thought Derek had seduced Michelle. He was so pure. They all believed Michelle had seduced Derek. I felt like a shit letting Michelle take all the guff, when it was me who caused all the trouble. I wanted to come out and tell everyone the truth, but I had promised Michelle I would let her break the news when she thought the time was right. It was hard, but I kept to my promise.

I didn't see how Derek could have known the truth. I hadn't opened my mouth. Michelle told me every time she started to say "there's something I've got to tell you," he would not let her talk about any mistakes in her past.

Then Michelle told me of one particular conversation she had with Derek.

"You won't believe it," she said. "He told me that he loves me as I am and doesn't care what I may have done in the past. That there's nothing that could change how he feels about me. Even if the baby I was carrying wasn't his."

"He really said that?"

"Yes."

"So you told him after that?"

"I started to, but then he just put his finger to my lips and said we need to concentrate on the future and not the past."

Michelle and I both were sure he knew, even though we could not figure out how he knew. I had always believed he was psychic even though he denied it.

The baby boy arrived in August. It was hard for me to tone down my excitement. Several people, including Derek, said you would think it was my baby. I'm telling you that son-of-a-bitch knew.

As time went by I fell hopelessly in love with Michelle, but I never touched her. I know she liked me and seemed to hold no resentment about my making her pregnant. She was so in love with Derek and he with her.

We never talked about being Mike's biological father, but he grew up to look like me.

Then late one afternoon I was outside talking to Michelle when Derek arrived home.

"I'm glad you're both here. Let's go inside," he said, lovingly putting his arm around Michelle's waist. He had a serious look on his face, so we knew it had to be something significant.

"What's the matter?" Michelle asked. Derek remained silent until we were seated on the back porch. Derek sat on his favorite swing.

"Last week I went to see Dr. Blake, the urologist," Derek began. "I wanted to find out if it was me who was the reason why you haven't gotten pregnant. He examined me, finding everything okay and arranged for me to have my sperm tested. I've just come from there. And I found out it's very unlikely I will ever father a child. Dr. Blake said things could change, but right now my semen is so acidic that it kills whatever sperm I produce and I don't produce all that much."

There was a silence as he stared at Michelle. The tears began to well up in her eyes.

Derek broke the silence, "Michael, I think you know that we have wanted badly to have another child so Mike wouldn't be an only child and would have a sibling to play with. I probably should have discussed this with Michelle first, but if Michelle is agreeable, Michael, would you be willing to donate your sperm?"

Michelle broke into tears and clutched Derek in her arms. "It's okay, Michelle, if you don't want to, it's okay," Derek said trying to calm her.

"Derek, I do *not* want another child if you are not the father. I don't. I don't. Maybe we'll be lucky. I'm willing to take that chance."

Her crying slowed and she finally said, "I love you, Derek, I really do. It would have been very beautiful to have a child together, but we will always have each other. Nothing can diminish our love." She, without realizing it, had said "a child" instead of "another child." Maybe Derek didn't respond because he already knew Mike wasn't his.

The night of Derek's accident, we found out that he did, in fact, know all along that Mike was my child. On his deathbed, Derek smiled and looked at me. "Funny, isn't it? Your son has my last name and my son will have your last name."

"You son-of-a-bitch, you knew about Mike all along, didn't you?" I responded.

"Only about an hour after you did. Josh told me. He overheard your phone conversation with Michelle and thought you were setting me up. I swore him to secrecy. I didn't want Michelle to think I might be marrying her because I felt sorry for her."

"Yes, but that was 15 years ago. Why didn't you tell us you knew?" I demanded.

He smiled, "I just did."

When Derek died, Mike was 16. When I told him Derek had asked his Mom and me to marry right away because Michelle needed me, I asked him if he would resent it. He replied, "No, that is the way it should be." I beamed with relief. Then he asked, "Should I call you 'Dad'?"

I replied, "No, Derek was your Dad."

He pulled me over to a mirror and stood next to me. He was my height, had my blonde hair and many of my features. "I know you're my father."

I gasped.

"You can call me Father if you like," I told him without denial or further explanation.

"When are you going to tell me the whole story?" he asked.

"Later," I replied.

"Mike persisted, "I can't wait. You've got to tell me now."

"Okay, I'll tell you now if you agree to let me or your mother tell your grandparents and anyone else who has a right to know." Mike agreed, so, I told him the whole story.

All he said was, "Thanks, Father," but he continued thereafter to call me Michael.

Michelle's Second Account

I tutored Michael in French so he would be eligible to play football for the rest of the season. Michael came to my apartment across the street from the school after football practice.

He showed up with his hair still wet from his shower. I sat him at my kitchen table and pulled my chair next to his. After going over some of the rules of grammar, I had him translate several sentences while I went into the living room to read the newspaper. From where I sat I got a side view of him. He had a powerful, perfectly proportioned physique. His tee shirt was form fitting and what a form! He had a full chest, slender waist, well muscled upper arms, large square wrists, little or no observable hair on his arms. His lips were full and sensuous, thoroughly masculine. His blond hair, not quite a tow-head, was tousled from running his fingers through it as he wrote. He was the sexiest man I had ever seen. When he had finished writing he came in to get me. I quickly glanced back at my paper pretending I'd been reading.

Michael paused in the archway with his weight on one foot, his right shoulder against the arch and his left hip extending sideward, watching me seductively. I glanced up. His jeans were tight fitting and revealing. I trembled wondering what I would do if he…and I wanted him to. And he wanted to. And we did.

As we lay there after our orgasms in the glow of the physical release that follows, my mind became really troubled. What had I done? What had I allowed to happen? What does the future hold? What if he brags and the school finds out? Oh, my God! I panicked.

"I'm sorry I let this happen. You have to go," I remember telling him.

I arranged for my star pupil, Derek Saul, to tutor Michael. When I saw Michael in the hall, I avoided looking at him and gave him the cold shoulder, although inside I flushed.

Then came the bad news. I missed my period and I had always been very regular. A week later I went to the doctor and learned my suspicion was correct. I was pregnant. I panicked, panicked, and panicked some more. I was totally frightened and angered! My Catholic indoctrination made abortion unthinkable. I called Michael. He came right over.

"How do you know it's my baby?" he asked.

"Because you are the only one," I answered, angry at the implication. Michael knew what he was doing. He was lusting after me as he had after a dozen or maybe dozens of other women. Adrenaline poured through my veins. I was angry. But I had lusted, too. Never, never again, I vowed! And I never did, at least not until we were married many years later.

Michael said he would somehow pay for an abortion, but he was in no way going to get married. He had already been offered football scholarships to several colleges. And I was not willing to jump straight from an affair into a marriage. We didn't really know each other at all.

Michael has already told how I resisted inviting Derek over to learn oral French. I truly did resist. I, in no way, wanted to trap him into marriage even though I loved him with a passion and wished I were carrying *his* child. Eventually I acquiesced and to my great surprise Derek took over, which I could not believe. We made love.

When he proposed, which he did in record time, he would not let me tell him anything about my past. I tried and tried to tell him I was pregnant and he always stopped me. When he finally knew I was pregnant, I tried once more to tell him, but he said he wouldn't even care if he wasn't the father.

He told me, "It's you I love, but if you want to try to spoil my happiness, go ahead." I told him it wasn't that important. And that's the way we left it. I was convinced he didn't care and I was happy to know I hadn't trapped him.

Part Four

Chapter Fourteen

Ken's Journal (May 1)

After receiving the revised versions from Michelle and Michael, I also finally got the account from Mike. I can't get over how mature he sounds at age 19.

It's amazing how well he has handled what could have been a very confused childhood. I think it goes to show how significant it is that he received strong love and support from Derek and Michelle, and also from Michael.

Mike really is great, too. Jenny and I took him out to the movies today and spent some "quality" time with him. I think we're actually going to have him come up and visit us over the summer. He seemed quite interested and we could really get to know him better then. I think it could be ideal for Jenny and me since we don't have any children of our own. We could enjoy our nephew for a few weeks over the summer. Jenny's definitely excited about the idea.

After we got Mike home, before we returned to Mom and Dad's, we went out for a walk to have some time to ourselves. We talked about everything that's gone on over the weekend and neither of us could believe how much Derek, Michelle, and Michael have gone through. Especially since we always thought they had no problems or issues to deal with. We've had issues of our own, but they don't seem as big anymore and they don't seem worthy of making ourselves unhappy. Jenny and I are talking the way we used to and it feels great. Believe me, it feels really great!

Mike's Account

It's hard for me to write about my life with Derek Saul without telling the end first. Until I was 14, almost 15, I believed Derek Saul was my father. He truly lived the part.

However, I was by then eight inches taller than him and had many other physical features of his best friend, Michael Bassett.

I was Michael's height, blonde, and in many other ways resembled him. I had my mother's dark eyes, however. I was sure Michael was my biological father which bothered me. It's not that I didn't like Michael, but it bothered me as you can well imagine. I just wanted to know for sure, or just to be told the truth. And what happened anyway?

After Dad died I confronted Michael with what I was already sure of and he confirmed my belief, but didn't want me to call him Dad.

Michael had always been very attentive to me, being like a second father. But Dad, by which I mean Derek, was such an exceptional person and father. To figure out he wasn't my biological father was probably as confusing as an adopted son finding out at age 14 that he was adopted and then finding his real father and finding out he liked him.

It's hard to explain my feelings. You'll have to use your imagination to understand how I felt. After the initial shock it was really like having two fathers and fortunately, in my case, loving both.

In this account I will refer to Derek as Dad and Michael as Michael. After all these years of calling him Michael, I think of him as Michael.

As far back as I can remember, Dad was always there when my brother and I or Mom needed him. He was always helping Mom one way or another. They truly loved each other. You could tell by the way they touched, the way he would put his arm around her and held her close. Or the way he held her hand, the way they talked, and their laughter as they looked into each others' eyes.

If Mom and Dad had something private to say to each other, which they didn't want me to hear, they would talk in French. Mom was born of French parents and spoke French at home. Dad learned French from Mom.

Dad spent a great deal of time playing with me. He read to me a lot when I was little. We'd ride our bicycles together and, as we grew older, Dad taught me how to fish, and we'd go camping. On most Friday nights, except in summer, we would go to family swim at the YMCA. In the summers we would frequently go to lakes or to the shore. Movies were another thing we all enjoyed together.

Dad encouraged me to go out for athletics at school. And so did Michael. Michael joined us in many of our activities and had dinner with us a lot, particularly after his divorce.

Dad would help me with my homework when I needed help. So would Mom. Dad would never do my problems for me, but would make sure I knew how to do them.

Dad would stay up late and get up early. I don't know how he could do that. I liked to sleep late whenever I could, particularly on Saturdays. Many a night I would hear Dad and Josh discussing things late into the night. Josh was Michael's younger brother who lived in the third floor apartment in our house most of my life. I asked them what they found so interesting to talk about so much. Dad replied "spiritual things."

I asked him if that meant religious things, but he said no. Dad warned us not to think of God as a divine person up in heaven. He said God is spirit and does not occupy space but is everywhere at once, everywhere, and is aware of everything all the time.

Dad believed a spark of God is in all of us and God has given us free will. So, when you combine the two, we can create. That is, let God work through us. Sometimes our creations don't work out well. That's because we didn't choose well.

Dad said the greatest law is to do to everyone what you want done to you. Another is "what goes round, comes round." That is, we get back what we dish out.

I remember once getting so mad at a guy I wanted to punch him out, Dad calmed me down by saying, "If you get mad, he's going to get mad. That's the law. One of you is going to have to forgive the other to keep peace. Then, if one of you does forgive, the other will also forgive or he will eventually have to pay the consequences for not forgiving. That's also the law, turn the other cheek."

There is nothing wrong with experimenting with free will. How else are we going to learn? However, if it doesn't work out well for everybody, then experiment some other way. Dad would say if we find someone who is experimenting badly, recognize that's what he's doing and forgive him for his bad choices and hope he changes the next time.

Dad was opposed to a large military. The armed forces are taught to kill without feeling guilty. Movies and TV also teach likewise. When discharged from the armed forces that ability to kill without guilt lingers on. It's terrible.

No one can win a war in the long run, anyway, because the hate in war and defeat lingers for years, generations even, and will eventually surface. In the short run, it may seem like we win a war, but unless the mind-set of the enemy is changed by our compassion and fairness, the hate will surface again. The best example of reducing hate Dad knew of was General Douglas MacArthur's treatment of the Japanese after World War II. There really never was a good war or a bad peace.

Getting back to life with Derek, I have already said he was an excellent father, but what do I mean? I think his greatest attribute was he taught by example. He showed his love for us by being interested in what we said and did without being too critical. He never made us feel inferior, but always showed us ways to do better.

One of my earliest memories was snuggling up to Dad when he sat on his favorite swing on the back porch. He would frequently just sit there quietly staring away or with his eyes closed. I would crawl up beside him. He would put his arm around me and we would sit there together quietly.

He played with me and my friends a lot. When we were young he would wrestle with me on the bed or on the floor. He tossed me around. He played hide and seek and would play ball with us, and later frisbee also. He would romp in the snow with us in the winter and swim with us in the summer.

He would read to me when I was small and taught me to read without pronouncing the words. He would take me to kids' movies. He helped the coach out when I was in the Little League. He helped the scoutmaster when I was in the Boy Scouts. In short he always was available to me and to Mom also. And he worked hard in grandpa's insurance agency, but came home on time to be with us.

Often Michael would join us fishing and camping. Hardly a day went by when Michael didn't drop over. He still lived next door with another divorced teacher. When I grew larger they taught me to play racquetball at the Y and I also went out for the Y swim team as they had done at my age.

I had a neat set of friends my age, and we all got along well together, probably because Dad and Mom took us places and did things with the whole bunch of us. Fortunately, we had a large van. It was a good vehicle when we went out camping, too. Often Mom and Michael camped with us and sometimes Josh.

Dad had a way of disciplining me so I wanted to do the right thing. He would talk about what would happen if I did something this way and what would happen if I did it that way. Sometimes he would leave me without an answer to figure it out myself, which was annoying. He would encourage me to think what would be best for most people and he was glad if that was the way I chose. He always used to say "What goes around, comes around."

Maybe a half-dozen times Dad spanked me when I had repeatedly done the same wrong thing or really stepped out of line, but he never did it in a moment of anger. He would use his belt, but over my clothes—never hard enough to do more than smart, or he would have me take down my pants, which was more humiliating, and use his hand. When I reached an age of reason, he didn't spank me anymore. He would reason with me. He was compassionate with me and my friends. With everybody, I guess.

Dad was always smiling, not grinning, but a happy smile. He said smiling was a way we could let God spread joy through us. Dad mentioned that history honors the glum-faced Pilgrims. Yet, they had no joy. Without joy, as observed through smiling faces, there is no love and God is love, the glue of the universe. So, why are the Pilgrims honored? It should be because they kept on with the struggle. They worked hard and survived.

Dad would say that it's better to tell a smutty joke than no joke at all. Dad also didn't disapprove of most swearing when used appropriately to get attention or to emphasize a point. But not just to be vulgar.

Dad would say God made it necessary for us to choose whether we wanted to be selfish or generous, good or bad, forgiving or not. If we chose right, things would go well for us. If things weren't going well for us, it is a clue that we are or have chosen wrongly. It's our own fault in other words and we should not look for ways to put the blame on others. We are attracting what we get by the way we behave and think.

Dad often said what we think is as important as what we do because thoughts are things. He also said that *why* we do what we do is even more important than *what* we do. People who measure themselves by the jobs they hold and the money they make are missing the point.

Dad said a good gauge to remember is, if it seems wrong, don't do it. What we do to others we do to ourselves because there is only one self and we all share in it. Dad had a neat way of looking at things. For instance, he believed we should reach down and lift others up. "It's the best exercise you'll ever get," he said.

Since God, being just spirit, is in all of us, what we do to others we also do to God. And he said God doesn't want a bunch of puppets in this world. He wants people to choose the right way, but that's up to us, not Him. God would have no joy if He made us do the right things, but there is joy for Him if we by ourselves choose to do the right things.

I remember Dad once said, "We don't go to heaven, we grow to heaven." And that heaven is really a state of consciousness and can even happen here on earth.

Dad didn't take me to church or Sunday School. He said what Christianity, actually every religion, teaches can be wrapped up in a few sentences which he made me learn. "Do unto others as you would have them do unto you." And, "He who knows not love, knows not God, for God is love," therefore, "Love God with all your heart, strength, mind, and soul, and your neighbor as yourself." How do we love God? "In as much as you do it to others, you do it to your God." And Jesus gave us the commandment, "Love one another as I have loved you."

I believe he thought it was important for me to know how he thought so I could ask questions or dig into spiritual matters on my own. I know he and my uncle Josh spent many hours talking about these sorts of things.

Dad told me to live every moment without expectations, but with expectancy. He called this "living in the now," allowing what is happening to happen, and watching life unfold. This attitude allows us to let go of things that separate us from God.

Dad used to always talk about "energy patterns." He explained how Einstein established that all matter is energy. Since we can measure brain waves they must be energy also. So, in our thinking we are creating energy patterns which can effect the energy of matter for good or for bad.

We can create sickness or good health by our thinking and don't usually know we are doing it. We can create prosperity or poverty and again we may not realize we are doing it, also good times or misfortune. Fear and guilt are good examples of energy patterns that can attract bad things.

I really wish Dad was still here to talk about all this stuff. I can't think of anything else to say except I really miss Dad.

Actually, I talk to him most every night before I go to bed. Well, of course, I don't actually talk to him, but I want to think he hears me. I just fill him in on what's going on in my life and I ask him what I should do when I have problems. It makes me feel better, even though I really know I am talking to my higher self.

When Dad died it was a tremendous, tremendous blow to us all. Then, when Mom told me Dad had asked her to marry Michael before the baby was born, I thought it was weird Dad would ask them to do such a thing so soon. I'm sure it would have happened eventually. I'm sure he reasoned that Mom needed a husband with her being pregnant and needing to raise me. Dad was full of fun, but he didn't act unreasonably, so, I went along with it.

Then, too, the very thought of Dad reincarnating into Mom's expected baby was also weird. Imagine being your own father. I wondered if Dad told Mom and Michael about his reincarnating into the unborn baby just so Mom wouldn't be so sad and maybe to make sure that Michael would be a good father.

However, I couldn't imagine Michael being anything but the best of fathers to Dad's child. Not only were those two closer than brothers, but look how well Dad had raised me, and I was Michael's son. Last year Mom and Michael had my cute little sister Anne.

Right from the start, baby Derek looked like the pictures of his father. He's smart too…and stubborn. It will be interesting to see how he turns out. Sometimes when I look into his eyes, it's like he knows something. It may be just in my head, but I guess I do think Dad is inside him.

Chapter Fifteen

Ken's Journal (May 3)

Jenny and I went out for breakfast with Mom and Dad early yesterday morning and then got an early flight back home to Massachusetts. We got home a few hours ago. Jenny had a wonderful time down there. She was very happy to see me getting so much closer with my family (and her).

Now I'm getting myself organized for my upcoming overseas assignment. Jenny and I were talking about her coming over to meet me at the end of it and then taking a brief vacation in the Mediterranean. I think it's going to work out, which will be wonderful. It's amazing how quickly we have gone from having our relationship look very dismal to being completely re-energized. I think she would thank my little brother if he were still around. Maybe he is. Who knows?

Based upon conversations and letters received, there is no question in my mind that Derek had a wonderful effect upon the lives of those who associated with him. It would seem to me Derek proved that a seemingly ordinary man can be a saint. He also proved we don't have to be a member of an organized religion to do what is right, to be a truly great soul. Derek was such.

Derek showed that God is not only love, as Christian churches teach. In as much as it would be unloving if the universe were unlawful, God must also be law and truth, which is the same as God's will. Derek believed that saying, "In the beginning God...," declares that, in the beginning, there was only God. So, what He created had to be created out of Himself. Since all matter is energy and all action is energy, including thinking, then God must also be energy. Therefore, God is all, but He has given us free will to choose how we will use Him (that is, the energy which is God). He has also given us consciousness that we might be aware of the results of our choices and choose again when appropriate.

"God is, therefore, my body, in and through me," Derek said. "That is where I must meet Him. It is written, 'Ask and you shall receive.' That is to say my free will can choose, consciously or subconsciously. I am, thereby, directing my energies, or the God within who does the good works, and it shall happen, if I don't doubt and if I haven't already set up conflicting desires or energy patterns."

Man's purpose is to express his free will so God can participate with us as co-creator, thereby better comprehending His diversity.

Derek claimed, "Jesus can be better remembered by the effect he had on those who actually knew him, rather than by what men have written years later about what they or others say he meant. Think of the courage his immediate followers must have had to go through the dangers of torture, even death, but also remember, death is not as important as we often make it out to be. It is just the passing from one room to another."

Account after account of those who contributed to the book about Derek, have quoted him as saying, "I do not proclaim what I say is truth." Hopefully, some or most is, but he did not want to be like many of the past religious leaders of all religions who have proclaimed "This is the truth and you must believe it or else...." Derek trembled at the thought that he might lead others astray from the truth. He believed it is everybody's duty to study what is called good and also what is called bad, as well as the motivations of both good and bad people to find out what rings true for them.

As to Jan Hall, I can only conclude that Derek considered her as a member of the family. She was so close, particularly with Michelle, that she belonged at the celebration of Michelle's pregnancy. I think Jan was driving because she was considering buying Derek's old car when he bought his new one. She was test driving it and it really doesn't matter who caused the accident.

I believe the improvement with Jenny and me is a result of our exposure to Derek. Our outlooks have changed remarkably. I believe that Jan similarly became a changed person by the same exposure. Her life was flowing and she was appreciated. Her sexual proclivity was not an issue. For instance, she had given up her night job in the gay/lesbian bar. She never made a pass at desirable Michelle. She was a loved and appreciated person, functioning well in society. In effect, you could suppose Jan had learned the lessons she needed to learn in this life and that it was okay for her to move on. Her purpose here had been accomplished. Her brother could care for their mother. It's possible he needs, thereby, to learn a lesson or two himself. Who knows?

When we were visiting in Falls Church, Michelle summarized Derek's belief about the differences between the body, the soul, and spirit.

"The soul is not perfect. It is the totality of all previous life good, bad, or indifferent that the present life (and past lives, if you can accept reincarnation) has experienced. Every act, conversation, thought, desire, fear, emotion has set up energy patterns or vibes and the totality of these constitute the soul. The soul can progress or backslide. Hopefully, by learning from experiences, the progress will be upward towards the awareness of the knowledge that "I and my father are one." The soul determines what lessons need to be experienced each life and sets it up accordingly.

The spirit is always perfect as we are part of God and God is spirit and God is perfect. There is only one spirit and we all share in it. When we are in touch with our spirit, we are in touch with God.

The body is the vehicle in this physical plane, and both the soul and spirit are passengers. The body goes through the experiences the soul is in need of.

Spirit is the life. Mind is the builder. The physical is the result. The soul is of all three. We need the physical body. It is our classroom, but what happens here is usually not as important as most people think. Some things like patience can't be learned except on the physical level.

Derek frequently said,

"I DON'T CARE WHAT RELIGION OR DENOMINATION OR CASTE, COLOR, CREED, OR GENDER PEOPLE BELONG TO AS LONG AS THEY ARE LOVING, JOYFUL, PEACEFUL, COMPASSIONATE, FRIENDLY, SHARING, NON-JUDGMENTAL, PATIENT, TOLERANT, FORGIVING, KIND, AND GENTLE."

Cannot it be truthfully said that many persons because of their associations with Derek became better people? Better souls?

One thing is for sure, God blessed us with Derek!

About the Author

Born in 1926 in New London, Connecticut, W. Lawrence Miner, Jr., completed studies at Harvard University and went on to Stanford University to get a master's degree in business administration. There he met his wife of 48 years. They have five children and eight grandchildren.

After three short-term jobs in California, Miner returned to Connecticut to enter his father's real estate, insurance and appraisal firm, which he took over upon his father's retirement. He has traveled to every continent and has led trips sailing, skiing, backpacking, canoeing, kayaking, rafting, houseboating, trekking and a safari. He also led wilderness retreats for several metaphysical organizations.

In 1992 at age 67 he retired from leading wilderness retreats and busied himself writing his first novel and screen play, plus doing much personal traveling with his wife and grandkids. He is an elected member of the Explorers Club and the American Alpine Club and is active with UFO investigation, hiking, racquetball and skiing.

MORE GREAT BOOKS FROM GRANITE PUBLISHING GROUP

Agents of Change

THE GODSPELL SOLUTION
Life, Love, Healing and Abundance
A trusty companion for the spiritual journey...
Bill Jason O'Mara
1-928992-02-1
$10

THE ESSENTIAL PATTERN
A Thesis on Cosmic Energy
Heavily illustrated with detailed diagrams
Rosalind Thorp
1-928992-03-x
$20

Wild Flower Press

ABDUCTION IN MY LIFE
A Novel of Alien Encounters
Bruse Maccabee, Ph.D.
0-926524-54-2
$15

THE VOYAGERS SERIES
Volume I: *The Sleeping Abductees*
1-893183-08-4 $13
Volume II: *The Secrets of Amenti*
1-893183-16-5 $20

SOUL SAMPLES
Personal Exploration in Reincarnation and UFO Experiences
R. Leo Sprinkle, Ph.D.
1-893183-05-x
$18

ZETATALK
Direct Answers From the Zeta Reticuli People
Nancy Lieder
1-893183-15-7
$14

OPENING TO THE INFINITE
Human Multidimensional Potential
Linda Seebach and the late Alice Bryant
0-926524-43-7
$14

CONVERSING WITH THE FUTURE
Visions of the Year 2020
Jenna Catherine
0-926524-45-3
$14

Swan•Raven & Co.

KINDRED SPIRITS
Animal Teachers and the Will of the Land
Jesse Wolf Hardin
1-893183-06-8 $20

THE VOICE OF THE INFINITE IN THE SMALL
Revisioning the Insect-Human Connection
Joanne E. Lauck
1-893183-10-6 $17

PLANT SPIRIT MEDICINE
Healing with the Power of Plants
Eliot Cowan
1-893183-11-4 $14

TAROT OF THE SOUL
A guiding Oracle that uses ordinary playing cards.
Belinda Atkinson
0-926524-32-1 $7

Granite Publishing Group

To receive a free catalog
please write to...

Granite Publishing Group
P.O. Box 1429
Columbus, North Carolina 28722

or call...

800.366.0264

or visit our web site at...

www.5thworld.com

Thank you.